# The Private War of Corporal Henson

E. Michael Helms

Also by E. Michael Helms:

*The Proud Bastards*

*Of Blood and Brothers* (Books One and Two)

*Deadly Catch: A Mac McClellan Mystery*

*The Private War of Corporal Henson*

ISBN 978-0-9897605-5-3

eBook ISBN 978-0-9897605-6-0

STAIRWAY≡PRESS

STAIRWAY PRESS—SEATTLE

Cover Design by Chris Benson, BensonCreative
www.BensonCreative.com

**www.stairwaypress.com**
1500A East College Way #554
Mount Vernon, WA 98273

*To the memory of my late father-in-law, Urban Anthony Cyruss, USN, WWII; and Dennis R. Mathena, USN combat corpsman, Vietnam.*

*… it was a savage, brutal, inhumane, exhausting and dirty business.*

—Eugene B. Sledge, *With the Old Breed: At Peleliu and Okinawa*

# Acknowledgements

A huge and belated "thank you" to the members of my combat veterans counseling group, and especially Team Leader Gregg Brown, USN, Vietnam. This is your story as well as mine. Semper Fidelis.

# CHAPTER ONE

IT WASN'T THE homecoming Nathan Henson had envisioned.

There were no cheering crowds or tickertape parades like his father experienced during America's last "good war." No long weeks of routine and camaraderie aboard a troop transport affording precious time to adjust from the insanity of combat for a triumphant return to a grateful nation. The best Nathan's war had to offer was a quick flight back to "the World" on a freedom bird to some West Coast airport where one could hopefully slip back into the heartland unnoticed by hostile demonstrators. Forty-eight hours from the jungle to the streets. Welcome home.

Nathan and the other wounded aboard the C-141 StarLifter were denied even that. For the past several weeks his world had been dogged with pain and suffering. When his physical agony found momentary respite in a fog of medication, his mind was still tormented by the cries of comrades left behind on the battlefield of Vietnam and the ward at Yokosuka Naval Hospital.

Nathan shifted position in his seat and grimaced for the effort. Just gotta hack it, he told himself. It had taken weeks to be declared ambulatory and he wasn't about to let a little pain get in the way. He'd had enough of lying flat on his back and staring at ceilings and counting endless dots in the tiles dancing before his not-quite-focused eyes. Whatever the cost, he would endure.

He glanced around the dim cabin again. Rows of ailing soldiers and Marines sat or reclined in ever-changing positions, seeking relief from pain or a bit of comfort as though part of a common, restless entity. Intravenous bottles hung above many of the patients, the clear liquid seeping almost imperceptibly drop-by-drop into veins. Nathan found himself staring at one bottle across the aisle, trying futilely to detect a change in the fluid level. After several minutes or hours he gave up the game. It was like watching an ocean evaporate.

Intermittent groans of the wounded blended in strange harmony with the muffled whine of jet engines. Nathan eased back his seat and thought of another flight, eight months earlier. How different that one had been! Like the other young Marines aboard, he'd been full of piss and vinegar, itching to get into combat and prove himself. But boyish bravado had quickly turned to fear, which in time grew to morbid resignation as the grim realities of war ripped away the armor of innocence. Finally, it had all come down to this—a big world of hurt.

Still, there was some solace to be found amid all the suffering. His battalion had been mauled in the fierce fighting along the Cua Viet River during the Tet Offensive. It seemed everyone around him was dying and he'd never expected to make it out alive. This pitiful flight of torn flesh and wasted youth was at least a step above the stacked silver coffins in which so many of his comrades had journeyed home.

The flight nurse was making her rounds down the aisle, taking temperatures, checking IVs and administering pain meds and cheerful words. Nathan's pulse quickened as she drew nearer. A hunger stirred inside him. It had been months since he'd felt the soft touch of a woman, and Lieutenant Evans was most definitely a woman.

Her sunny smile and southern accent reminded him of Laura, though strangely he could no longer clearly picture his fiancé's face. During pre-flight rounds he'd nearly mustered the courage to ask Lieutenant Evans for her first name and where she was from. But the silver bars on her olive drabs and the thermometer in his mouth stopped him. Still, when her soft hand held his wrist while checking his pulse he'd almost melted. Her scent, the sound of her breathing and the subtle rising and falling of full breasts beneath the utility jacket were almost too much to bear.

Lieutenant Evans was only a row away when a shrill alarm pierced the calm. She turned and sprinted for the rear of the plane with two medics and another nurse at her heels. They disappeared through the drawn curtains separating the ambulatory patients from the more serious stretcher cases. As many eyes as could manage followed them. Ears took up the vigil, straining above the droning engines at the voices, trying to discern what was happening.

Nathan knew. They all knew. That icy fist gripped his gut again; the terrible cold dread when a buddy lay dying and Nathan was pinned down and helpless to do anything but try to survive. He pressed his hands over his ears to shut out the sounds but the voices were within and the screams of the dying continued unabated.

And then he saw it all again— Roberts shot to hell and sprawled across the rice paddy dike and Doc Dunn sprinting towards him . . .

"No Doc, stay down, he's dead! Stay down you crazy bastard!"

But Dunn didn't listen or didn't hear and his head exploded in a red geyser.

"I told you to stay down but you wouldn't listen goddamnit, you wouldn't listen, damn you."

"Shh, calm down Corporal . . . take a breath; everything's okay."

Nathan moved his clenched fists from his eyes and blinked to clear his vision. A pretty face framed by auburn hair smiled at him. "You were dreaming again," Lieutenant Evans said as she wiped his brow. "I'm gonna give you something that'll take care of the pain and help you get some rest."

She pushed the pajama sleeve above his right biceps, swabbed a spot with alcohol and with practiced hand injected a shot of

Demerol. She lowered the sleeve and brushed a wisp of blonde hair from Nathan's damp forehead.

"You rest easy now. I'll check on you again in a little while."

The drug was already taking effect as Nathan watched his angel of mercy disappear down the aisle. He settled deeper into the cushions; he feeling drowsy and heavy, and yet as though he could float up and fly away without the airplane if he wanted to. But he had no desire to leave. He was going home, back to the World.

The World. That magical place he'd dreamed about and longed for so desperately during the months of madness. Back to the real World, back to Laura.

He was giddy now, euphoria in command. With weary eyes he searched the cabin for the nurse, who in his stupor had become Laura. His buddies may have deserted him but Laura was there, and she would be there for him when he woke up. Yes, Laura was waiting. He sighed and surrendered to a deep sleep.

# CHAPTER TWO

HE KNEW IT would be a bad day. *"Beware the Ides of March!"* the ancient soothsayer had warned Julius Caesar. Like an unrelenting predator, the fifteenth of March had stalked Nathan Henson for days, and now it was upon him.

It was dusk when he turned onto the long driveway leading past his landlady's house. He saw Mrs. Ard in her kitchen. The aroma of fresh baked bread wafted from the open window, making his mouth water. Sometimes she would drop by after a day's baking with a loaf or two still warm from the oven. Tonight, maybe? He could sure use the company.

Nathan parked the van in front of his house. Beyond the trees bordering his yard the western sky was a shimmering canvas of aqua, gold and pink. Layers of steel-blue clouds glowed orange as if they had swallowed fire from the sun before it deserted the horizon. A strange feeling swept over him as though time had halted for a moment and that it would never again be measured in pain and disappointment. He wished the feeling would last forever, but it was gone in a rush.

He unlocked the front door and switched on a light, chasing some of the gloom from the house. He flipped on the hall light as he made his way into the kitchen for a beer.

He'd spent the afternoon driving around town, trying to reestablish contact with some of his customers. In the winter months when yard work and landscaping came to a virtual standstill he was able to scrape by on his VA disability check. But there was money to be made when cold weather eased its grip on the Florida panhandle in March or early April. It was best to get a head start scheduling regular customers as a safeguard against the competition.

He'd visited four residences in the affluent Bayview Heights area where he'd established a good clientele the past few years. The Holloways were touring Europe and weren't due back for several weeks. The Nelsons had relocated to Atlanta; a realtor was handling the leasing and upkeep of their property. Ed and Anita Barnes were now living in a retirement villa in south Florida and the daughter and son-in-law occupying their home made it clear his services would no longer be required. And when Nathan learned that sweet Mrs. Parnell had passed away during the winter, he'd given it up for the day.

He sat at the table drinking beer and watching the TV on the kitchen counter. Vanna White was turning letters as only she could. Nathan tried to get interested in the puzzle but couldn't concentrate. He drained the beer and opened another.

"This time we're looking for a phrase," Pat Sajak said. Nathan gulped beer and tried not to think. Outside, a whippoorwill announced its return from a winter's absence. "I'm gonna give the wheel a final spin," Sajak continued, "vowels are worth nothing, consonants will be worth—hey, not too bad—fifteen hundred dollars!"

Three empties were on the table by the time Vanna waved "Bye-bye." Night had consumed all traces of color in the west. Crickets serenaded the coming spring and moths flew in tight erratic orbits, taking turns thumping the bare bulb outside the back door. To the north distant thunder rumbled a salvo across the black sky, sending a shiver up Nathan's spine.

He was restless and couldn't sit still. Why bother? he reasoned. He got up and opened another beer. Seventeen years without fail. It would always be this way. No matter how hard he tried not to think about it his mind kept replaying the night of 15 March 1968. There was no escape.

Nathan chugged his beer, hoping to drown the memories before they overwhelmed him again. He stared out the window into the darkness, dreading the night. . . .

The attack came two hours before daylight. Corporal Nathan Henson and the other sleepy grunts on watch in their foxholes heard the muffled report of artillery firing far to the north. Fatigue fled, banished by fear. Palms sweated and dry lips mouthed silent prayers as they waited the awful seconds that seemed to drag on forever, hoping against hope that some other poor bastards were about to catch hell.

And then it was upon them—*Incoming!*—shrill whistling followed by earthshaking explosions and the hideous hum of whirring shrapnel filling the night with terror. Instinctively, Nathan opened his mouth to counteract pressure from the concussion of the blasts. He rued taunting the gook gunners a few hours before and mentally kicked himself in the ass.

Nathan and Betz cowered in the hole, trying their best to disappear beneath the frail protection of helmets and flak jackets. He wished they had dug-in deeper though he knew it wouldn't make a difference if their hole took a direct hit.

The North Vietnamese had done their homework. Like all the villages the NVA occupied along the Cua Viet River, this one was zeroed-in perfectly. Already the fierce pounding was taking its toll and casualties mounted. Cries of "Corpsman up!" sounded from several sectors of the vill amid the roar of the barrage.

A hundred meters to Nathan's right one of third platoon's fighting holes took a direct hit. Private Higgins and a new replacement no one had bothered getting to know yet disintegrated in a blinding flash. A boot-covered foot, half a torso and scattered chunks of charred flesh and shredded utilities were all that remained in the smoking crater.

Several meters to the rear of Nathan's position Lieutenant

Simonson, who had left his hole to answer nature's call just before the shelling began, lay writhing and screaming in agony, his right leg and both buttocks sheared away by shrapnel. Ignoring the intensifying explosions, Staff Sergeant Chambers sprinted to the platoon leader's aid. Just before reaching Simonson shrieking metal smashed through Chambers' forehead, launching his brains and skullcap skyward.

Now the incoming slackened. Parachute flares from Marine artillery batteries at Dong Ha popped overhead and bathed the vill in orange. Nathan and Betz raised their heads above the crest of the hole and peered across the eerie landscape.

"Oh shit," Betz muttered. His hand flashed across his chest in the sign of the cross. "Oh Jesus, oh shit."

Nathan had expected it though he tried hard to make the moving figures mere wavering shadows like he'd been fooled by months before. He knew better now and began straightening the pins from the half-dozen grenades piled in his corner of the fighting hole. He and Betz emptied their bandoliers of magazines and stacked them within easy reach.

Barely a hundred meters away lines of shadowy figures trotted toward them behind the final explosions of the covering barrage. Small arms and automatic weapons began to pop and crack and chatter, sporadically at first, and then building to a continuous crescendo like the unleashing of a violent thunderstorm upon a tin roof.

Like cornered animals the young Marines watched the dogged enemy close the gap. *Closer.* Sweating hands clutched the detonators of claymore mines set forward of their fighting hole. *Closer.* The black air sizzled with the evil hissing and buzzing of fiery metal singing the serenade of death. *Closer.*

Now the moving shadows took shape. Nathan saw them clearly in the shimmering light of the flares—pith helmets camouflaged with leaves and brush; legs pumping up and down faster and faster as they drew nearer; arms cradling AK-47s and rocket launchers and light machine guns and other bundles of death; the faces, the faces, the faces—

"Die, you bastards!" Nathan screamed as he squeezed off the claymores. A wall of bodies tumbled like scattered bowling pins. Blinding flashes and booming explosions and tongues of fire and streams of green and red tracers swept back and forth across the killing ground.

Still they came. Closer, closer, and Nathan hurled grenade after grenade at clusters of darting figures until there were no more to be thrown and then he sprayed burst after burst into the bodies and they kept falling and screaming and dying but even more were coming coming coming—

"God! God!"

The enemy was on them now, filling their hole, violating their space. The clammy touch of strange flesh; limbs entwining; the mingling of panting breath like forbidden lovers in the surrealistic intimacy of death. The muffled bark of weapons exploding point-blank into flesh. Animal screams fed on adrenalin and fear and desperation. Rifle torn from hands, kicking and stomping, choking and gurgling. Hand clutching KA-Bar, striking out and plunging deep, deeper, again and again into the void, hot and wet and sticky. . . .

Through a gray mist Nathan stared across the scene of carnage. Bodies lay everywhere. Dozens and dozens of them. More bodies than he'd ever seen at one time. Between him and Betz two NVA soldiers lay in frozen poses of violent death. The foxhole reeked of blood and shit. Already flies were swarming and feasting on the gore.

To Nathan's right Gabby and Walker stood outside their hole and waved. Gabby flashed his wide-mouthed grin. Nathan waved back and tried to return the smile but couldn't. There wasn't enough left in him.

He slumped back in the hole and stared across the bodies at Betz who was splattered with blood. Betz gazed back at Nathan with hollow eyes. He shook his head as though he still didn't believe what had happened or that he was really alive.

"Don't make sense," Betz mumbled, "it just don't make no fucking sense."

Nathan fumbled for a canteen and noticed his own hands and arms were covered with black sticky blood. He took a deep swallow of the foul tepid water and then passed the canteen to Betz. He tried to think of something to say, but gave up. Leaning his head against the dirt wall, he closed his eyes. . . .

Soft fingers of sunlight crept through the kitchen window. On the sill outside, Clarence, Mrs. Ard's big yellow cat, arched his back high against the screen, stretching and yawning. From a nearby budding sycamore a cardinal welcomed the day with song.

Awakened by Clarence's meowing, Nathan lifted his head from the table. He got up and let Clarence inside and filled his bowl with Cat Chow. He limped down the hallway to the bathroom, turned on the shower and undressed and stepped into the stall. The hot spray pelted his body. With great deliberation he lathered the washcloth and scrubbed his hands and arms over and over.

# CHAPTER THREE

NATHAN SQUIRMED IN his chair and stared at the clock above the doorway. Three-twenty. Black dude's been in there almost fifteen minutes, he noted; my turn next.

His palms sweated and his pulse raced like a school kid next in line for an oral book report. Relax, this is no big deal, he told himself, what's there to be nervous about anyway? He took several deep breaths to calm himself, unaware that his right leg was pumping up and down.

He sat in the corner with his back to the wall beside a large filing cabinet. He glanced to his right at the others seated in the room. A gaunt man clad in bright green trousers and yellow polyester shirt was absorbed in a paperback novel. The garish colors reminded Nathan of unripened bananas.

At the far wall next to the room's lone window a husky man with balding head and trimmed beard puffed on a plastic-tipped cigar. Dress shirt, tie, gray slacks and polished shoes. Officer material, Nathan guessed.

The door to the inner office opened. Nathan's stomach tightened as the Vet Center counselor stepped from his office with a burly black dude.

"I'll see you next week," the counselor said as he and the man shook hands. He paused to pick up a file folder from the stack on the table beside the door.

"Victor Guerino?"

A wave of relief swept over Nathan as Officer Material stood up and crushed out his cigar and followed the counselor into the office. The door closed behind them. Nathan sighed. A reprieve. He'd been sure he was next. Shit, what was that guy's name? Geramio, Geronimo, something like that. Must be going in alphabetical order. Damn, I'm next for sure.

His stomach cramped and he fought back another wave of gas pains. Seventeen years since an NVA rocket cut short his tour of duty and his wounds still bothered him. They always would, but he'd been lucky, very lucky. That is, if spending several months in a hospital ward filled with abdominal injuries and surrounded by colostomies could be considered lucky. The ward had a smell all its own, like medicinal shit. Many a night he'd lay awake unable to sleep and listening to the grotesque serenade of groans, snores and liquidy farts emitted from over-expanded colostomy bags. But he was fortunate. He was fully functional again while many of his former ward mates would carry a bag with them to their grave.

From the reception room down the corridor came the rapid-fire *tap-tap-tapping* of an electric typewriter. A heavyset woman in her late thirties popped gum as her fingers flew over the keys. Sarah Potter was responsible for Nathan being here today. As secretary and part-time case worker at the county Veterans Service Office, she'd seized the opportunity to contact the Vet Center in Tallahassee, a hundred miles northeast. She convinced their staff of the need for an outreach counseling effort in Bay City. Then, like a mother hen, she'd rounded up several veterans to come in for interviews.

Nathan didn't want to be here. He was uneasy meeting new people, and besides, counseling was for psychos and he wasn't crazy. But Sarah was okay in his book. They had attended the same high school though she was a couple of grades ahead of him and he hadn't really known her well back then. But she did seem to care about vets and their problems, one of the few people Nathan knew who really gave a damn. So as a favor to Sarah he'd agreed to stop by.

"Nathan Henson?"

Nathan looked up to see Officer Material leaving the room and the counselor standing in the doorway. "Shit," he muttered as he stood and walked stiffly across the room. Thanks a lot, Sarah.

"I'm George Browne," the counselor said, shaking Nathan's hand and motioning for him to take a seat. "What can I do for you?"

Nathan slid the chair back several inches farther from the desk. He sat down and eyeballed the counselor for the first time. The young man's casual attire didn't match Nathan's idea of a shrink. Browne leaned back in the plush swivel chair and plopped his feet on the edge of the desk. The corduroy trousers and well-worn western boots sealed the deal. This wasn't the straight-laced authoritarian Nathan had expected.

"I heard there was some sort of a group for Vietnam veterans starting up. Figured I'd come by and check it out."

"I see," George said, stretching his arms upward and clasping his hands behind the long curly hair covering his neck. He rocked back and forth. "Do you feel you need to talk about Vietnam?"

"I don't know. I'm not one of those crazies you hear about that gets up on some building or tower and starts sniping at people. But I do think about it a lot."

"About sniping at people?"

Nathan laughed. "No, about Vietnam."

"Anything in particular?"

"What do you mean?"

"Are there any specific people or events you seem to think about more than others when you think about Vietnam? Any particular buddies, firefights, ambushes? Anything that stands out in your mind?"

Nathan frowned; he resented the intrusion. He tugged at his moustache and felt as though he were sitting on tacks. "Yeah, I lost some close friends over there. I think about it a lot. I mean, it's always there, you know?"

George nodded. He scribbled a few notes in the folder in his lap. "Give me a brief rundown of your military service. What branch you were in; were you drafted or did you join; when and where you served in Vietnam; your duties over there; how much combat you saw."

Nathan leaned forward and rested his arms on his thighs. "I joined the Marines right after high school. Actually it was a couple of months later. My parents wouldn't sign so I had to wait until I turned eighteen. After boot camp and infantry training they sent me to Camp Lejeune. They made me an office pogue." He forced a nervous laugh. "Can you believe that shit, an office pogue? Hell, I joined the Marines to fight, not to push pencils.

"Anyway, this buddy of mine from boot camp was stationed at Lejeune with me. He wanted the grunts too. We worked in the same office together and kept putting in requests for change of MOS to the infantry. It took a couple of months but we finally got orders for FMF WESPAC. That's Fleet Marine Force, Western Pacific. That meant an automatic free ticket across the big pond to Vietnam."

George stopped writing and took a sip of coffee. Nathan cracked his knuckles. "Go on," said George.

"We arrived in-country in October '67. I was assigned to Second Battalion, Fourth Marines. My buddy wound up with Two-Twenty-six. Those unlucky bastards caught all that incoming up at Khe Sanh a few months later during Tet.

"My outfit operated all along northern I CORP just below the DMZ. We saw our share of the shit, mostly against North Vietnamese regulars. The NVA were hard-core; they really had their shit together. Wasn't a bunch of rice farmers like a lot of people think. They were outstanding fighters.

"Anyway, I only lasted six months. I got hit in April and was medevacked to Japan. I spent a couple of months there and then they sent me back to the World." Nathan hesitated a few seconds. "That's about it."

George grabbed the pen again and wrote something else in

the folder and then looked up and smiled. "That's fine." He drummed the pen across a knee. "What we're planning here isn't some loose rap group where a bunch of vets sit around bullshitting each other with war stories. I'm looking for vets who are serious about wanting help, those who want to be part of a structured group and are willing to work hard on their problems. I think you're a good candidate, if you're interested."

Nathan frowned. He didn't relish conjuring up painful memories and old ghosts. He'd spent too many years trying to put the war behind him, trying to forget about the whole mess. But he was tired of the sleepless nights and the almost constant thoughts running through his mind like a bad never-ending newsreel. He took a deep breath and let it out. "Yeah, I'd like to give it a shot. I don't guess it'll hurt."

"Good," George said, "but I can't promise you it won't hurt." He stood up and extended his hand. I'll see you here next Friday then, three-o'clock sharp."

They shook hands. "I'll be here."

Nathan backed carefully from the parking space in front of the Veterans Service Office. There was just enough room for him to clear the cars parked on either side before cutting the wheel hard to avoid hitting the wall of an adjacent office building.

"The county really outdid itself with this parking lot," he said, shifting into first and turning onto Oak Street, "good thing I don't own a Cadillac."

The weak attempt at humor drew no response from his passenger.

Great, a stoic. Now Nathan wished he'd made up some excuse when Sarah cornered him and asked if he could wait around and give one of the other guys a ride home.

"Sure, be glad to," he'd said. It was a lie.

It turned out to be the man dressed in the unripened banana colors. Nathan had forgotten his name almost immediately after their awkward introduction. Why couldn't he just tell people "no" instead of worrying about hurting their feelings or disappointing them? Why was he always getting himself caught up in these uncomfortable situations?

Nathan stopped for the red light where Oak dead-ended at Bayview Drive. He looked left, then right, sizing up his passenger as he checked traffic. He turned right and headed west on Bayview. *Doesn't look unfriendly*, Nathan thought; *maybe he just didn't hear me. This old clunker's awful loud.*

"Mind if I smoke?" The gravelly voice was much deeper than Nathan thought should come from such a frail-looking body.

"No, go ahead," Nathan said. He shook his head when the man extended the pack of Kools. He hated cigarette smoke but didn't want to complicate matters. He was glad the guy had a least said something to ease the silence.

It had been an unusually cold winter for the Florida panhandle and the mild March breeze flowing through the van's windows felt good. Nathan watched a flight of pelicans gliding low over the glassy waters of St. Martin Bay. In the distance, near the gulf pass, sunlight cast a golden glow on the white bluffs of Hurricane Island. It was nearing low tide and shallow pools lay along the bay's shoreline like shards from a shattered mirror, reflecting the late afternoon sun. He remembered the happy times spent as a kid with his friends gliding over those same tidal flats on homemade skim boards.

"Who were you with in 'Nam?" Nathan said, feeling pressured to keep the meager conversation going. He'd already decided from the man's appearance that he was probably in supply or an office pogue. Air Force, he guessed.

From the corner of his eye Nathan glimpsed the thin, almost cadaverous face turn and blow a long stream of smoke out the window. "I was a Navy corpsman with Third Battalion, Third Marines."

Nathan was thunderstruck. *Corpsman; Third Marines?* He let the words sink in. "Three-Three? No shit? I was with Two-Four!"

The tenseness inside the van flew away as right arms lifted and fists clasped together.

"When were you there, Doc?" Nathan felt camaraderie growing like he'd known this former corpsman for years.

"November '67 through May '68." The drawn face had gained some color and the gray eyes seemed to come alive. "They sent me to Okinawa after my third purple heart."

"I'll be damned. We were there at the same time. I got there in October and medevacked out in April. Ain't that some shit?"

A horn blared. Nathan was so mesmerized by the conversation and his racing thoughts that the van had drifted across the center line. He jerked the wheel and brought the VW back into the proper lane.

"Three-Three. Weren't you up around Con Thien?"

"Alpha-Three mostly," Doc said, "and Gio Linh. We operated all along the Trace."

Nathan nodded. "MacNamara's famous line. Dumbass politicians really believed that plowing a few hundred meters of ground was gonna keep the gooks from coming south. Can you believe that shit?"

He braked for a car turning ahead. "Then you were in on Operation Kentucky and Lancaster." He shot Doc a big grin. "Real fun time."

He slowed for the sharp curve where Bayview Drive ended and became Bedford Avenue, and then down-shifted to second gear. The four-cylinder engine strained to climb the steep hill that led inland.

"My company lost a lot of men during Operation Kentucky," Doc said. "Damn near my entire platoon."

Nathan's mind drifted. Kentucky had been a bitch but Napoleon-Saline was even worse—the frontal assaults day after day against fortified villages; the pounding from enemy artillery and rockets; the night they were overrun by hordes of NVA.

He snapped back to the present. "I don't remember exactly where Sarah said you live."

"Straight for a few more blocks and then turn right on Eighteenth Street. Third house on the right."

Nathan pulled into the driveway of a small red brick house with white trim. The yard was well-tended, he noted, with several ornamental bushes and flower gardens. A hedge of mixed azaleas was in full bloom. The winter lawn had a smattering of green patches. At the far end of the drive a lone citrus tree stood naked in death, victim of the cold winter.

Doc opened the door and climbed out of the van. "I appreciate the ride, Nathan," he said, using Nathan's name for the first time.

"No sweat. Uh, I can't remember your name. My short term memory's about shot. Too many cold ones," Nathan said, grinning.

"Dan Matthews." He extended his hand through the window.

"Semper Fi," Nathan said as they shook hands. "Hey Doc," he called as he backed into the street, "be glad to give you a ride next week if you need one."

Dan signaled thumbs-up. Nathan waved as he coaxed the old VW into low and drove away, unaware of the smile spread across his face. It had been a long time since he'd made a friend.

Doc grabbed the entrenching tool and dug furiously. Grimy sweat ran down his face in muddy rivulets. His eyes burned in the darkness; his mouth and ears were packed with dirt. Silent screams stabbed his brain.

He tunneled like a madman; earth flew in great showers from the e-tool. The faster he dug the quicker the hole filled again. He tried screaming for help to the shadowy figures surrounding him but the mouthful of dirt strangled his cry. Accusing fingers pointed at him from the black night.

Suddenly he noticed the shovel had no blade. He flung the useless handle away and began scratching and clawing at the unyielding earth with bloody fingers.

Finally the earth gave way to timbers and the timbers to the rough weave of sandbags piled like rubble from a demolished building. Frantically he heaved sandbag after sandbag from the pit.

"Guilty!" screamed the silent voices. "Guilty!" echoed the pointing accusers encircling him.

He reached the last sandbag and with great effort lifted it from the hole. He groped desperately into the void. His hand touched something. He clutched it and pulled it from the abyss and prayed he was not too late.

"Guilty!" shouted the skull filling his hand; it leered at him with hollow eye sockets, its jaws locked in a hideous grin. "Guilty! Guilty! Guilty!". . .

He bolted upright in bed and gasped for breath, his pulse racing. The twisted sheets were soaked with sweat. His hand fumbled across the night stand and knocked a stack of paperbacks to the floor. He found the pack of cigarettes and with trembling hands lit one, inhaling deeply and blowing clouds of smoke into the darkness.

After a while he switched on the lamp and searched the drawer of the night stand. He found the bottle and twisted off the cap and downed four red and gray capsules with the dregs of a warm beer. He lit another cigarette and turned out the light and lay back staring into the darkness.

Dan Matthews would sleep no more this night.

# CHAPTER FOUR

THE PHONE WAS ringing. Nathan opened his eyes and squinted at the alarm clock. Nine o'clock. He started to sit up and then eased his head back on the pillow.

"Oh, shit." His head ached and his stomach churned and his mouth was dry.

The phone kept ringing. He rolled over and sat on the edge of the bed. Through bloodshot eyes he saw he'd already shut off the alarm set for six-thirty. He limped down the hall into the kitchen; the worn linoleum was cold beneath his bare feet. Empty beer cans littered the table.

He grabbed the receiver and reached for the coffee pot. "Hello," he muttered while rinsing day-old coffee grounds down the sink.

"Did I wake you up?" It was his mother with her usual greeting if the phone rang more than once, day or night.

He cringed; he didn't want to give her the satisfaction of catching him asleep, and he dreaded the family gossip he knew was coming. "No, I was outside working on my van."

"I was just calling to see if you were still alive," she said. "I haven't heard from you since I don't know when."

Nathan spooned fresh grounds into the pot and added water and turned on the burner. "Yeah, I'm still kicking. Been real busy working."

"Eddie and Sue are still having their problems. I loaned them the money to finish paying off that hospital bill. I'll probably never see any of it again though, not the way Sue squanders money. That girl is spoiled rotten if you ask me. She can't fix regular meals like normal people. She's always buying that prepared junk."

Nathan rinsed out a coffee cup while his mother rambled.

"I do believe your brother is losing weight. You'd think Sue's mother would have at least taught her how to cook. And those diapers; she won't hear of using cloth diapers like people used to use. I'll bet she spends twenty or thirty dollars a week on those throwaway things. That's just good money down the drain if you ask me. She could buy a couple of dozen cloth diapers for what she spends a week on those plastic things and never have to buy any more. But will she listen to me? No, and your brother doesn't have enough backbone to stand up to her and put his foot down. He lets that girl walk all over him if you ask me."

"That's nice," Nathan mumbled, bored and only half listening. He stared at the clock in the stove panel. Ten after ten. He hadn't bothered to set it back last fall for standard time. No need bothering now, he decided, it would be correct again in a few weeks anyway.

"That little Eddie Junior is just the cutest thing you ever saw," his mother said. "He's growing like a weed and already has two teeth."

Who gives a shit? The coffee was beginning to perk.

"Looks just like his daddy did when he was a baby . . ."

Must have ears like Dumbo the elephant.

". . . a real joy, but oh Lord, what a responsibility being a parent is . . ."

Better him than me.

His mother droned on for several more minutes, bringing Nathan up to date on all the latest family news. He was well into his second cup of coffee when she abruptly changed the subject.

"Guess who came by to see me yesterday?"

"The Pope?" It was a pointless conversation and Nathan was in no mood for guessing games.

"You shouldn't be making fun of religion like that," she said "and besides, you know good and well we're not Catholic."

"Sorry. Billy Graham?"

"Nathan Henson! You better watch your tongue. You know what the Bible says about mockers. No, it was Tommy Carter."

The name seared him like a branding iron.

"He said that Jennifer will be graduating this year. Can you believe that; little Jennifer a senior? Why, it seems like just yesterday that she was—"

"I really don't give a damn what he had to say. Listen, I gotta go; I was changing the oil in the van and I'm expecting a call about a job any minute now."

"Oh, son, can't you find it in your heart to forgive them? All that happened so long ago. You and Tommy used to be such good friends."

"God's in the forgiving business, not me," Nathan said and slammed down the receiver.

Tom Carter this and Tom Carter that! His arm lashed out and beer cans flew in a dozen directions.

Emma Matthews tapped lightly on the door. There was no response. She tried again a little harder. Still no answer. She opened the door quietly and peeked in. Sunlight filtered through the partially closed blinds and cast zebra patterns across the floor and over the bed. Colorful posters and maps covered the walls. Fighter planes from four wars hung from the ceiling, suspended in mock dogfights. Mounds of books and magazines littered the furniture and dirty clothes lay everywhere. It was a child's room.

She touched the bare shoulder and gave it a nudge. "Daniel? Wake up, dear."

"Huh? What is it?"

"You have a phone call."

"Tell whoever it is I'll call back later." He rolled onto his side and pulled the covers over his head.

"It's long distance, dear; it's Linda."

Dan winced beneath the covers. "Oh hell, I can't talk to her now. Tell her I'm sick or I'm not here."

"But Daniel, you can't keep avoiding her like this. I can't keep making excuses. She really needs to talk to you."

"I just got to sleep. Tell her I'll get back to her later, okay?"

"All right then. I'll tell her you'll call tonight." Emma Matthews patted her son's shoulder and turned and walked toward the door.

"Mother?"

"Yes?"

"Close those blinds before you leave, will you?"

"Yes, dear."


Nathan was restless. He had intended to drive up to the dam and try for speckled trout on the morning tide but oversleeping blew that. There was nothing on television except the usual Saturday morning offering of kiddy drivel. Football was over and baseball was still a month away. Another hunting season was past and it was too cold for swimming. To Nathan, March was a limbo filled with nothing but boredom and bad memories.

His stomach rumbled. He'd had a twelve-pack for supper the night before and now his belly demanded something more substantial. He opened the kitchen cabinet and stared at the mountain of canned goods. His VA check had come last week and he'd restocked his cupboard.

It was a ritual he performed every month. One time in Vietnam his company had been surrounded and pinned down for several days. Their rations soon ran out and bad weather combined with intense enemy fire made resupply impossible. Hunger finally drove some of the Marines to sample immature bananas from the trees scattered throughout their position. It was like eating unripened persimmons and those who managed to swallow soon fell victim to stomach cramps. Nathan swore to himself then that if he made it back to the World alive he'd never go hungry again. It was a vow he kept religiously.

He opened a can of chili with beans and spooned it into a pot and turned on the gas burner. Through the window above the sink he saw Mrs. Ard hanging wash on the clothesline in her back yard. She was portly with stooped shoulders but still rather spry for a woman nearing eighty. Her round face was lined and speckled with age spots and her silver hair was pinned back in a tight bun. She wore one of her usual sack dresses and open-heeled slippers. Clarence alternately rubbed against her stout legs and the big wicker basket of damp laundry. In Nathan's mind Mrs. Ard hadn't changed in the twenty-five years since he first delivered newspapers to her house as a boy.

While stirring the chili he remembered he hadn't paid the month's rent. He started to raise the window but Mrs. Ard was already disappearing around the corner of the house with Clarence at her heels. Nathan pulled five twenties from his wallet and placed them on the counter. He set his keys on top of the bills and sat down to eat. He added Tabasco sauce to the chili and glanced at a pamphlet he'd picked up from the Veterans Service Office after his interview. On the cover a soldier in combat gear shouldered an M-60 machine and waded through a rice paddy. The booklet was entitled: POST TRAUMATIC STRESS DISORDER AND THE VIETNAM VETERAN.

He flipped through a few pages and laid it aside. Already he was having second thoughts about getting involved in the group. He'd gotten along just fine by himself all these years and wasn't looking forward to meeting a bunch of strangers and listening to their sob stories. Yeah, he'd promised Sarah, but what the hell? She'd get over it.

Nathan thought about Dan Matthews. The few minutes they'd spent together had rekindled a sense of camaraderie and belonging he'd almost forgotten existed. Maybe this group thing wouldn't be too bad if Doc was going to be there.

He finished the chili and put the dirty bowl and spoon in the sink and grabbed his keys and the rent money. He'd give it a few days before making a decision about the group. Right now there was rent to pay and beer to buy.

# CHAPTER FIVE

THE FOLLOWING FRIDAY Nathan drove to the Veterans Service Office for his first group meeting. He arrived a few minutes early, apprehensive but looking forward to seeing Dan Matthews again. In the reception room Nathan saw George Browne standing near Sarah's desk. He was flipping through a folder and looked up and nodded. Nathan returned the greeting.

"Back room," Sarah said as he walked past them and down the hall.

Inside the meeting room several chairs were arranged in a semi-circle before a desk. Dust particles danced in the sunlight streaming through the room's lone window. Nathan grabbed a chair and positioned it so his back was to the wall and away from the window.

A portable blackboard stood next to the desk. COMMON SYMPTOMS OF PTSD was printed in large letters. Nathan scanned the board. Been there, done that, he thought. He checked his watch. Almost three. He'd better not be the only one to show up.

Footsteps clicked in the hallway. Nathan glanced up, hoping it was Dan Matthews. Officer Material stepped through the doorway and glanced around the room. He was dressed the same as before except a blue patterned tie and socks replaced last week's red. He appeared tense and was puffing a small cigar.

"Oh, hi," he said when he finally noticed Nathan. "I didn't

see you sitting there." He offered his hand. "Vic Guerino."

"Nathan Henson." Vic's grip was firm and his voice seemed friendly enough.

A few seconds passed as Nathan searched for something to say. "What outfit were you with in 'Nam?" he said, choosing the obvious but safe common ground to build the conversation.

"Army. I flew slicks."

"Slicks . . . what are slicks?"

Vic arched his bushy brows. "You must not be Army. Slicks are Hueys. We carried troops and supplies, 'Ass and Trash.' We inserted troops into landing zones, extracted them, carried supplies and ammo, whatever the brass handed down."

"Nathan nodded. "I was a grunt in the Marines. The only Hueys we had were gun ships. We flew mostly in UH-34s, sometimes Sea Knights. Most of the time we just humped."

"Those old '34s were around during Korea, I think," Vic said. "Good birds in their day, but I'm glad we didn't have to fly 'em. Seems like you Marines always got the leftover junk."

Nathan was relieved by Vic's easy-going manner, but he knew pilots were officers and it felt strange talking to an officer on equal terms. "You were an officer, right?"

Vic blew a bluish cloud of smoke into the air and laughed. "Yeah, Well, sort of. I was a Wobbly-One."

"A what?"

"A warrant officer, WO-1. The bastard rank. Commissioned officers looked down on us like we were second-class citizens and enlisted men despised us like any other officers."

Nathan laughed just as Dan Matthews walked in. He stood to greet him and was grateful for a third party to join the conversation. "Doc, how's it going?"

Dan looked drawn and his eyes seemed slightly unfocused. "Hell, I never felt this good when I was alive." He and Vic exchanged introductions.

"Ol' Vic here was a chopper pilot with the Army," Nathan said. "A real live semi-officer flyboy. Reckon we ought to salute him?" He nudged Dan in the ribs with an elbow.

Vic grinned. "Yeah, you lowly peons show some proper respect here. And while you're at it, my shoes could use a little spit-shine."

All three burst out laughing. This crap might not be so bad after all, Nathan decided.

It was happy hour at the PUB 'N CUE. Nathan, Dan and Vic sat at a corner table working on their third pitcher of beer. At one of the pool tables in the center of the barroom a husky biker with a bushy beard and ponytail lined up a break-shot. His leather vest nearly covered the end of the table. The cue shot forward and sent a white blur crashing into the triangle of striped and solid balls. From a jukebox Hank Williams Junior extolled the virtues of Texas women. Clouds of cigarette smoke hung in layers over the room and reflected a rainbow of fluorescent bar lights.

Nathan emptied his mug again. He grabbed the pitcher and poured and watched as the golden liquid explode into white foam up and over the rim of the mug. "Aw, shit." He leaned over and slurped spilled beer off the table and looked up and grinned. "Waste not, want not," he said and laughed at his own joke. He was feeling no pain.

While Vic visited the men's room and Dan went to feed the jukebox, Nathan's thoughts drifted back to the meeting that afternoon. . . .

All-in-all things had gone okay. First, George Browne reintroduced himself to the group and thanked them for showing up. He gave a quick rundown on the history of the VA's Vet Center Program and then laid out a few guidelines for the group.

"There's just a couple of rules we have to agree to," he said, "but they're important ones. First, nobody shows up under the influence. If anybody comes to group messed up on booze or drugs you're out of here for that meeting. If it happens again you're gone for good. Agreed?"

Everybody agreed.

He lit a Marlboro. "Rule number two. Anything and everything that's said or done inside these walls stays inside these walls, understood? I don't mean you can't discuss things among yourselves outside the group. But I do mean we have to have absolute confidentiality. Nobody says anything to anybody outside the group about what goes down in here." He paused and made eye contact with everyone in the room. "If we can't trust each other then we don't need to be here. Clear?"

To Nathan it was crystal clear. Trust? Sounds like this guy's got his head and ass wired together. I haven't heard this shit since the 'Nam.

George then asked each of them to give a brief biographical summary. By way of example, George gave the group a brief sketch of his background. Born and raised in Arkansas, his was a typical small town beginning. He was an average student who was active in sports and had been somewhat of a hell-raiser through high school. A draft notice in 1970 prompted him to join the Navy. He served in the Mekong Delta during '71 and '72 as part of a naval advisory group. The war was winding down as far as America's involvement in that area and he'd seen little actual combat. After being discharged he entered college to study psychology and social sciences. He hired on with the Vet Center Program while still in school and became a full-time counselor after graduation.

Nathan was too busy formulating his own bio to remember much of what any of the group members revealed about themselves. The black dude's name was Andrew or Andrews; Nathan wasn't sure if it was his first or last name. Vic was married and had moved to Bay City from somewhere in Alabama. He'd worked as a pilot for a small airline but was now selling insurance. Dan was divorced and had flunked out of college or medical school, Nathan couldn't remember which, and now worked at the local hospital as a lab technician.

Nathan hadn't seen Rene Boudreaux before. He was short

and wiry with a dark complexion and deep-set eyes. His black hair was frosted with gray and matched a bushy moustache and eyebrows. His nose was large and hooked and Nathan couldn't help thinking of costume horn-rimmed glasses with the attached fake nose. He wore ragged jeans and a faded flannel shirt and despite the cool weather he was barefoot. He seemed withdrawn but George had managed to coax out that he'd been in the Army and served as team leader in a LRRP unit—Long Range Reconnaissance Patrol.

Nathan was the last to speak. He covered his thirty-six years in a few awkward minutes.

"I grew up here in the Bay City area," he said, his voice a little shaky. "I played a lot of baseball and football and joined the Marines right out of high school. I thought it was the right thing to do at the time, go fight for your country and all that patriotic John Wayne crap."

He paused and took a breath. "I got to Vietnam in late '67. I was a grunt." He paused again and fidgeted in his chair. "We operated up north mostly against the NVA. We really hit the shit during Tet."

He glanced out the window and wished he hadn't come to the meeting. "In April I got hit three times in one day." He gave a nervous laugh. "Guess it just wasn't my day. They medevacked me to Japan. I spent a couple of months there and then they sent me back to the World to the naval hospital in Pensacola."

He rambled on for a few minutes, recalling how after the service he'd grown his hair down to his shoulders and spent a year traveling and camping in his Volkswagen van. He had wound up in California writing songs and playing guitar in a band that went nowhere.

"Then I moved back here and tried college for a couple of semesters. Thought I might be a park ranger or a journalist or whatever. I did okay for a while but then I started screwing up and wound up dropping out. I don't know. I just didn't seem to fit in. It was like I didn't belong. I felt like I was twenty years older than the rest of the students.

"After that I worked on fishing boats and painted houses and swung a hammer for a while. Then a few years ago I started my own lawn care business. . . ."

Something white flashed before Nathan's eyes and snapped him back to the present. He looked up to see the attractive young barmaid wiping the table. She wore tight jeans that made her shapely legs and rear look as though they were cast from a denim mold. The top three buttons of her western blouse were undone and when she leaned over he saw she was braless. His groin ached. It had been months since he'd been with a woman.

"Keep the change," Vic said, handing the waitress a ten dollar bill after she placed a full pitcher and three fresh frosted mugs on the table.

"Why thank you, hon," she said in a heavy southern twang. Her red-painted lips spread in a wide smile. "Thank you so much."

The three half-looped vets stared transfixed as she sashayed across the room and behind the bar.

Vic broke the silence. "Oh, man." He smacked his lips. "If I wasn't married I'd—"

"A perfectly poetic posterior," Dan said, "an absolutely astounding anatomical attachment."

"Five dollars?" Nathan said. He was well on his way to being sloppy drunk. He leaned across the table and eyeballed Vic. "You gave that broad a five dollar tip! Christ on a crutch, there ain't no pussy on the face of this earth's worth a five-dollar tip."

"You dumb grunts don't know anything about women," Vic said. He took another swallow of beer and puffed on his cigar. "Trouble is, all that damn ground pounding has messed up your sense of reasoning. Now, us officers and gentlemen know how to handle women. You treat 'em right now and they'll treat you right later. Sure I tipped her a five-spot, but there's no telling what kind of return my five buck investment might bring in the future."

Nathan took a big swig from his mug. "You hear this shit, Doc?" He snorted and stared across the table at Dan who was singing along with George Jones about how if the drinking didn't kill him his memories would. "Ol' flyboy here thinks that broad is all impressed 'cause he just laid a five spot on her. Shit. And he thinks we done lost all our powers of reasoning.

"Tell you what Mr. Geronimo, sir," Nathan said, flicking Vic a middle-finger salute. "I reason I'll give her five dollars, too—if she'll promise to come over here and squat on my face!"

Dan and Nathan pounded the table and roared with laughter.

Vic shook his head. "You two a-holes are totally uncouth." Then he broke up and howled with them.

# CHAPTER SIX

NATHAN KEPT BUSY the following week contracting with several homeowners and businesses for his lawn care service, and by Friday his work schedule for the spring and summer was close to full. That afternoon he drove to the counseling session feeling good about what he'd accomplished and looking forward to seeing Dan and Vic.

"Today's subject is first impressions about Vietnam," George Browne said to open the meeting. "I want to know what it was like when you first arrived in-country. What you saw, the sounds, the smells, the people. What were your first impressions?" He looked from face to face. "Anybody? Nathan, how about you?"

Nathan's pulse quickened. He fumbled with his coffee cup. Shit, I knew I should've gone first last time, he thought. Might as well get it over with.

He glanced out the window and then back at George. "It was dark when we landed so there really wasn't much to see." He looked up at the ceiling as though he'd find a script written there. "We flew into Danang on a commercial jet. I remember thinking it was weird going to war in an airliner. My old man was a Marine during World War Two and he'd told me all about how they were crammed like sardines in troop transport ships for weeks, and how the trip over was just about as bad as the actual combat, and here I was, going to war aboard a commercial airliner." He paused, searching for words.

"On the flight over from Okinawa everybody was talking and joking around with the stewardesses and shit like that. But when we landed it was like a funeral parlor. We sat there a few minutes staring out the windows and wondering if the gooks were somewhere out there watching us. Then we got the word to disembark.

"When I stepped out the door I half expected to get shot at by a sniper or hear mortar rounds going off, but it was mostly just quiet. You could feel the heat and humidity. It wasn't as bad as I'd expected, but this was in October and we were in northern I CORPS. After being inside that air conditioned plane for so long the air felt heavy and it was hard to get a good breath. It stunk like diesel fumes." He paused again and glanced around. Probably boring the shit out of 'em, he thought.

"Go on," George said.

Nathan took a sip of tepid coffee. "Once we got off the plane we grabbed our sea bags and headed for these big Quonset huts for processing. On the way we passed this long line of guys waiting to board the plane we'd just flown in on. Now that was weird; the same plane that delivered us to Vietnam was going to be their freedom bird back to the World. Some of 'em were hooting and hollering and saying shit like, 'You'll be sorry,' and 'No sweat newbies, you've only got thirteen months to go.' Man, I wanted to turn around right then and get back on that plane." He looked at George. "You want me to go on?"

George finished lighting a cigarette. "Did anyone ask you to stop?"

Nathan shrugged. "Okay. So we filed into this Quonset hut and it was the usual hurry-up-and-wait while they processed us in and we got our orders. I can picture it like it was yesterday. I guess it's because it was so unlike the rest of my in-country experience. Everybody was clean and squared-away and looking like barracks Marines in our stateside utilities. Wasn't long before that scene changed."

Nathan glanced at George again. "You sure you want me to keep going? I'm probably boring the hell out of everybody."

Vic grinned. "You're not boring me. How about you guys?"

"He's got me on the edge of my seat," Dan said.

Nathan flicked Dan a one-finger salute. "Up yours."

"You're doing fine," George said, "keep going."

Nathan let out a breath. "Okay, so we'd just gotten our orders. The reason that sticks out in my mind is because that's when me and my buddy Brimley got separated. We'd been together since boot camp and we were really tight.

"I opened my orders and saw I was going to Two-Four. That's Second Battalion, Fourth Marines. When Brimley said he was assigned to Two-Twenty-six, man, I just felt lost. It was like the whole place suddenly changed."

He hesitated and looked around the room. His words seemed to have struck a chord of recognition with the others. They looked at him as though remembering their own sense of feeling lost or helpless when first arriving in-country. Only Rene Boudreaux seemed indifferent. He stared at the wall as though he were in another place or time.

"I felt like an orphan," Nathan said. "I couldn't imagine how I was going to get along without Brimley. We'd been together done everything together since boot camp. He was like my security blanket.

"A couple of hours later Brimley shipped out. It was just after daylight. I remember standing there in this big crowd of Marines ten thousand miles from home in a strange place where strange people would soon be trying to kill me and my only friend was gone. Man, that's a lonely feeling." For a moment Nathan was back in that long ago steamy Asian dawn.

"But I'm glad now that we didn't wind up in the same outfit. If Brimley had been with me he probably would've gotten his ass zapped." He paused and smiled. "Lucky bastard. He was at Khe Sanh during Tet. Made it through his whole tour with just a little shrapnel wound. I ran into him at Camp Lejeune after I got out of the hospital. We were going to get together and have a few beers and make plans to keep in touch and all that shit. Never did, though." Nathan breathed a sigh of relief. "That's about it."

"Good job," George said. "Who wants to go next?"

There was an uneasy pause as eyes flashed about the room, avoiding contact. The air conditioner clicked on and swirled the thin haze of smoke hovering near the ceiling. Nathan tilted his chair back against the wall and enjoyed the fresh air blowing from the overhead vents.

". . . it was the bodies." The voice was barely audible.

"Speak a little louder, Andrew," George said to the husky black man who sat hunched over with his arms resting on thighs; his hands were clasped as though in prayer.

Andrew hesitated a few seconds and then looked up. "I said I guess what I remember most when I first got there was all them bodies."

He hesitated again.

"Tell us about it," George said.

Some of the color seemed to drain from the dark face. "I don't remember nothin about gettin to my unit or nothin like that. It was like I just woke up and I was there, and they was all these bodies layin stretched out in rows. Some of them was covered up with ponchos, but some of them was just layin there like they was starin up at the sky."

"How did you feel seeing all those men lying there?" George said.

"Don't remember. Bad, I reckon."

"Do you remember what was going through your mind at the time?"

Andrew hesitated and stared at the floor; his fingers were twitching. "I was thinkin somethin like, 'Wow, this is real! And it ain't nothin like they taught us in trainin.' And I was thinkin that they was a good chance that I could die over here. Like, if all them troops could be dead, I could be too." He pulled a pack of Newports from his shirt pocket and tapped one out with shaky hands. He fumbled in another pocket for a light. George passed him his lighter. Andrew lit the cigarette and exhaled a cloud of smoke.

"They was all these dust-off choppers that kept flyin in, one after the other, like they was playin follow-the-leader. They was all loaded down with bodies. Some of 'em had wounded on board and these medics kept screamin at us new guys. We was carryin ponchos and stretchers and layin the wounded in this one place and they had us puttin the dead guys in another place."

Andrew stopped. He leaned back and staring at the wall and took a deliberate breath. "We carried them bodies for . . . I don't know how long it was. Seemed like it was all day long. Them choppers just kept comin and comin. And them bodies, it seemed like they was no end to it. They just kept on pilin up."

Dan Matthews reached over and laid an arm across Andrew's broad shoulders. "Christ, that was one hell of an initiation. I know where you're coming from, bro. Being a corpsman I was trained to deal with situations like that. But for somebody new in-country to be thrown into circumstances like you described sounds like too much for anybody to handle."

Nathan was curious. "Where was this at, man?"

Andrew looked at him. "Don't know if y'all ever heard about it or not. Happened in November '65, place called the Ia Drang Valley."

Nathan had heard. Elements of the Army's First Cavalry Division had stumbled into a large force of North Vietnamese Army Regulars and were nearly wiped out before reinforcements were able to save them. Over three hundred Americans were killed during this first pitched battle with the NVA. He looked Andrew in the eye and nodded. "Yeah, I heard about it. That was some bad shit."

Andrew sucked in a breath. "I never did no actual fightin at Ia Drang. By the time they flew us out there it was mostly over with. But them bodies, I won't never forget that."

After Andrew finished the group took a ten-minute break.

Rene Boudreaux disappeared down the hall toward the restroom. The others gathered around the coffee maker in the small lounge. Nathan had learned to drink coffee black while in the Marines, and when he saw Dan and Vic dumping spoonful after spoonful of sugar and powdered creamer into their cups he couldn't resist:

"Jesus H. Christ, Doc, I thought only officers and pussies drank sweet-titty coffee."

"You uncivilized grunts could never figure out what that white stuff was for," Vic shot back.

"Low blood sugar," Dan said with a straight face.

Nathan wasn't sure if he was kidding or not.

"How about you, Andrew?" Nathan said. "You were a grunt. You doggies use cream and sugar in your coffee?"

Andrew held up the Pepsi he was drinking and grinned. "My mama told me never to drink coffee. Bad for your health."

Nathan shook his head. "Christ on a crutch, you people are hopeless."

# CHAPTER SEVEN

"PHONE CALL, DAN."

Dan Matthews glanced up from the microscope at Rick Simmons' bulky figure filling the doorway. "Be there in a minute; I have to finish up this blood count."

He looked back into the eyepiece and slightly adjusting the focus. His left hand eased the slide across the viewing field while the fingers of his right hand flew over the buttons of the cell counter. Then he pulled a pen from the breast pocket of his lab coat and jotted down the readings on a lab slip.

Dan got up and walked across the room and rubbed at the bright spots dancing before his eyes from the glare of the microscope. Carefully placing four test tubes filled with equal amounts of blood into the holding receptacles of a centrifuge, he switched on the machine. The high-pitched humming increased as he adjusted the dial to twenty-five hundred RPMs. After setting the timer for five minutes he walked down the hall to his office.

"Hello?" he said, cradling the receiver against his ear with a shoulder. He unzipped his lab coat and fished a pack of Kools from his shirt pocket.

"Dan, hi, it's Linda."

Damn! His mind began searching for excuses. "What's up? There's nothing wrong with Danny?"

"No, he's fine. We're all fine."

"That's good." Here it comes, he thought.

"I'm calling about the child support. I hate to bother you at work but it seems like you're never home when I try to reach you at your mother's."

There was a long silence. Dan blew a stream of smoke and inhaled again.

"Are you there?"

"Yeah. Sorry, I was jotting down a reading on some blood work-up before I forgot it. What were you saying?"

"I was wondering when you were going to send Danny's check. You're three months behind, you know."

"Three months? Are you sure? I thought it was only two," he said, trying to buy time while conjuring up a reasonable excuse.

"No, it's three. We really need the money. I realize Emma's operation set you back some but you know John's been laid up over a month now from his accident, and his workman's comp is all we have to live on right now. And with the new baby coming and Amy and Danny's tuition at school—"

"Why can't they go to public school like everybody else?" Dan was aggravated; he didn't care hear family news about someone else's family.

"You know how the public schools are nowadays," Linda said, "with all the drugs and violence. Besides, the public system hardly teaches kids anymore. There's no discipline and most of the teachers are inept."

"How does Danny like the chemistry set I sent for his birthday?" Dan said, hoping a change of subject might help.

"He loves it. Of course John hasn't had much chance to help him with it since he broke his leg, but Danny's just tickled to death with it."

Dan felt like he'd been slapped. He was tired of hearing about John. I should be the one helping my kid with his chemistry set, he thought, not that son-of-a-bitch.

Ten years had passed since Linda married John Waldrop and moved to Virginia. For a while Dan saw his son several times a year, but as time passed and circumstances changed, the frequency of the visits decreased. It had been nearly two years since he had last seen Danny.

"About the money; when do you think you'll be able to send something?"

"I intended to have it paid by now, but with Mother's hospital bills . . . and I totaled my car a couple of months ago. The insurance only paid eighteen hundred. I had to have wheels to get around."

"Were you hurt? Emma didn't mention anything about an accident."

"Some woman broadsided me. I got a few scratches and bruises, nothing serious. I missed a few days of work." He was lying about the accident, but Linda had always been an easy mark. The ruse might buy him a little more time.

"I know you well enough to know you're trying to keep Danny and me from worrying. Now tell me the truth, are you really okay?"

"I'm fine. All right, I spent a couple of days in the hospital, but the doctors say I'll be okay. I should regain full use of my arm if I keep up with therapy. You sure Mother didn't say anything to you? I told her not to."

"No, not a word. Don't worry; I won't say anything to her about it."

"Thanks Linda, I appreciate it. Listen, I get paid again next Friday. I'll try to send at least a payment and a half then and catch up the rest in a few weeks. Will that do for now?"

"That'll be fine. You sure it won't put you in too much of a bind?"

"I can make do. I need to get back to work. Tell John and Amy I said hello, and tell Danny his daddy loves him and hopes to come see him this summer."

"I'll be sure to. Give Emma my love."

"Will do."

"Vic, could I see you in my office a moment?"

Vic Guerino had been staring blankly at a policy for several minutes, daydreaming. Now he glanced up to see his boss standing in front of his desk. "Sure, Mr. Peterson. I'll be right with you." Sure dickhead, anything you say. He followed Will Peterson, branch manager of Gulf Central Insurance Company, down the hallway and into his spacious office.

Mr. Peterson sat behind a large oak desk and motioned for Vic to take a chair. On the wall behind him a sailfish arched in full flare; the blues and silvers of the six-foot body glowed in under the room's lighting as though it were yet trying to throw the hook.

Peterson flipped through a folder. "Vic, you've been with us now, let's see, about six months isn't it?"

"Yes sir, since October." He cringed. Sir, my ass! I was an aircraft commander in Vietnam when this dipshit was still in high school trying to chase down his first piece of tail.

Peterson looked through the folder and rubbed his chin. "Hmm. You seem to have done quite well for the first couple of months but it looks like things have fallen off a bit lately." He stared across the desk. "How do you account for that?"

Vic squirmed and sweat popped out along his brow. Sure, he'd done okay for a while. It was a cinch to persuade most of his relatives and friends to change companies and buy policies of one type or another from him. But he'd soon run out of personal contacts. He found it hard to talk to people about buying something so intangible as insurance. It was easy enough to bilk an occasional newlywed couple into purchasing a policy they really couldn't afford yet, or convince beaming grandparents to invest in a policy that could be converted later to finance a college education for their new grandchild. But there were only so many of those types to go around. And besides, he just couldn't manage to get excited about the insurance business. If the truth be known, it was damn boring. It certainly wasn't like flying. There was nothing on earth like flying.

"I don't know, Mr. Peterson, I guess I've been in a little slump lately."

"A little slump? Your records show you haven't met your quota for the last three months and you haven't made a single sale in six weeks. That's a bit more than a 'little slump,' as you put it." His voice was cold and stern like a teacher reprimanding a delinquent student.

Vic flushed. His temples throbbed and his nostrils flared. Why am I letting this pipsqueak son-of-a-bitch talk to me like that, he thought. I ought to jerk that scrawny motherfucker across the desk and beat the living shit out of him! "I wrote a policy just this morning that I'm sure I'll have finalized by Wednesday. And I've got several other prospects in the works." His voice was shaky and apologetic. The sound of it disgusted him.

"Mr. Larrimore tells me your hours have been erratic," Peterson said, ignoring Vic's explanation. "He says you're habitually late in the morning, and that, quite frankly, your sales don't justify the hours you supposedly spend in the field with prospective clients."

"What do you want me to say?" Vic said. He was tired of this beating-around-the-bush bullshit. "I've been trying. This is all new to me. When you've been doing one thing that you love for almost twenty years and then suddenly you're told you can't do it anymore, it's just not that easy to adjust to something else overnight. It's not like changing clothes or—"

"Six months isn't exactly overnight. We've had many people who've changed careers come to work for us and turn out quite successfully. To be honest with you Vic, Gulf Central is a progressive and vibrant company. We need go-getters, not dead weight. The bottom line is, if there's not a marked improvement in your performance by the end of the month we'll be forced to let you go."

Vic sat still for several seconds trying to compose himself. He gripped the arms of the chair so tightly his fingers grew white and his jaw was clenched so hard it ached. He took several deep breaths and then stood and pointed across the desk.

"Hey Peterson," he said, his voice deliberate and controlled, "go fuck yourself!"

Karen Guerino set the bag of groceries on the table and stared incredulously at her husband. "What do you mean, you quit your job?"

"I mean I no longer work for Gulf Central Insurance Company. What the hell do you think I mean?"

"Kendra, go out back and play honey," Karen said to the fidgeting four-year-old she'd just picked up from daycare. "Mommy and Daddy have to talk."

"How could you?" she said after their daughter closed the back door. "You know what that job means to us. Do you think our bills are just going to magically disappear? How are we supposed to make the house payment?" She slumped into a chair; her face was pale and she close to tears.

Vic stared out the window at his daughter playing on the swing set in the back yard. Her long brown hair nearly brushed the ground as she leaned back in the seat and pulled and kicked herself higher and higher. He turned to his wife.

"They were going to fire me anyway. I saved them the trouble."

"Fire you? Fire you for what?" Karen said, her voice trembling. She lit a cigarette.

"Peterson is a son-of-a-bitch," Vic said. "That whole office is full of assholes."

Karen slapped the table. "Everyone's a son-of-a-bitch according to you! It's the same everywhere you go—the whole world is full of assholes." Tears streamed down her face and smeared her mascara. "It's been the same ever since you were grounded. Why can't you ever get along with anyone you try to work for? Why can't you learn to take orders like everybody else?"

"I tried honey, I really did." He reached out to hold her but she shrugged away. "That Joe Larrimore kept getting on my case and filling Peterson's ears full of shit. I can only take so much."

Karen looked up and wiped her face with the back of a hand. She took a quick drag on the cigarette. "*You* can only take so much? What about me, what about the kids? How much of this crap are we supposed to take? I'm working and scrimping, trying to put food on the table and take care of two kids and a house, and you can't handle it when somebody tells you what to do. No, you just quit!"

She stood and stared out the kitchen window with her arms hugging her chest. After a moment she turned to face her husband. "This isn't Vietnam. You're not a hotshot pilot flying helicopters anymore, Vic. This is the real world. You're not God. Vietnam is over, flying is over; you hear me, over! Why don't you face up to it and start acting like a man for once? Just how are we supposed to live?"

The words stung. "I'll tell you how we're supposed to live," Vic shouted. "By drawing the goddamned money out of savings to pay the bills like I've been doing for the last six months!"

The blood drained from Karen's face. She leaned back against the counter. "You've been using our savings?"

"That's right," he said, pouring a drink from the bottle of Wild Turkey he'd grabbed from a cabinet. "I haven't made enough money from that fucking job you insisted I take to even meet my expenses."

"How much is left?" she said weakly.

"I don't know, a couple of hundred or so. Don't worry about it, I'll find something soon."

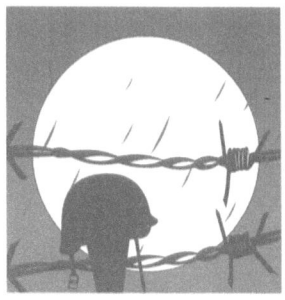

# CHAPTER EIGHT

IT HAD RAINED steadily for three days because of a low pressure system brewing a few miles offshore in the Gulf of Mexico. To Rene Boudreaux it was the monsoon. He sat inside the crude cabin and stared through the only window at the gloom. Low clouds fluttered like shredded curtains from nature's ceiling, and the normally aqua waters of Mashburn Lake had turned pallor gray. Sand pines and cedars ringed the lake like an ominous black wall. It was a world of dreary monotone where indifference reigned; a place like all the places Rene had existed for the past twenty years.

A brilliant white flash cut the darkness as lightning ripped a nearby tree. The thunderclap rattled the window and shook the cabin's thin walls and echoed across the lake.

"C'est la vie," Rene muttered, the same saying his grandmother would use when confronted with something over which she had no control. It was Friday but there was no way he could make the meeting. The day before, after tending his marijuana patch, he'd checked the abandoned logging road and nearly got his battered Chevy pickup stuck twice before covering a third of the distance to the highway. It would be several days before the rutted road was passable, if the rain stopped soon. He smiled and rolled another joint.

"It happened on my first combat assault." Vic Guerino snapped his lighter shut and slipped it back in his pocket. The group's topic for the week was initial combat actions and he was the first to speak. "It was my second or third day in-country. I'm pretty sure it was my second day. We got there at night and saw a gunship go down. The next morning the squadron commander held a briefing and they had the 'dink of the week' laying out there and—"

"You told us all that last week," George said. "We're concentrating on first actions today."

"Oh yeah, right," Vic tapped cigar ash into an empty Styrofoam cup. "Anyway, we got our gear and had our checkout flight and the next morning I flew as co-pilot with this guy we called J.J." Distant thunder boomed like the faraway report of howitzers. The afternoon was dark as dusk. "J.J. had been there a long time and was due to rotate home in a couple of weeks. Real cool guy, but crazy as hell. He used to buy drinks for the house all the time at the O' club. When he wasn't flying he was usually shit-faced."

"First actions," George said. "Let's stay focused on the topic and save the sea stories for your own time."

"First actions, right. Okay, so we got up that morning at early-thirty. It was still dark when we got to the flight pad for pre-flights. The crew chief and door gunner were walking around the bird rubbing their hands all over the fuselage. I didn't know what the hell they were up to—we never did anything like that during pre-flights at Fort Rucker—so I asked 'em what they were doing. The crew chief stared at me like I was some sort of dumb fuck and said they were checking for shrapnel holes from last night's mortar attack. Oh, did I mention last week that the VC hit us with mortars the first night?"

"Yeah, don't you remember?" Nathan said, winking at Dan. "Poor baby had to leave his nice warm bunk and clean sheets and run all the way to the bunker in the dark."

Dan snickered.

"Up yours," Vic said. "You ground-pounders are just jealous."

George laughed. "All right, let him continue. We need to at

least get Vic into the chopper before our time is up." He was glad to see the interplay between these three. It was a sign they were beginning to bond, but it needed to be kept in check.

He glanced at his watch. The heavy rains had caused him to be late and his daughter's dance recital began at seven. If he'd known the weather was going to stay like this and Andrew and Rene weren't going to show he'd have canceled. "Go ahead. You're at the chopper."

"Yeah. So everything checked out okay. We're sitting there and J.J.'s got the bird warming up. We're going through some final checks. It was getting light by then and these deuce-and-a-halfs drove up full of troops."

"You hear this shit, Doc?" Nathan said. "The doggies rode to the choppers before they flew into battle. Damn, we missed our calling. If we would've joined the Army we wouldn't have had to hump everywhere."

George silenced him with a sharp look.

Vic puffed on the cigar and leaned forward. "So the troops get off the trucks and start forming up. We were finished with our pre-takeoff checks so we just sat there for a while. I'm looking out my window at all these grunts standing around smoking and talking and looking bored. I'm thinking, man, these guys are loaded for bear. They had M-60s and crisscrossed belts of ammo and rockets and grenades hanging everywhere. They were some bad-looking dudes. And I'm thinking, these guys are about to go into combat and I'm going to fly them there. I guess reality was sinking in—training is over and this is the real show.

"So they finally load up. J.J. torques it and we take off. There were maybe six or eight slicks in our flight. I don't remember much about the flight to the LZ except I know I was really excited. Hell, I was going to war. We were somewhere near the middle of the formation. I could see a couple of other birds ahead of us. There was the usual radio traffic and talking back-and-forth with the crew chief on the intercom. I remember J.J. telling one of the other ACs that he had a 'peter pilot' with him. That's the helicopter pilots' version of an 'FNG.' You guys remember what that was, don't you?"

Nathan and Dan nodded. Every grunt remembered having the distinct displeasure of being the "fucking new guy" in his unit.

"We were airborne for about twenty minutes and then things started happening real fast. Suddenly we were sweeping in real low and fast. Then there were all kinds of voices on the freq like everybody in the whole damn flight was trying to talk at once. It was totally confusing to me but J.J. seemed to know what was going on. He looked at me and said, real calm, 'Hot LZ.'

"The next thing I know we're flying between two tree lines maybe a hundred-fifty, two hundred meters away on either side and there's red and green tracers flying everywhere." Vic bent down and crushed out the stub of his cigar against the heel of his shoe.

"So we're slowing down and starting to flair and the ground is coming up *real* fast. I'm wondering what to do. Should I just sit there or should I have my hands on the controls just in case, or what? Then I hear this *bam-bam-bam-bam-bam-bam!*" Vic said, slamming his fist into his open palm, "like somebody beating hell out of the chopper with a hammer. The crew chief started yelling, 'We're taking rounds.' Well no shit, I'm thinking, even a new dumb fuck like me could figure that out.

"Then the bird started flying funny. I could feel it even though I didn't have the controls. It was like the tail wanted to spin around to the front and we were leaning way over to my side. J.J. was fighting the controls. He had this odd look in his eyes. I can't describe it but I remember that look like it was yesterday. Then he yells, 'We're going down!' I think that's when I pissed in my pants."

Lightning flashed and illuminated the parking lot and thunder clapped a second later. Rain pounded the roof in torrents and blew through the open window. Nathan got up and lowered the window, leaving just a crack for some fresh air.

"It's funny when I look back on it," Vic said. He fished in his pocket for another cigar but came up empty. "Here I am on my very first combat flight and it's a hot LZ and the aircraft is taking hits and I feel something warm running in the crack of my ass and down my legs. I was scared shitless for a second thinking it might be blood. Then I realized what I was doing but I couldn't stop. I went ahead and emptied my bladder right there in the middle of getting shot down."

"Had you already landed your troops?" Nathan said. His right leg was pumping up and down. He'd had his own experiences with hot landing zones.

"No, we didn't have a chance to get 'em off. They were going down with us. So now we've lost all power and it's like we're sinking all of a sudden, like the feeling you get on an elevator. I'm not sure how far we dropped, maybe ten or fifteen feet. For a few seconds everything was quiet. I can't remember hearing anything, not even gunfire. It was strange.

"Then we jolted hard and everything went dark with all the smoke and dust. The hit wasn't nearly as bad as I thought it would be. Hell, I thought we were gonna explode in a big ball of fire like you see in the movies."

Vic paused to catch his breath. An English sparrow bumped the windowpane and fluttered on the sill and flew away. Vic groped in his pocket again and then bummed a Kool and a light from Dan.

"The next thing I know the crew chief is dragging me out of the chopper. He pulls me out and we start crawling for this dike about thirty meters away." He took a heavy drag on the cigarette and wiped sweat from his brow. "The grunts are already spread out behind the dike busting caps toward the tree line like there's no tomorrow. There were four guys lying behind the dike in this one spot. A couple of 'em were moving and groaning but two were dead. I think they were killed before we crashed.

"So we're lying there behind this paddy dike and the grunts are blasting away and our crew chief and door gunner are using an M-60 they took off the chopper. I didn't see J.J. at first. He was on the other end of the line of grunts. For a while I wasn't sure if he'd gotten out of the bird or not. Everybody was shooting back at the dinks but me. I had my .38 but I hadn't bothered to load it. Then one of the grunts shoves this M-14 at me; he'd got it from one of the dead or wounded I guess. Hell, I'd never fired an M-14 in my life. We'd trained with the M-16.

"So I lifted it over the top of the dike and pointed it at the tree line and pulled the trigger but nothing happened. I'd forgotten to take the damn safety off. I fumbled around and found the safety and pushed it off. Then I pointed the rifle back at the tree line and held it up over my head with just my hands, like this." Vic held his hands slightly above his head. "When I pulled the trigger that damn rifle flew out of my hands. It had been set on full automatic and——"

Nathan broke up laughing as he pictured the scene. The M-16 was easy to handle on full automatic mode but the heavier caliber M-14 was a different matter altogether. Dan was bent over and turning red in the face. Even George couldn't escape the contagion of the moment. Vic stared at them straight-faced for a few seconds and then joined in.

For Nathan it was the unconscious resurfacing of a survival technique common among combat-hardened soldiers—the ability to find humor in the midst of seemingly desperate situations. During the war it had enabled him to cling to a semblance of sanity while immersed in an insane world.

Several seconds passed before George restored order to the group. He glanced at his watch again. "Okay Vic, finish up."

"Nothing much happened after that. A gunship team arrived and started working over both tree lines. The M-14 had landed behind me so I just said 'fuck it' and kept my head down."

Nathan choked back another laugh.

"There wasn't much I could do with an unloaded pistol anyway," Vic said.

Nathan snorted.

"Not long after that the other slicks landed and we jumped

on one with the dead and wounded from our chopper. The gunships had pretty much taken care of the dinks in the tree line by then.

"After we got back to Ban Me Thuet the medics checked us over and then I followed J.J. to debriefing. Later on I went to the O' Club and was trying my best to get smashed. J.J. beat me to it. All this happened in just a few hours. It was around two o'clock or so and I'm sitting there starting to get a real good buzz, still amazed at everything that had happened that morning. Then this other AC from our flight comes in and tells us to be ready because we're going again in a couple of hours. J.J. just sits there nonchalant and keeps drinking like there's no tomorrow. I'm thinking, how can they do this to us? Don't we get a few days off now? We just got shot down! And how the hell is J.J. supposed to fly drunk?

"But he did. By the time we took off that afternoon you wouldn't know he'd even been drinking. It was amazing."

"How did you feel about having to fly again so soon after what you'd just been through?" George asked.

Vic shrugged. "I don't know."

"Were you pissed off? Scared?"

Vic shook his head. "No, I wasn't scared, not that I remember. I guess I hadn't been there long enough to be scared. I figured after getting shot down not much more could happen to me. Boy was I ever wrong about that, but that's another story."

Rene looked around the interior of his cabin with satisfaction. Let it rain, he thought, I've got everything I need. It was a good hooch, one of the best he'd ever lived in. The two-by-fours and plywood were compliments of a construction job he'd worked a few weeks; the rolled roofing, nails and window were additional fringe benefits he'd picked up after hours. A Coleman lantern hissed from its hook near the center of the room and cast soft shadows that flitted on the bare walls. Along one side a heavy nylon and canvas hammock seemed to float in the dim light. A crude table and bench fashioned from other salvaged lumber stood next to the opposite wall. The floor was bare earth that was packed hard and kept dry by a sloping trench dug along three sides of the outside the cabin walls.

The wind rose and moaned through the treetops like some invisible entity. A pot of beans and smoked ham pieces simmered on the camp stove and filled the cabin with a pungent aroma. Rene stirred the beans and tasted them. Another hour or so; no need to hurry.

Thunder boomed, more distant this time. The wind howled and rain drummed against the slanted roof. A gray mist hung low over the lake, rising like ghostly fingers clutching at wavering black curtains. Rene lit a joint and stretched out in the hammock. He held the acrid smoke in his lungs a long time and then exhaled and watched the cloud dissipate into the shadows.

Would they come tonight? It had been a while since their last visit. He drew in deeply again and held the smoke. He stared at the glowing ash lighting the palm of his cupped hand. He hoped they would come. It would be good to see them again.

# CHAPTER NINE

THE RAIN TAPERED off the next day and by nightfall clouds began moving out. Sunday dawned clear and cold with a brisk northerly wind. Nathan drove Mrs. Ard to church that morning. After services she would travel with her seniors Sunday school class to a three-day conference and retreat in Alabama.

"Are you sure you won't come along to church with me?" she asked as he helped her from the van and handed her suitcase to the bus driver. "It might do you a world of good."

"No ma'am. If I went in there the roof might cave in and I wouldn't want to spoil your trip. Besides, I'm a heathen, not a Baptist. It's against my religion to worship on Sundays."

"Oh, shoo," she said, and chuckled. "What am I going to do with you, boy? Now you be sure to feed Clarence and don't forget to keep the birdbath full. Those birds will be wanting to use it after all this cold weather. And Clarence likes to drink out of it, too."

"Don't you worry about a thing. Just enjoy your trip. I'll take good care of Clarence and your place."

"Now don't you be giving him beer, you hear me?" She tugged at the shoulder of the shapeless dark print dress. "Poor thing was just a-staggering the other night when I let him in. I swear, that tom weren't good for nothing next morning."

Nathan grinned. "Baptists shouldn't swear, Miss Ard. I'm

sorry about Clarence getting loaded, but he kept begging me with them big yellow eyes. You know how he is. But I'll make sure he stays on the wagon while you're gone. You better get on in there before they start without you and you miss an amen or a hallelujah or something."

"All right then. I'll see you in a few days." She lumbered up the steps to the front entrance.

"Have a good trip," Nathan called, and then added, "Hey, Miss Ard?"

She turned to face him.

"Try to keep your hands off them Alabama preachers."

"Oh, shoo," she said and waved him off.

"Gee Doc, you look like warmed-over shit," Nathan said as Dan climbed into the van. Vic had invited them to his house for a Sunday afternoon cookout.

Dan stared at him through bleary eyes. "Why, thank you. I feel better than I ever did alive." He leaned back against the headrest and groaned. "Don't drive this thing so damned loud."

Nathan reached into the Igloo on the floor between the seats and handed Dan a can of Busch. "Here you go. Sure-fire cure for what ails you."

Dan stared at the can for a few seconds and then popped the top. "Remember the Alamo," he said, and then tilted the can and chugged the cold brew.

Nathan laughed. "There it is." He tapped his can against Dan's in a toast and took a long gulp. "Ah, liquid bread, the nectar of life."

Vic lived in the upper-middle class North Shores subdivision. Nathan drove along Airline Drive which skirted the northern arm of St. Martin Bay. Strong winds whipped the water into dancing steel-blue chops. Frothy whitecaps topped the waves. On the distant shore a tall forest of slash pine stood black against the cloudless blue sky. The smell of salt rode the wind. Nathan stared at the distant tree line and thought about the open spaces they had been forced to cross to assault the hostile villages north of the Cua Viet River.

"How's the world been screwing you," Nathan said as he dropped the empty can into the ice chest and fished for another beer.

Dan took a swallow and stared out the passenger-side window. "Let's see; my ex-wife is threatening to call the law on me for past-due child support; my mother thinks I should move out; I'm about to lose my job; my car's been repossessed; my dog died and my sister's got the clap. Other than that, things are just dandy."

Nathan laughed, but Dan was only half-joking. His car had been repossessed last month and his job was in jeopardy—too many missed days and an excess of botched procedures had him walking a thin line at work. His mother would never think of kicking him out of the house, but his sister, who was married to a prominent real estate broker, rode him incessantly to "get out and make something of yourself, like Charles." He had smoothed over the situation with his ex-wife for the time being, and he didn't have a dog. Still, he felt the world was closing in on him much of the time and sought escape whenever he could.

Nathan glanced at the used envelope on which he'd jotted down Vic's directions. "You know what me and you should do?" he said, making a right turn before answering his own question. "Become mercenaries. I was reading this magazine, *Soldier of Fortune*. Them guys make some serious money doing the same shit we did in the 'Nam for almost nothing. They live a hell of a lot higher on the hog, too. They're like advisors. They give the orders and let the locals do all the dirty work. Think about it man, we could be kings. And this time we'd know what the fuck was going on. We'd be the ones running the show. Couple of hardcore grunts like us could do a bang-up job at that shit. We could go to Central America and zap some Sandinistas. 'Course there's always the chance we might get our own asses blown away, but what the hell?"

Dan stared at Nathan. "You're more fucked-up than I originally diagnosed." He reached over and felt Nathan's forehead. "A definitive case of delirious delusion," he said, shaking his head. "Critical cranial corruptus. No hope and no cure."

"Up yours, Doc."

Nathan sat in a lawn chair drinking bottled Michelob on the Guerinos' stone patio. He'd volunteered to watch the grill while Vic and Dan tossed horseshoes in the back yard along the chain link fence. Dan was losing badly. Near the patio, Kendra and a little blonde-haired girlfriend were sliding tandem down the board attached to the swing set. Next door, twelve-year-old Vic Junior was playing Whiffle ball with several neighborhood boys. The wind had calmed down and the mid afternoon sun flooded the yard with light and warmth.

Karen Guerino reclined on a chaise lounge reading a romance novel while working on an early tan. A thin stream of smoke rose lazily from a cigarette in the ashtray beside her. Catching Nathan's eye, she peered over the rims of the sunglasses perched on her nose. "Can I get you another beer?"

"Sure, if you don't mind." Nathan still found it awkward talking with people he didn't know well, but a good buzz made socializing easier.

"No problem at all." Karen smiled and leaned over as she sat up and swung her shapely legs off the recliner. "I could use a refill myself." She held up a glass with the remnants of melted ice and rum and Coke. "Be back in a jiff."

Nathan's eyes tracked her across the patio and through the sliding glass door into the kitchen. He couldn't help but notice the ample cleavage above the bikini top when she'd gotten up. And those legs—firm and glistening with suntan oil. Stop it asshole; that's Vic's wife, not some slut you're trying to hit on.

"Ringer!" Vic shouted as the solid clanging of metal against metal filled the air. Dan mumbled something Nathan couldn't make out. In the lot next door a heated argument arose over whether a runner was safe or out. Nathan heard the sliding door open and bump shut.

"Here we are," Karen said. She handed him a cold Michelob. Nathan thought her fingers lingered just a bit provocatively along the neck and lip of the bottle.

"Thanks," he said, dismissing it as a figment of his overactive imagination. "You want me to put barbecue sauce on all this chicken?"

"You might leave a couple of wings and drumsticks without," Karen said. "Sometimes the kids can be picky. They'll probably just have hotdogs or hamburgers anyway."

Nathan watched as Karen sipped the rum and coke with her full red lips puckered around the straw and thought how nice it would be to curl up with her for just one night. A few minutes later he got up to check the grill again. He flipped the burgers on the top rack and gave the hotdogs a half turn. Black patterns branded their reddish skins. On the lower rack chicken pieces sizzled when he turned them and aromatic smoke filled his lungs as dripping fat exploded on the hot coals. Golden brown blisters rose from the skin.

Whenever he grilled chicken Nathan never failed to think of the napalmed dead from a village along the Cua Viet. They had swept through the vill after an air strike and rooted out pockets of hardcore NVA soldiers who had refused to di-di. Dead gooks lay everywhere and many were genuine crispy critters. Hideous blisters rose from the charred bodies like grotesque yellow balloons and protruded upward several inches from abdomens or eye sockets. He and others from his squad strung one of the bodies on a pole behind their fighting holes and dubbed him Charcoal Charlie. They had taunted and dared the NVA in the next village several hundred meters away to use Charlie as an aiming stake for their artillery. That was the night of the heavy barrage when the company was overrun.

Nathan snapped back when he realized Karen was talking to him. "I'm sorry; what'd you say?"

"I asked if you've ever been married." Karen shifted the recliner to a more upright position. She drew her knees up close to her chest and wrapped her arms around them.

Nathan forced his gaze from between her legs and concentrated on the brown eyes above the shades.

"Vic mentioned you were single. I was wondering if you'd been married and divorced, or what?"

He hated the question but forced a smile and shook his head. "Nope, never been hitched. Never found anybody quite worthy of me," he said, hoping she would take it as a joke. His smile faded. "I almost did once, but that was a long time ago."

A long time ago; a lifetime ago since his world had come crashing down. . . .

"Yo, Henson."

Nathan glanced up from the hospital bed where he and two other patients were playing poker. It was Doc Rickards, one of the corpsmen working the day shift on Ward Eight-C.

"Yeah Doc, what can I do you for?" he said and raised the bet a quarter.

"You got a visitor. Outside. Who's winning?"

"Johnson, who else?" Nathan said. He pointed a finger at a burly young black man. "That damn card shark would cheat his own mama. Who is it, my mother again?"

Doc Rickards grinned. "If that's your mother I'm going to marry her and adopt your young ass. No disrespect to your dear sweet mama, but nobody that good looking could've produced something as butt-ugly as you."

Laura, he thought, his heart pounding, it's got to be Laura!

Nathan had spent six months in-country and then another couple of months in the hospital at Yokusaka, Japan. And then one morning the naval doctor stopped by his bed told him he was going back to the World. No more Vietnam. No more humping and no more killing and no more loading the bodies of his friends aboard choppers. He was going home!

He'd been a patient at Pensacola Naval Hospital for almost two weeks now. His mother and younger brother and sister had visited twice already; but no Laura yet, not even a phone call. His mother tried to explain that she was probably tied up with final exams at Florida State in Tallahassee. Nathan had a hard time reasoning how anything could be more important than seeing each other again after so many months of separation. What was the big deal with college and grades anyway? Hell, he'd been to war; didn't Laura understand that? The intensity, the hardships, the terror; everything else paled in the light of that experience. Couldn't she see that?

But now she was here, at last. Just a few more minutes and he'd see her again and hear her sweet voice and look into those beautiful green eyes and wrap his arms around her.

"Deal me out guys. Here, finish my hand," Nathan said, handing Rickards his cards. "Watch out for the splib; he's probably got an ace shoved up his useless asshole."

"Fuck you, chuck muddafucka," Johnson shot back.

"Yo, Henson."

"Yeah?"

"Bring me back a fingerful."

Nathan laughed. "No way squid; she's mine, all mine."

Nathan hobbled down the hallway. His shuffling footsteps were magnified by the empty corridor. His foot ached like hell but he didn't care. He stopped at the door and pulled his bathrobe open to make sure the bandages covering the drainage holes in his abdomen weren't leaking. They were clean. He retied the belt and pushed open the heavy glass door and stepped out onto the veranda that separated two wings of the hospital. The May air was warm and carried the scent of flowering gardenias. Songbirds chirped and flitted high in the branches of a great live oak which shaded the brick veranda. Nathan glanced about and then sat at one of several concrete tables to wait. He watched two bushy-tailed gray squirrels scamper around and around the oak's broad trunk.

"Nathan?"

Was he dreaming or did he really hear her voice? He was afraid to turn and face it, afraid it would disappear like some mirage. Afraid that after all the killing and death and horror, one more cruel joke was waiting to be played out.

"Nathan, is that you?"

He turned. "Laura?" The word broke in his throat. "Laura?" He still couldn't make himself believe it. She walked toward him and her heels clicked on the bricked deck. She was coming to him but he was still trapped in that faraway place, a place where dreams quickly grew old and then faded into obscurity. No, this couldn't be real.

But still she came. He reached out to touch her, as though doing so would make the vision real at last and bring him home—truly home.

She stopped short and placed her hands in his and stood at arm's length looking into his eyes. "How are you? Your mother said you're doing well." The voice sounded strange, hesitant somehow.

He sensed it immediately. Something was wrong; a trip wire along the trail or an ambush just ahead. Color drained from his already pale face and his mouth went dry. A cold shudder danced along his spine. He tried to shake it away. "You can hug me." He tried to sound cheerful and hoped his instincts were wrong. "I don't have a bag anymore, and I promise I won't break."

Laura drew closer; her arms encircled his neck in a half-hearted hug and her cheek rested lightly against his chest.

Nathan buried his face in Laura's auburn hair and devoured her scent and for a moment there was hope. He tried to pull her close. He longed to feel the fullness of her breasts pressed against him, but she placed a palm to his chest and gently pushed away.

"What's the matter?" It was a fruitless question because now there was no doubt something was wrong. "I know I look like sh—sorry. I know I look bad. I've lost a lot of weight but I'm doing better now. I'm getting stronger every day and putting on weight and—"

"You look fine. Let's sit down, okay?" Laura sat without waiting for a response.

Nathan slumped onto the bench; he felt numb and drained, like he'd just humped ten klicks with full gear. Laura fumbled in her purse and produced a pack of Benson & Hedges and a lighter. "You don't mind if I smoke, do you?" she said and placed the cigarette between her lips. Nathan watched dumbfounded as she flicked the lighter before he could answer.

"Smoke? You don't smoke," he mumbled and then realized it was a stupid statement as she lit the cigarette.

"I do now," Laura said. She turned her head aside and exhaled a stream into the spring air. "Bad habit from college," she said with a nervous laugh.

For a moment Nathan just sat there stunned; his mind was racing but nearly blank at the same time. It wasn't supposed to happen like this. Over Laura's shoulder he noticed the squirrels going at it again. Thunder rumbled as clouds gathered in the northwest. The air grew cooler. He'd dreamed about this moment for months. It was what had kept him going when he had nothing else to cling to. What had happened to the Laura he'd known?

"What's going on?" he finally managed.

Laura took a quick drag on the cigarette. "You never answered my last several letters," she said as smoke escaped her lips and nostrils. "I wrote you all about it but you never answered. I thought you knew, until your mother called."

'It?' Nathan thought, just what the hell was 'it?' "I don't know what you're talking about. We didn't get any mail the last few weeks I was there. We were in the bush. Don't you know what was going on over there? The Tet Offensive? Didn't you hear about that? Write? Hell, we were busy just trying to stay alive!" He was pissed now and losing control. "What the hell do you think? That we had all the time in the world to just sit around and answer our mail? I wasn't away at college for all those months. I was fighting a war, remember?"

Laura looked away. Her hands trembled and tears began to well.

Nathan grabbed her shoulder. "Look at me goddamnit. What the hell's going on?"

She faced him and dabbed at her eyes with her fingertips and drew in a raspy breath. Nathan's chalky face had turned red, almost purple around the temples and eyes. "Calm down, please. Just calm down." She placed a hand on his and lifted it from her shoulder and touched it to her cheek.

"I'm sorry. I didn't realize you hadn't received my letters until your mother called me at school." She avoided his glare and took another puff on the cigarette. "I don't know how to tell you this except to just come right out and say it. Tom and I have been seeing each other for several months now, and . . ."

Nathan heard the voice but the words sounded like some strange foreign language, hollow and far away.

"We didn't know it was going to get this serious . . ."

Thunder clapped and drowned out the unwelcome message.

". . . realized we were in love, and . . ."

The words were a vicious bolt of lightning that seared his heart.

". . . never meant for you to be hurt . . ."

Leaving him all hollow and burned out and empty.

". . . going to be married next month. And we're expecting a baby."

Baby? She's having a baby? Nathan laughed, slowly at first, and then it grew and grew until he was roaring; a maniacal laughter at himself, at Laura, at the World, at the God who allowed him to survive all he had endured only to face this final cruel joke.

A baby, he thought, that's a good one. My virginal Laura. The same Laura I loved so much I wouldn't go all the way with just in case I didn't make it back. I didn't want her to be spoiled goods for someone else. Ha ha, good one, God, the joke's on me.

I'm up to my elbows in some gook's guts and shit, killing him before he can kill me so I can get home to Laura. And what's she doing? Waiting for me? Wrong! She's screwing the socks off Jody. And who does Jody turn out to be? Why, none other than my best friend, closer-than-a-brother buddy from childhood—good ol' reliable Tom Carter. That's a real good one, God. You fucking outdid yourself with this one, ha ha ha ha ha ha!

"Nathan, please." Laura's voice shook and tears rolled down her cheeks and smeared her makeup.

Nathan stopped the forced laughter and stared across the table. His eyes were tight slits and his fists were clenched in rage. "Go!" He turned his head and spit. His teeth ground together so hard his jaws ached. "Get out of my sight. Get the *fuck* out of my sight, you bitch! Get out of here before I rip your heart out and shove it up your ass!"

Laura knees almost buckled as she stood. Her lips quivered and she tried to speak but her voice failed. She ran crying and disappeared around a corner of the building.

"Go, slut," Nathan hollered after her, "you worthless bitch!"

Dark clouds draped the sky and the wind smelled of rain as it whispered tauntingly through the leaves of the big oak.

He pounded his fist against the tabletop. "Bitch!" He punched it again and again, leaving bloody smears and shredded skin across the abrasive surface. "Bitch, bitch, bitch!" . . .

"Hey grunt, is that chicken done yet?"

Nathan was jolted back by Vic's voice from across the yard. Karen lay dozing on the recliner. He picked up a drumstick with the tongs and turned it. "A few more minutes."

"Come on over. I need some competition," Vic called. "Let this sorry sawbones watch the grill. Maybe he can do that. He sure as hell can't pitch horseshoes."

Nathan set the tongs down and grabbed his beer. "That's your ass, flyboy. Horseshoes are just like hand grenades, and I'm the best there is!"

# CHAPTER TEN

"I'D BEEN IN-COUNTRY about two weeks," Dan Matthews began, continuing the theme of first combat experiences. "I was with Kilo Company, Third Battalion, Third Marines. We were at Gio Linh at the time, near the coast just below the DMZ. Word came down that the company was moving west to Alpha-Three, a new firebase the Seabees were constructing. We started out just after daylight humping all our gear with us which meant we were loaded down like pack mules.

"I had my Unit-One with me, the medical bag all corpsmen carried," he said, "and my full field pack like all the grunts. Plus I was humping some rocket rounds for the old bazookas our rocket teams were using at the time. Later they switched to LAWs but when I first arrived in-country they still had the big tubes."

"What are laws? Vic said.

"Light Anti-tank Weapon," Dan said. "Disposable one-shot rocket launchers about the length of a baseball bat. You unsnapped some clips and they telescoped out like a small bazooka."

"They were a badass weapon," Nathan said, remembering how he'd silenced an NVA machine gun with a well-placed round through the bunker's gun port. Like shooting gooks in a barrel, Betz had said after they'd checked the bodies. "We still had the old bazookas when I got there, too. There was this little spic dude with our rocket squad. We called him Short-round. I remember how funny he used to look humping that big tube. Damn thing was longer than he was." He smiled at the memory. The smile faded. "He got hit at the Cua Viet. Fucked him up big-time. I saw him in the hospital in Japan. They had his stomach laid wide-open with all kind of tubes and shit sticking in him. He looked bad. I don't think he made it."

"So, your company is about to move to a new location and you're all loaded down with gear," George said, steering the topic back on course.

Dan tapped the ash from his Kool into the dregs of his coffee. "This was around the second week of December. It had rained nearly every day since I'd been there. We were constantly wet and cold. A lot of people look at you like you're crazy when you tell them it was cold in Vietnam. They have this Hollywood concept that it was all steaming rice paddies and sweltering jungle. But it got cold too, especially up north."

"Cold as a well digger's ass," said Nathan

"Let's keep it focused, guys," George said.

Dan took a deep drag on his cigarette. "We moved out along the Trace. That's what they called McNamara's Line. The Seabees used Rome plows to clear-cut this huge swath just below the DMZ from the coast all the way to Con Thien. It was supposed to prevent the NVA from infiltrating across the DMZ. The idea was that the gooks wouldn't cross it because they'd be exposed in the open if they tried. So naturally the brass picked that route for the move to Alpha-Three."

"How did you feel about moving over exposed ground like that?" George said.

"I didn't give it much thought at the time. I was too new to know better. Some of the salts were bitching about it, but it's natural for Marines to bitch about everything."

Vic reached for his cup of coffee on the vacant chair between him and Dan. "Why didn't they just fly you guys there?"

Nathan rolled his eyes. "Old Marine Corps rule: never fly or ride when you can walk. Hell, if they'd been able to figure out a way for us to walk on water they would've shitcanned our amtracks."

Dan laughed. "There it is. The weather was too bad for choppers to fly except for emergency medevacs. Somebody said we were having a dry monsoon, but the Trace was nothing but muck. Every step we took the mud bogged us down."

"Man, I remember that shit," Nathan said. He pointed at the floor and made a swirling motion. "It seemed like that mud was alive, like a red-blob monster trying to suck you under. I remember one time we——"

"Let's let Dan tell it," George said.

Nathan shrugged and sat back in his chair.

"Nathan's right," Dan said. "It was like something alive trying to pull you down. That old adage of war, about nature being your enemy too, is true."

Dan stood and walked to the window and stared across the parking lot. After a moment he returned to his chair and lit another Kool from the butt of the other.

"We humped for what seemed like hours. The weather was really socked in; you couldn't tell where the sun was. I was too tired to check my watch. All I could think about was to keep moving because if I stopped I'd sink down and might never get up again.

"Then the gooks opened up on us from our right flank. It sounded like all hell was breaking loose but it was only a quick firefight. It was my first time under fire, and at the time it seemed a lot worse than it was."

George swallowed a sip of coffee. "How did that first burst of gunfire affect you?"

"It scared me shitless," Dan said. "Everybody hit the deck. We'd been cursing that damned mud just a few seconds before and now we were hugging it like lovers. The rounds were snapping just above our heads. It was mostly AK-47s, but there were some tracers so I assume they had a machine gun, too. They also hit us with a few mortars but they were ineffective because of the mud.

"There was a lot of yelling and confusion. I didn't know where the gooks were. Their fire was coming out of the fog. Our guys were returning fire but a lot of the weapons jammed because of the mud. I only carried a forty-five at the time but I had an M-16 cleaning rod thanks to a corpsman I'd met in Phu Bai before I joined the company. He told me it would come in handy and he was right. I started moving around and helping people clear their weapons."

Dan paused and took a deep breath. "Then somebody to my left yelled 'Corpsman up!' I thought, Well, here we go—here's what you've been training for. I took off running toward the voice. That is, I was trying to run; plodding would be more like it.

"This tall skinny Marine named Conners had taken a round in the calf. By the time I got there another Marine had already tied a battle dressing over the wound. I removed it and checked the wound. It was filthy so I dug some gauze and peroxide out of my Unit-1 and cleaned it the best I could. It was a simple through-and-through in the muscle without much bleeding. I sprinkled sulfa into each hole, put on a fresh bandage and jabbed him with morphine. Then I wrote his tag."

"Tell us what you felt when you first heard the call of 'corpsman up,'" George said. "Were you excited? Scared? Worried about what you might find or how you'd handle the situation?"

Dan thumped the ash from his cigarette and took a long drag. "I was fairly calm about the whole thing. I was a little shaky when the NVA first opened up but I don't recall being scared after I heard the call for a corpsman. I don't even remember hearing the rounds after that. I suppose I was concentrating on getting to the wounded Marine and doing what I was trained to do. I'm glad it was routine. I came away feeling confident. I believed I could handle anything after that. Of course, that was just wishful thinking. There were a lot of things later on that I didn't handle very well at all. But it's good the first one was so easy. If it had been a sucking chest wound or a head shot I don't know how I might have reacted."

"Sure you do," Nathan said. "You would've said, 'This poor dude's brains are hanging out.' Then you would've patched him up the best you could. I never once saw a corpsman fuck-up under fire." He laughed and added, "Then you would've told him to take two aspirins and see you in the morning."

George shot Nathan a glance. "I know you're trying to rescue Dan, but let's let him tell his story. That's what we're here for." He leaned back in his chair and nodded to Dan. "What happened next?"

"One of our platoons managed to flank the gooks," Dan said, "and then the rest of the company got on line and assaulted their position. There was a lot of yelling and firing from our side but the NVA had already di-di'd. We found a couple of bodies and searched them for documents, took what weapons they left behind and left them there lying in the mud. Then we moved on to Alpha-Three like nothing had happened. I was still hyped but those grunts just slogged on through the mud like zombies. It was business as usual for them.

"We had two WIAs if I remember correctly. Both were minor wounds so we didn't request a medevac."

Vic toyed with the knot of his tie and turned to Dan. "We used to feel bad for the grunts when the ceiling was too low and we couldn't fly," he said, sounding almost apologetic. "There was this one time some grunts were really in the shit near a place we called the Volcano. I was carrying a load of ammo and C-rations for them but on the way the weather socked in. Their CO was on the radio pleading for me to land. They had some seriously wounded who needed to get out in a hurry." He paused and tore the cellophane wrapping from a new pack of Tiparillo cigars.

"I told him I couldn't land because the ceiling was too low." Vic lit the cigar and exhaled bluish-gray smoke. "He started cussing me out over the radio for everybody to hear. He called me a chickenshit coward." Vic's face was pinched.

"But hey, I really couldn't land." He spoke as though trying to convince himself. "Visibility was zero and I knew there were a lot of trees down there. I would've crashed for sure if I'd tried to land. I had my crew to think about, and the ship, as well as those guys in the shit. I might've killed people on the ground if I tried to put it down and didn't make it."

Nathan glanced at George and wondering why he was letting Vic go on when the subject was first combat actions. Vic had discussed his last week. Then he looked at Vic and understood. The anguish in his eyes told him Vic needed to get this matter off his chest now.

"So, what did you do?" George said.

Vic pinched the bridge of his nose but said nothing.

George sat upright and rested his arms on the desk. "How did you handle the situation?"

"What?" Vic said. He looked puzzled as though he were somewhere else.

"After the commander on the ground called you a chickenshit coward. What happened then? Did it make you mad or what? How did you respond?"

"I don't know, I guess I . . ." Vic seemed confused. "Yeah, damn right I was mad but I understood how he felt. He needed to get those wounded out of there. I tried to explain again that I couldn't land. Then he starts screaming that I better get the fuck out of there or he would shoot us down." Vic held his palms open. "What the hell was I supposed to do?"

"You tell me," George said, "you're the pilot."

Vic paused for several seconds. His face was flushed. He puffed on the cigar. "I told him I was sorry but there was nothing I could do in that weather. Then I told the crew chief and door gunner to kick the shit out the door and got the hell out of there."

"And?"

"And what?"

"And how did you feel about your decision then? How do you feel about it now?"

There was a long silence. "I guess I did the right thing."

"You guess?"

"Well hell, I wanted to land and get those wounded troops but I couldn't! Chances are I would've lost my bird and maybe killed my crew and people on the ground too. I just couldn't risk it."

George leaned back again and propped his boots on the desktop. "So, what you're telling us is that as aircraft commander you were confronted with a problem. You weighed the pros and cons of that problem. And then you made a command decision based on the best interests and welfare of everyone concerned—yourself, your ship, your crew and the troops on the ground."

Vic thought it over. "Yeah, I guess I did."

"You guess?"

"I did."

"Right, you did." George allowed a few seconds for his message to sink in. He checked the time and then announced a ten-minute break.

Relief covered Vic's face as he followed the others to the lounge.

After the break Andrew spoke briefly in his quiet reserved manner about coming under sniper fire while searching the Ia Drang Valley for any dead or wounded left behind in the confusion of the big battle. No one had been hurt, and after the trauma of handling all the dead bodies a couple of days before it had seemed almost uneventful.

Nathan then recounted at some length his baptism of fire during Operation Kingfisher. He recalled watching a Marine with whom he'd gone through infantry training being blown treetop level after tripping a huge booby trap, and how the blank expression on the dead Marine's scorched face haunted him as he tried to sleep that night.

The next day his company was ambushed and a big firefight ensued. An attached company of ARVNs—South Vietnamese soldiers—fled the fight and left the outnumbered Marines to battle on alone, forever earning Nathan's scorn. He recalled not being afraid during this initial action, but instead fascinated and excited and proud he'd performed well.

Finally, George prodded the reticent Boudreaux into talking.

"My first tour was in '66," Rene began. He was smoking a non-filtered generic brand cigarette. "I was regula infantry then, ya see." His voice with its thick Brooklyn accent was surprisingly soft in contrast with his sharp, almost cruel features.

"We were at some firebase in the Central Highlands. I don't rememba the name. I don't rememba any names except my last team, but that was my second tour, ya know." He kept the cigarette in his lips as he spoke and it bobbled up and down beneath the bushy moustache and hooked nose. He slid down in his chair and extending his legs and crossed his bare feet at the ankles. His hands were shoved in his jeans pockets.

"They sent us on a squad-size patrol, maybe ten or twelve of us, mostly newbies. We were in thick jungle not very far outside the wire. The point man tripped a booby trap and the dinks opened up and wasted the whole damn squad when they tried to get to him. Only me and one other dude lived through it. I crawled out of sight under some bushes. Dinks came out of the jungle into the clearing and started popping heads to make sure. They stripped the bodies and took the weapons and beat feet. They didn't know I was there. They shot the other dude who lived in the head too, but only creased him. It was a couple of hours before a reactionary force found us. The radio was wasted, ya see, and anyway I wasn't about to come outta my hiding place. I figured the dinks might've left a sniper behind to watch the place. End of story."

Rene's voice was matter-of-fact and void of emotion or expression. He sat quietly and smoked his cigarette.

"That's some heavy shit, man," Nathan said.

"There it is," said Dan.

Rene remained silent and stared blankly at the wall ahead.

George waited for him to continue. When it became evident to the group that Boudreaux wasn't going to volunteer any more to the story, he said, "What was running through your mind while the VC moved in and finished off your buddies?"

Rene's eyes narrowed. "They weren't my buddies. I didn't have no buddies. They didn't mean nothin to me."

George straightened. "You're telling us it didn't affect you to see all those people being killed? I don't believe it. You had to feel something."

"I already told you. I just got there, ya see. I didn't know 'em. They were nothin to me." He ground the cigarette butt on the callous of his bare heel and glared at George. "Don't mean nothin."

# CHAPTER ELEVEN

"WHAT'S THE MATTER, Doc, you get a Dear John letter or something?"

Dan Matthews seemed unusually quiet and withdrawn as he and Nathan rode along Bayview Drive after the meeting. The sinking sun drove shadows from the tall trees across manicured lawns and up the facades of the fashionable homes fronting the bay. Near the shore a flock of black skimmers sailed low over the smooth surface dipping their uneven beaks into the scarlet water. The scent of pine and sea mingled in the cool air.

"I've just been thinking," Dan said. He lit a cigarette and continued staring through the windshield into the distance beyond.

"About what?"

"Hell, I don't know. All this . . . life." Dan paused a moment and then looked at Nathan. "What's it all about, Alfie?"

"You been smoking wacky tobaccy? You ain't making much sense lately."

"This life is what doesn't make sense," Dan said. "Do you ever stop and think about it? Really think about it?"

"Christ on a crutch, think about what?"

Dan drew on his cigarette. "What I mean is, you're here, I'm here, but where are we really? Think about it for a minute. We're both reasonably intelligent people, more intelligent than most, probably. And yet, where are we?

"Look at you. You do yard work for other people. Mow their lawns, rake their leaves and haul away their trash. It's all menial labor. You're probably smarter than ninety percent of the people you work for. But what are you? A common laborer."

"Gee thanks, everybody needs an ego boost now and then."

"You're welcome. But hell, you're a smashing success compared to me. I was planning to be a doctor. Relieve the suffering of my fellow man. Win the Nobel Prize for medicine. Christ, I'm almost forty years old and where am I? A half-assed lab technician who's in danger of losing his job, lives with his mother and doesn't have a pot to piss in or a window to throw it out of. Now there's a real success story. And you know why?"

Nathan gave Dan a pitying look. "Because we're poor Vietnam veterans who went off in our innocent youth to fight for our country, wound up getting our asses shot off and came back home to the big bad World where nobody gives a shit."

"There it is. You can joke about it all you want, but there's a lot of truth in what you just said. It is the war. It's in our bones, like a cancer. That's why we're so screwed up." The tip of Dan's cigarette glowed against the twilight as he inhaled and illuminated his waxen face.

"Oh, bullshit. You can't keep blaming the war for everything," Nathan said. "What difference does it make if people give a shit or not? It's not going to change a damn thing. Okay, so maybe we did get a raw deal. So what? Hell, I joined the Marines because I wanted to fight in a real war. It's something I'd wanted to do ever since I was a kid watching all them John Wayne flicks. I wanted to be a big league baseball player, too. Okay, I didn't make the majors, but I did get my shot at war. I asked for it. I could've skated and gone to college like most of the people I went to school with. But even knowing how it all turned out I'm glad I didn't. I couldn't live with myself if I hadn't done what I did. Vietnam's the only worthwhile thing I ever did in my life."

"It's easy enough for you to say that. You get a disability

check every month. Maybe I'd see things a little differently too if I could sit on my ass and get paid for doing nothing. Anything you earn from that half-assed business of yours is gravy."

Dan flicked his cigarette butt out the window. "You've got it made. You can sit on your can the rest of your life and not have to worry about paying bills and making ends meet. I've got three purple hearts and I don't get a damn penny from the government. You think that's fair?"

The unexpected tirade sliced through Nathan like a sharp bayonet. "Well excuse me for fucking living. What the hell do you expect me to do, tell Uncle Sam 'No thanks, I don't want the money, keep it and give it to someone who really deserves it.' Screw that.

"Let me tell you something, Doc," he said, his voice rising. "I almost bought the farm over there. Another inch higher and my heart would've been scrambled like so much hamburger meat. Body bag city. The government would've handed my mother ten thousand dollars and a folded flag and told her 'Thank you very much,' and my young ass would've been history."

He steered the van near the center line to avoid a bicyclist in his lane. An oncoming car blew its horn. Nathan flipped the driver a finger and muttered, "Asshole."

He gathered his thoughts for a moment and then glanced at Dan. "You ever wear a shitbag? Try it sometime and see how much you fucking like it. And while you're at it go live on a colostomy ward for a couple of months. Watch all the little curlicues of soft shit ooze out of them abdominal assholes like a cake decorator while you're trying to eat. Then lay awake at night and listen to all the liquidy farts—it sounds like a bunch of frogs croaking in a pond of shit. And don't forget that wonderful smell of medicine and shit that you can't get rid of.

"So screw you and your three skating-ass purple hearts. And screw anybody else who's got a bitch about me getting that check. It wasn't free goddamnit, I earned it!"

For a moment nothing was said. Only the steady hollow

whine of the engine penetrated the silence and twilight that lay heavy in the van. Finally, Dan broke the silence.

"I apologize, man; I had no right dumping on you like that. I was talking out of my ass. You deserve every penny of the disability you get. You damn well earned it."

Dan sighed. "I've been under a lot of pressure lately and you were a convenient target. Things are going to hell and I can't seem to get a grip on anything. It's all just coming apart." He broke off in mid sentence and stared out the window as though ashamed to look Nathan in the eye.

"I'm sorry too, Doc." The car ahead slowed and signaled for a right turn. Nathan eased off the gas and checked the side view mirror and made the pass. "I know you didn't mean all that crap. And I didn't mean what I said about your three hearts. We've both seen our share of the shit. Hell man, we're brothers. We're all we've got."

"There it is," Dan said. "But doesn't it ever bother you that nobody seems to care about what we went through?"

Nathan shrugged. "I don't think it's that people don't care, I think it's that they just don't understand. I mean, how can they?

"We've been through something special, something the World can't even begin to comprehend. It's alien to them. They can't understand it no matter how hard we try to explain, so what else can they do but go on as if it never happened? Hell, it didn't happen to them. So for them life goes on just like it always has."

He braked and turned onto Bedford and downshifted to climb the hill. "There's always been wars, and it's always been the same. Those who go to war and are lucky enough to come back alive are changed forever. Nothing's ever the same for them again. And for those who don't go, the world keeps right on turning like it always has. The sun rises and sets. The tide comes in and goes out. The seasons change. Damn, I'm waxing poetic."

Nathan stopped at an intersection and waited for the light to change. "It's a paradox, Doc. Everything is constantly changing but nothing ever really changes." The light turned green; he toyed with the clutch that had been slipping for a few days and the van lurched ahead. "Every night I get up to check the locks and take a leak. I go outside to piss because I like to look at the stars. I'll see Orion climbing up there in the southeast and I'll think, this is the same sky that people living thousands of years ago saw. All those years—eons—and nothing that matters has really changed. Man, does that ever make me feel small and insignificant."

The van got up to speed and Nathan shifted into fourth. "And then I'll think about my buddies who got killed over there. Seventeen years. They've been dead for over seventeen years now, and the sun and the moon and the stars and the seasons and the world are still the same. And when it's been seventeen hundred years it'll still be the same."

"So what difference does it make if I run a yard service and you're a lab tech?" he said, easing off the gas for a dog ambling across the street. "Would anything really change if you were the next Albert Schweitzer and I was the president? What difference would it make? What we are doesn't matter. And you know why? Because in the long run it don't mean shit. Being here, just being alive, is enough."

It was nearly dark by the time Nathan pulled into Dan's driveway. Dan had remained silent and deep in thought. Now he turned and lifted a hand which Nathan grasped.

"Thanks, bro. Thanks for the ride and thanks for the talk. I needed that."

Nathan grinned. "No sweat. But I'll tell you what you really need, what we both need. We need to go out and get good and drunk and then get laid. How about it?"

"I don't think so. I think I'll turn in early tonight. I've had a headache most of the day and—"

"Oh, bullshit. You spend more time in bed than a bear in hibernation. Every time I call you your mother tells me you're in bed. Not tonight. You know what this is? Spring Break weekend."

Dan looked duly unimpressed. "So?"

"Hell, I forgot, you weren't raised around here. All the high school and college students from the southeast get out of school for the week and come down here to party at the beach. There'll be more poontang than you could ever dream of shaking your stick at."

Dan's eyes narrowed. "Uh, excuse me, but don't you think we're just a little long in the tooth to be chasing after high school and college pussy. Unless my memory fails me we could get arrested for that."

"Ah, but that's where you're wrong, Doc. Spring Break is a great tradition. It's like homecoming. It won't just be the current crop of students coming down. There'll be plenty of old alumni from our generation, too. It's a party pilgrimage. It would be damn near sacrilegious not to be there. So, how about it? I know a couple of good places to hang out. It'll be like shooting gooks in a barrel."

Dan mulled it over for a few seconds. "Okay, I'll go, but you better not get my ass in trouble. I'm in enough hot water as it is."

Nathan slapped the dashboard. "All right! It'll be fun, you'll see. It's gonna do your young ass a world of good, too. I'll pick you up around nine. Don't go falling asleep on me."

Dan rolled his eyes and nodded.

Nathan backed the van into the street. "Hey Doc," he called as he pulled away, "you still remember how to cure the clap don't you?"

Nathan and Dan sat at a table near the dance floor of the Silver Saddle Lounge talking with two women they'd met an hour earlier. The crowded room was uncomfortably warm and the air was heavy with smoke. Nathan was relieved they'd found a table beneath an air conditioning vent.

The lounge was alive with the murmuring of a hundred meaningless conversations. The band was on break but a few couples swayed across the hardwood dance floor to Buddy Holly's "True Love Ways" blaring from the jukebox.

"What did y'all say y'all did for a living?" said Darlene, a buxom blonde school teacher from a small town outside Birmingham which Nathan had already forgotten. She was in her late thirties, Nathan judged, and not particularly pretty, but he liked the way she'd pressed her breasts against him the first time they'd danced.

He drained the last swallow from a can of Budweiser and signaled to the cocktail waitress at a nearby table to bring another round. He and Dan had polished off most of two six-packs before they arrived at the nightclub and Nathan was feeling no pain. He glanced left and then right. Holding an index finger to his lips, he leaned close to Darlene. "Shh. Me and ol' Doc here are a dying breed." He paused to let the suspense build. "We're mercenaries . . . soldiers of fortune . . . professional killers."

"Really?" gasped Gloria, Darlene's friend. She had mousy hair and was slightly plump but pretty, and appeared to be a couple of years younger than Darlene. Both claimed to be divorced but Nathan had noticed a telltale pale circle on Darlene's ring finger when they danced.

"Oh, y'all are just putting us on. Y'all aren't really mercenaries, are you?" Darlene said.

Dan caught Nathan's quick wink. "Ladies," he said with feigned hurt on his face, "Nathan and I are among the last of true southern gentlemen. You've wounded our pride with your insensitive inquisition of our integrity."

Nathan coughed to keep from laughing. Dan seemed to really be enjoying himself and eager to play along.

"It's usually beneath us to do this," Dan said, "but now our honor is at stake. Show the ladies, Nathan," he said, and pulled up the right sleeve of his blue oxford shirt.

Nathan took Dan's lead. He reached down and worked the trouser leg above his left calf revealing an ugly fist-sized scar. Several purple dots were scattered about the scar, small pieces of shrapnel from an NVA rocket that continued to work their way to the surface.

The women gaped at the scar. "Ooh," Darlene cooed, "that

must've really hurt." She ran her fingers lightly across the old wound.

"I got this one in Nicaragua back in '79 fighting with the Contras," Nathan said straight-faced. "It was nothing."

"I caught this one in the hills outside Manila during the Huk uprising," Dan said, pointing to a nearly round depression on his biceps. "AK-47 round. Broke the bone."

Nathan gurgled and faked another coughing spell. He swallowed hard and struggled to maintain his composure.

"You poor thing," Gloria said. She leaned over and kissed Dan's scar. "There," she said, patting his arm, "all better?"

He grinned. "Much."

The waitress arrived with the drinks. Nathan paid and left a dollar tip on the tray. The band members were making their way back to the small stage. From the jukebox Loretta Lynn sang about the hardships of being a coal miner's daughter. An overweight couple clung to each other and swayed out of step to the tune.

"How long have y'all been soldiers?" said Darlene.

Nathan spread the most soulful look he could muster across his face. He turned slowly and stared into her eyes. "It's all we know."

Darlene's eyes shone like the soft glow of a nightlight. She placed a hand on Nathan's forearm and gently stroked and squeezed the muscled flesh.

Jesus H. Christ, Nathan thought, I missed my calling. I should've been an actor.

"Nathan and I first fought together with the Marines in Vietnam," Dan said, continuing the farce. He tapped a Kool from his pack and offered it to the ladies. Both accepted.

Uneasiness came over Nathan as Dan struck a match from a club matchbook and held it for Gloria and Darlene and then used it to light his own cigarette. It wasn't the fact that Darlene was smoking that troubled him. He was drunk enough already that it didn't matter; besides, it was only sex he was after. But something bothered him. Something was wrong, something he couldn't quite pinpoint. Then he remembered—three on a match—a bad omen.

". . . had us pinned down until Nathan assaulted the machine gun position and destroyed it single-handedly," Dan was saying in a deep and serious voice. "He was awarded the Silver Star for that action."

The women beamed at Nathan. He suddenly felt uncomfortable with all the bullshit he and Dan were spreading. The medal was the truth but still he felt dirty and cheap, as though he were defiling the memory of Roberts, Dunn and Betz and so many others he'd fought with, suffered with and watched die. For a moment he contemplated leaving, just standing up and walking away from it all. But Dan was having a good time, and he'd started it himself with that crap about being mercenaries.

"Ol' Doc here is the real hero," Nathan said. He swigged his beer and reached over and grabbed Dan around the neck and hugged him. "He saved my young ass more'n once." His lips were numb and his tongue felt thick. "Hell, he don't like to brag about it but one time he saved our whole damn platoon from a VD assault. Wiped it out, all by his little ol' self!" He grinned at Dan who was trying to keep a straight face.

"Tell us about it Dan, please?" Gloria said. Neither woman seemed to have caught on to Nathan's joke.

Dan bit his lower lip. "Later ladies," he said. "We've got a whole sea bag full of stories to tell and scars to show. But this isn't the time or place, if you get my drift." He winked at Gloria.

The women looked at each other and giggled. Gloria cupped a hand and whispered into Darlene's ear and both giggled. "Y'all excuse us a minute, okay?" Darlene said as she grabbed her purse. "We gotta visit the ladies' room. Now y'all sit tight."

Nathan watched as they wiggled through the rows of tables and disappeared around a corner to the restroom. Then he slipped off his right shoe, took most of the money from his wallet, folded it and placed the bills inside his sock.

"What the hell are you doing?"

Nathan looked up and grinned. "Hell, don't you remember? Tijuana? Okinawa? Old Marine Corps rule: never carry big money in your wallet when you shack up with whores. They'll roll your young ass every time after you fall asleep. Better put your folding stuff in your sock."

Dan followed Nathan's example.

"Hey Doc, just what the hell was the Huk uprising?"

Dan snorted. "Damned if I know. That sounded pretty impressive though, didn't it?"

"Out-fucking-standing," Nathan said, "simply out-fucking-standing."

For a moment after waking Nathan didn't realize where he was. Then he remembered. Vertical bands of sunlight bordered the closed curtains of the motel room. The window air conditioner hummed noisily and the room was cold.

Someone stirred beside him. It was Darlene, pulling the covers over her bare shoulders. Even in the poor light Nathan could see the betraying dark roots in her hair. Crow's feet crept along the corners of her eyes. Her breath reeked of stale tobacco and booze. She was better looking last night, he tried to convince himself, or else I was drunker than I thought.

From across the room came muffled snoring. It was Dan, in the other bed with Gloria. Oh shit, not in the same room, Nathan thought, trying to remember details from last night. But everything beyond the Silver Saddle was either a faint blur or non-existent.

He eased to a sitting position on the side of the bed and realized he was naked except for his socks. He reached down and checked that the money was still there. He smiled in spite of the pain and wondered what Darlene must have thought about him keeping his socks on and what excuse he'd given. He glanced at his watch. Almost ten. Damn, we must've partied till at least three or four.

On the night stand next to the bed an empty bottle of Johnny

Walker Red stood beside the telephone. No wonder I feel like shit, Nathan thought, I don't even like Scotch. He looked around the room. Beer cans of various brands were scattered about, intermingled with plastic cups and wine bottles. No way we could've done all this damage by ourselves. It must've been one hell of a party. Sure hope we had fun.

Nathan speared another forkful of the western omelet on his plate. It was just past eleven o'clock. He and Dan were having breakfast at the Waffle House. They had managed to dress and slip out of the motel room without disturbing their slumbering bed mates. "You know something, Doc?"

"What's that?" Dan said. He'd ordered his eggs sunny side-up and was mashing and mixing them into a mound of grits.

The sight nearly made Nathan gag. He averted his eyes and sipped more black coffee. "I've never made love in my life."

Dan stopped mangling his eggs and stared at Nathan as though he'd lost his mind. "Say again?"

"I said I've never made love in my whole life. Not once."

Dan tore open another packet of sugar and poured it into his cup. "You seemed to be doing a fairly competent job of it a few hours ago if I remember correctly," he said, adding creamer to the coffee and stirring. "Surely that couldn't have been pushups, not the way Darlene was moaning." He shook his head and gave Nathan a pitying look. "No hope, no cure."

"Hell, that wasn't making love, that was just screwing. And that's exactly what I'm talking about. That's all I've ever done, ever. I had this steady girlfriend all through high school. I told you about her before, didn't I? Laura?"

Dan nodded as he chewed.

"Well, we never fooled around, not all the way I mean. We did just about everything else you could think of except that." Nathan traced a finger around the rim of his cup. "I had this chivalrous attitude back then. I knew I was going to join the Marines when I graduated, and I didn't want to spoil her for somebody else in case I didn't make it back. I loved her and respected her too much. At least I thought I did." He laughed. "What a sucker, huh?"

Dan shrugged.

"Anyway, right after I got back to the World Laura dumped me and married my used-to-be best friend. Turns out they'd been shacking up at college the whole time I was in Vietnam getting my ass shot at. Who needs enemies when you've got Jody, right?"

Dan's eyes widened but he said nothing and kept on eating.

"Yeah, well screw me once shame on you, screw me twice shame on me, right? You can bet your young ass I learned that lesson. Ever since then it's been nothing but the kind of shit we did last night." He spread a dollop of grape jelly on his toast. "So, I've never really made love, not even once. There it is.

"Know what that makes me?" He didn't wait for an answer. "A virgin, Doc. I'm a genuine emotional virgin."

# CHAPTER TWELVE

THE NEXT MORNING Nathan sat at his kitchen table eating breakfast and reading the Sunday edition of the *Bay City Herald*. A mild breeze and the musical tinkling of a love-struck Parula warbler drifted through the open window. Clarence, who had schmoozed his way inside and to breakfast, batted a sausage link across the floor.

Nathan flipped through the sports pages, passing over the basketball results and glancing briefly at the box scores of the spring training baseball games. He laid the sports aside and reached for the local/state news. When he saw the headline he bolted upright.

### Carter Named Assistant State Attorney

*State attorney John Canaby has appointed prominent Bay City lawyer, Thomas Carter, to replace Richard Farrell of Palm Meadows who resigned earlier this week amid a storm of controversy. . . .*

*Carter, 37, a lifelong resident of the area, graduated from Bay City High School in 1966, where he excelled in sports, being named to all-state honors his junior and senior years in both football and baseball. . . .*

Nathan's mind drifted past the drab existence of the last seventeen years and beyond the dismal months of the war to the bright days of invincibility and innocence. Days of waiting to take the world by the horns. Those had been wonderful days, glorious days. Nathan quarterbacked the Hurricanes to the conference championship, but Tom Carter grabbed the headlines with his record-setting performance at halfback

It was much the same during baseball season. Nathan was catcher and team captain. He excelled at the position, playing every inning of every game and leading the team in hitting. But Tom Carter was the Hurricane's ace pitcher and again received the lion's share of the glory, hurling a no-hitter and consecutive one-hitters. But it was Nathan who'd spent hours studying the opposing batters, learning their strengths and weaknesses. It was he who'd called the pitches and positioned the fielders to best defense each hitter and situation. He led the team to three straight conference championships, but Tom Carter was the headliner and the local hero.

Nathan's achievements hadn't gone unnoticed. The local junior college offered him a baseball scholarship but he turned it down to enter the Marine Corps after graduation. Tom, meanwhile, headed for Florida State University and fame on the gridiron with a full four-year scholarship. Tom was a good runner Nathan conceded, a hell of a runner in fact. He smirked. *Yeah, a real good runner, running away from the war by staying in school for six years, the fucking coward.*

The thought gave him a certain satisfaction. Tom Carter may have been the Big Man on Campus but Nathan Henson had been a warrior. A participant in the age-old sport of war, he had closed in mortal combat with a determined and worthy foe and stared Death in the face and come through victorious. . . .

>  *A graduate of the Florida State University College of Law, Carter has been married to the former Laura Annette Johnson for the past seventeen years. . . .*

Good ol' Laura. After she'd delivered her Dear John in person at the hospital, Nathan learned she and Tom had been sharing an off-campus apartment near the university for several months. Not the star player at college he'd been in high school, Tom eventually gave up his scholarship for political views unacceptable to the administration and football program. He and Laura became leaders in the campus anti-war movement.

Yeah, Nathan thought, while I was getting my ass shot off in Vietnam those two blue-blooded American patriots were out chanting "Hell no, we won't go!" Assholes.

Nathan suddenly felt nauseous. He got up and scraped the remainder of his scrambled eggs and sausage into Clarence's bowl. The big yellow cat rubbed against Nathan's legs and purred. His sausage had disappeared under the refrigerator. He sniffed the bowl for a moment and then began pawing at another link. Nathan poured himself another cup of coffee.

> . . . daughter Jennifer, 17, and son Joshua, 11. The
> Carters are very active in community and social
> affairs and members of . . .

Well isn't that just wonderful, Nathan thought, the all-American golden boy and his all-American family. Mr. and Mrs. Perfect. Why don't they mention how the draft-dodging bastard and his socialite slut were shacked up together and had to get married? Why don't they tell how he hid from the war by staying in school for so long, the coward son-of-a-bitch. Why don't they mention how little Miss Perfect was fucking around on her fiancé while he was overseas fighting for his country? Why don't they print any of that shit?

He flung the paper across the room in disgust. Clarence darted into the hallway. For several minutes Nathan sat staring into the blackness of his cup. In the distance he heard voices and a car door slam. Mrs. Ard was back from church. In a few minutes she'd be over inviting him to lunch and wanting to know when he was going to till her garden like he'd promised.

Clarence crept back into the kitchen. He stared up at Nathan with quizzical gold eyes. Nathan reached down and stroked his back and tail. "Come on Clarence," he said, sweeping the big yellow bundle into his arms and heading for the door, "we've got work to do."

"Dan, could I see you a moment?" Brenda Lewis, a registered nurse at Bay City Memorial, expected to find Dan Matthews alone when she walked into his office. His supervisor was usually at lunch from twelve to one. Instead, Dan and Rick Simmons were double-checking some lab results before sending them out.

Dan glanced up. "Be right with you." He frowned and motioned with his eyes for her to wait outside the door. "We're almost finished."

Brenda paced nervously in the hallway and hugged the black cardigan she wore over her white uniform. It was always too cold down here in the basement. She craved a cigarette but decided against it. Mr. Simmons was a stickler for rules.

A moment later Simmons exited Dan's office. Brenda forced a smile and exchanged a casual greeting as they passed in the corridor.

"Ah, just what the doctor ordered," Dan said as she entered the office. "Do you have it?"

Brenda nodded. "I'm about to die for a cigarette," she said, groping in the pockets of her cardigan. Dan quickly produced a pack of Kools from his desk drawer. He held the lighter steady as she drew smoke deep into her lungs.

"Well?" Dan said, growing impatient. There was no time to lose. Rick was lunching in the cafeteria today and might return any moment.

Brenda walked to the door and peered down the hallway. It was deserted. She slipped a hand into a pocket of her uniform and produced two small vials partially filled with clear liquid.

"Demerol," she said.

Dan took the vials. "Shit, these are half empty. What's the deal?"

"Or half full, depending on how you look at it."

"Okay. How much?"

"Same as usual."

"Oh, come on, I'm not going keep paying you full price for this stuff. You're starting to shortchange me every goddamn time. I can't afford it."

She dragged on the cigarette. "Listen, it's getting harder and harder to come by. Half the patients on my floor are complaining about pain after their shots. I'm giving them half saline as it is." She paused, arms folded and fingers kneading the wasted flesh of her biceps. "Crawford's getting suspicious. The old bitch isn't stupid, you know."

Dan stared hard at the thin nurse. Drugs had made the once-pretty Brenda Lewis old beyond her thirty-two years. He reached for his wallet. "Thirty-five," he said.

Brenda laughed and shook her head. "Fifty, take it or leave it. I don't have time to waste dicking around with you."

"Damn," he muttered, handing her the bills. "Next time I want my money's worth."

"You always get your money's worth," she said, counting the money and placing it carefully inside a pocket, "otherwise, you wouldn't keep buying."

"Godamn, you know when you've got somebody by the balls. You'd make a great hooker."

She drew on the cigarette and laughed. "You'd be surprised what a person will do for the right price." Her eyes seemed to burn through him. "Then again, maybe you wouldn't." She turned to leave and then paused when she reached the door. "And thanks for the smoke."

Wednesday evening when Nathan came over to pay the month's rent Mrs. Ard insisted he stay for supper. "Nothing fancy," she said, "just plain poor folks' food."

Nathan gorged himself on ham and collard greens, the last pickings from the winter garden he'd just plowed under. There were field peas with snaps, sweet corn Mrs. Ard had put up the past summer, and golden brown wedges of crackling cornbread.

"There's homemade apple pie and coffee soon as I wash up the dishes," she said.

Nathan offered to help but as usual Mrs. Ard shooed him out of the kitchen and into the parlor. He sat in an overstuffed chair, uncomfortably full but satisfied. Mrs. Ard's home cooked meals were a welcomed respite from his usual canned fare, and as always, he'd eaten too much.

From the kitchen came the sounds of running water and clinking dishes. The old woman hummed a church hymn. She always seemed to be humming or singing while she worked. Nathan wished he felt that way.

He surveyed the room. He liked this old house with its high ceilings and spacious rooms. It exuded warmth and a certain something Nathan wasn't sure he'd ever really known. Somehow, it felt like home.

Across the room a gas heater stood in the recess of an old fireplace. The evenings were still cool and blue flames danced against the glowing ceramic honeycombs. On the mantle above the fireplace, captured in frames of various shapes and sizes, was the essence of Louise Ard's life.

Nathan walked over to get a closer look at the photos. At one end of the mantle a stern father and stoic mother stared from a large oval frame of antique brass. A round-faced, plain girl of about six sat between them and stared bewilderedly at the camera. Next, was a photograph of Louise and Harold Ard on their wedding day. The young man had rugged features and a suit that hung loosely on his lanky frame. The smiling young bride wore her hair in thick braids coiled atop her head. She held a bouquet of white flowers that blended with the front of her flowing dress. Her round face was pleasant, almost pretty. Nathan had never met Mr. Ard. He'd passed away in the mid '50s a few years before Nathan began delivering the newspaper to the Ard's residence.

At the far end were pictures of Donna, the Ards' daughter. In one photo the little girl was dressed in ladies' clothing replete with hat and high heels, pushing a baby carriage. From another frame a pretty cheerleader sporting a short skirt and sweater with a large B smiled and waved pom-poms. And from a polished silver frame a young lady dressed in formal gown beamed on the night of her senior prom. Donna Ard was prettier than her mother and had married well. Nathan had only seen Donna a few times over the years, the latest several months ago. At fifty she was still an attractive woman.

And then there was Billy. A cowboy wearing a pair of six-shooters and a wide grin with missing front teeth; a determined twelve-year-old racing the wind on his brand new Western Flyer; the high school football star, number 42, one hand on hip and the other cradling a helmet with no face guard. And in the very center of the mantle stood a young soldier with intense eyes and a burning look of one ready to fight in defense of God and country.

Corporal Billy Ard was twenty years old and had not returned home from Korea.

A faded yellow telegram occupied one side of the double frame, regretfully informing the grieving parents their son was missing in action and presumed dead. Harold Ard never got over the loss of his only son. It had destroyed him. Mrs. Ard once told Nathan that her husband died of a broken heart. The official cause of death was congestive heart failure, but who could really say she was wrong?

Nathan understood. His own war had taught him about loss, a lesson repeated over and over until grief turned into numbness; until feelings morphed into a cold callousness of self-constructed walls. Inside those walls it was no longer life and future one clung to, but survival. It was a desolate place void of meaning and purpose, a place where hopes and dreams faded like fleeting shadows on the horizon.

"My Billy was a fine boy," Louise Ard said, startling Nathan. She set a tray with pie and coffee on the table fronting the sofa. "A fine boy," she said wistfully. "You would've liked him, Nathan. You remind me of Billy sometimes."

Nathan stood in front of the mantle and looked closely at the photograph and telegram. Years ago while collecting money for his paper route he'd asked Mrs. Ard about the soldier in the photo. Tears had welled in the woman's eyes as she told young Nathan that the soldier was her son, and how God had called him home to Heaven from the battlefield. Nathan never forgot how he'd felt miserable for days afterward, knowing he'd caused the nice lady pain.

Now he felt a strange bond of kinship with the young man staring back at him, an intimacy formed from common hardship and suffering. A brotherhood sealed with blood that was unfettered by bounds of time or place—the fraternity of the warrior.

Nathan felt uneasy. Several times over the past years he'd wanted to ask Mrs. Ard about Billy but was afraid of opening old wounds. Now it appeared she wanted to talk about her son. He seemed at a loss for words. Finally he said, "We don't look anything alike."

"Oh, shoo" she said, "I don't mean that a'tall. You act like Billy used to sometimes, the way you're always a-joking and a-teasing. The things that young'un used to pull." Her eyes twinkled at the memory.

"I remember one time when Billy was about ten. I was still working at the green stamp store then. It was a Saturday and we only worked half a day. It was about this same time a year, and I'd planned to put in my garden when I got home that afternoon. Billy's father was working out of town and I'd spent the better part of three weekends turning that garden under by myself. Weren't no gas tillers back then. I done the whole thing by hand with a shovel and a hoe."

She sat on the sofa and poured coffee into the cups. She added milk to one from a little china creamer. "You want cream or sugar?"

"No ma'am, black's fine. He walked over and sat at the other end of the sofa.

Mrs. Ard smiled. "I got home that day and changed into my old work clothes. Then I went to the shed to get my seeds and hoe to do my planting. Lord, I nearly died when I seen that garden. That boy and his friends had done dug holes and trenches all over. They had laid some old boards over the trenches to make tunnels. They was playing war and they done turned my whole garden and all my hard work into a fort."

Nathan laughed, as much at seeing Mrs. Ard's eyes lighting up as from hearing the story. "What'd you do then, wring his neck?"

"Lord, I sure felt like it. 'William Harold Ard,' I said, 'you get out of that tunnel and up here this instant.' He climbed up out of that hole and there weren't a clean spot on his whole body, nary a one. There was dirt everwhere. A body could've growed taters in that boy's ears.

" 'What is the meaning of this?' I hollered. All his friends had done run off by this time and poor Billy just stood there all by hisself trying to think of something to say. 'How come you little varmints dug my garden all up?' I said. "

Mrs. Ard chuckled and dabbed at her eyes with the corner of her apron as the scene replayed in her mind. "I won't never forget what he said to me. He looked up at me with them big brown eyes and that muddy face and said, just as innocent as you please, 'Well Mama, we tried digging in other places but we kept hitting roots.' He said it like I wouldn't have minded a bit if I'd come home and found the whole front yard dug up and my garden left be.

"That boy," she said, smiling and shaking her head, "that boy. Well, I give him a whupping he wouldn't soon forget. Then he went and rounded up all his friends. They had that garden all filled in and smoothed over by dark." She laughed again. "Lord, it sure made planting easy that year. Them boys had that garden turned under fine as beach sand." She sighed and sipped her coffee.

Nathan laughed. "Sounds like Billy was a handful all right. I used to play war when I was a kid, too. You must really miss him." Nathan hated himself the instant the last words slipped out. The last thing he wanted was to upset Mrs. Ard again.

Mrs. Ard set her cup down, and to Nathan's surprise and relief she was smiling. "Oh, Lord, yes. It's been thirty-three years since we got word about Billy. Sometimes it's hard to believe that so much time has passed."

She sighed. "It's something a body never quite gets over, not completely no how. Even after all these years I sometimes still get the feeling that muddy little boy will walk through that door tracking dirt through my clean house." She glanced toward the mantle.

Nathan set his cup down. He leaned forward and rested his forearms on his legs and stared across the room. "I think I know what you mean. I lost a lot of good buddies in Vietnam. It's been seventeen years and I still think about them every day." He looked up at Mrs. Ard. "I know it's not the same thing as Billy. What I mean is . . ." He paused, struggling for the right words.

"What I'm trying to say is, I only knew them for a few months but we got to be real close in that short time and it really hurt bad when I lost 'em."

The old woman smiled warmly. "I know what you're a-trying to say. Lord knows, I've surely played it all out in my own mind enough times through the years. But you're wrong about one thing. It's not how much time you have with someone you love that counts. It's what you do with the time you have that matters."

She reached over and placed a hand on his arm. "Life is so precious, son. Don't go a-wasting yours, you hear?

"Now, how about a slice of apple pie? It's still nice and warm from the oven."

## CHAPTER THIRTEEN

"ANDREW WON'T BE with us anymore," George announced before opening the meeting. "He's left the group. He called yesterday and we discussed it. He has some personal matters he needs to work out. We decided it would be best if he saw me on an individual basis, at least for now."

Silence ensued.

"Does anyone have anything they'd like to say about it?"

Nathan leaned forward in his chair. "Did one of us piss him off or something?"

"No." George took a sip of coffee. "It's strictly a personal matter. I really can't go into detail, but I can tell you it has nothing to do with the group or anyone here."

Another silence.

"No other questions, comments?"

"I think it sucks," said Nathan.

"Okay, why?"

"Hell, he could've told us about it instead of just skying out like that."

"I agree," Dan said. "It was pretty goddamn thoughtless of him not to at least talk it over with us first."

George leaned back. "What about you, Vic?"

Vic blew a stream of smoke into the air. "It ticks me off, too.

I thought we all agreed when we started this thing that we'd make all the meetings. And now he drops out, just like that."

George nodded and turned to Rene Boudreaux. "Rene?"

Rene slumped lower, propping one bare foot atop the other and sweeping his graying mane back with both hands. He shrugged. "Don't mean nothin to me."

Nathan jabbed a finger at Rene. "What's your fucking problem? We come here every week and lay our shit all over the table and all you ever do is sit there on your ass and say, 'It don't mean nothin,'" he said, mimicking Boudreaux's accent. "Well that's bullshit. If you're not gonna join in like everybody else then what the hell are you doing here? 'It don't mean nothing' ain't gonna hack it anymore."

George kept a straight face but smiled inwardly. He'd wondered when it would come to this, when someone in the group would get fed up with Rene's lack of participation and call him on it. It was this way in every group he'd conducted, and now it had finally happened with this one.

"Yeah," Vic said, "what gives you the right to just sit there while the rest of us spill our guts in here?"

"Put out or get out," Dan said, his gravelly voice making it unanimous.

"Fucking-A," Nathan said, his fists clenched.

Rene was silent but his jaw tightened and his olive complexion deepened.

George saw that Nathan was livid and knew he'd better step in before talk led to blows. He ground his cigarette into the ashtray and stared at Boudreaux. "Well, Rene?"

Rene glanced at him and then stared ahead at the wall; his eyes were mere slits.

George motioned to the others with a sweep of his hand. "These guys have made it clear they don't think you're carrying your share of the load in this group. It's your choice. You can either start contributing your fair share, or there's the door."

George looked at Nathan, and then Dan and Vic. "Is that

how you feel about it?"

"Hey, I just want him to do his part and—"

"Don't tell me," George said, pointing at Rene, "tell him."

Nathan turned and faced Boudreaux. "All we ask man," he said, his voice calmer now, "is that you carry your own weight. We've been busting our tails in here and you've just been sitting there saying nothing. If we've got to drop our drawers in here then so do you. That's all we're asking. It's like the 'Nam, man. We've got to know we can trust you."

Rene squirmed. He wanted to tell them all to shove it, and walk away. He didn't belong here. These weren't his people, they weren't his team. But he was caught in a no-win situation; that goddamn judge had seen to that. It was either this group counseling gig or six months in the county slammer for the theft charge. Six months for petty theft. And they had never really proven the charges. Goddamn redneck judge. He'd been lucky that George Browne had taken a chance on him. Well, he was up against it now. No choice but to eat shit.

"I need this group," he said finally, staring at the floor and trying to sound apologetic. "I'll try to do betta." The words left a nasty taste in his mouth.

"Well?" George said, glancing at the others.

"Fair enough," Dan said.

"That's all we want, man," Nathan said.

Vic nodded his assent.

"All right," George said. "We'll consider the matter closed and put it behind us."

George was far from convinced of Boudreaux's sincerity. He'd seen the type before, vets in trouble with the law, out to save their own asses from hot water instead of really wanting help for their underlying problems. But the others seemed willing to give him a chance, and there was the occasional vet in trouble who managed to turn things around through counseling and hard work. Those few who made it were worth the risk. Still, he wondered if Nathan and the others would feel the same if they knew the circumstances that led Rene to the group.

George lit a Marlboro and leaned back and propped his feet on the desk. "Okay. Subject for the day is losses. This seems like an ideal time to talk about it considering your reaction to Andrew's leaving." He paused and waited for someone to voluntarily take the lead.

After a moment Vic said, "Just what do you mean by losses?"

"Whatever it means to you," George said. "Remember, we're dealing with war and your experiences in the war. Losses can be many things, tangible or intangible; people, relationships, emotions, concepts, whatever you feel was destroyed or lost or taken from you by the war experience. That's what we're after. How these losses affected you, how you dealt with them then, how you're dealing with them or not dealing with them now."

He looked from face to face. They seemed collectively uncomfortable. It was a tough and painful subject, a topic that no one seemed willing to attempt. He understood their hesitancy. It was as if he were asking them to tear away a thick scab that took years to form and expose an old festering wound. But it needed to be done; the poison had to be drained.

"How about you, Nathan? I noticed something interesting in the way you reacted to the news about Andrew."

Nathan sat up straight and took a sip from his cup of coffee while he tried to figure out what George meant. "What did I do?"

"Think back to what you said when I first told you Andrew left the group."

Nathan tried to remember but drew a blank. He didn't feel like thinking. He didn't feel like sitting here for the next hour trying to dredge up shit he'd tried so long to forget. He wanted to get some beer and go home. If he got drunk enough he wouldn't have to think. Why was George dumping this shit on him, anyway? "I don't remember what I said."

George reached for the ashtray on the desk and set his cigarette on the edge. "I believe your words were, 'Did one of us piss him off or something?' Does that tell you anything?"

Nathan shifted restlessly; his fingers tapped the Styrofoam cup. God, he thought, I hate it when he plays these fucking mind games. "I don't know, maybe I'm stupid but I don't have any idea what you're trying to get me to say."

George picked up his cigarette and tapped off the ash. "Okay, you said 'Did one of us piss him off or something?' Think about it for a minute. What do you see in those words?"

Nathan rolled his eyes and stared at the ceiling. He tugged at his moustache and his right leg pumped up and down. "I was asking if it was my fault or somebody else's that Andrew left?"

"Which means?"

Nathan hesitated. His brow furrowed as he wracked his brain. "I don't know; that I'm trying to take the blame or something?"

George nodded. "That, and how about guilt?"

Nathan thought for a moment. "Yeah, I guess I do feel a little guilty about him leaving. I mean, how do I know there wasn't something I could've said or done that might've made a difference, maybe caused him to stick with the group or—"

George bolted upright and nearly came out of his chair. He slapped the desktop with an open palm. "Good, that's exactly it!"

Nathan was dumfounded; he wondered what he'd said to cause such a reaction.

"Don't you see?" George said. "It's a classic example of arrested behavior, a clear link from how you dealt with things as a nineteen-year-old in Vietnam to how you still react to things today nearly twenty years later. You're assuming guilt or taking responsibility for circumstances beyond your control."

Nathan sat there for a moment, confused, and then shook his head. "I don't get it."

George rested his arms on the desk. "Okay. Andrew was a member of this group; better yet, let's say a member of this squad. Suddenly he's gone. That's a loss. You're feeling that you possibly said or did something that might've contributed to his loss. Or maybe it was something you didn't do or say. An act of omission. Now, you're back in Vietnam. A buddy in your squad gets wounded or killed. It all happens in a flash and suddenly he's gone, flying away aboard a medevac chopper. And you start to wonder, 'Maybe if I'd checked out that tree line better,' or, 'If only I hadn't told him to walk point, then poor Joe wouldn't have gotten hit.' Sound familiar?"

Unpleasant memories swept through Nathan's mind, dark, questioning shadows of doubt that he'd wrestled with for years. What if? Yes, it sounded familiar, painfully familiar. "Yeah," he said, "shit like that happened. A lot."

"And you've been carrying the assumed guilt around with you all these years," George said.

Nathan massaged his eyes with a thumb and forefinger and then looked at George. "Well goddamnit, maybe it *was* my fault."

"Then tell us about it," George said, grabbing the coffee cup on his desk.

Nathan breathed deeply. He leaned back and stared at the ceiling. "Shit," he muttered, looking around the room and shaking his head, "I don't know if I can."

"We're with you, grunt," Vic said.

"Right here for you, bro," said Dan.

Even Rene seemed to be paying attention, though he said nothing.

Nathan looked at the others and wondered how he managed to keep putting himself in such spots. Screw it, he decided, might as well get it out and over with. George won't let it drop till I do.

He took a deep breath and slowly let it out. "All right," he said "this happened in February of '68 during Tet. We were on a squad-size patrol below Camp Carroll. Our company was providing security for the Army 175s that were firing support for Khe Sanh. We had a gun team with us and a corpsman of course." He pictured Doc Dunn's smiling face as they moved through the wire that morning. The sky was overcast and a cold drizzle chilled them to the bone, but nothing could put a damper on the young corpsman's spirit. Three more days and he'd leave for R&R;

Australia, hot food, clean sheets and round-eyed women.

"I'd just taken over the squad. Mendoza had rotated back to the World a couple of weeks before, and then Lukens and Calder both got their shit blown away within a couple of days of each other. Hell, I'd only been there five months and just made corporal." He looked up with a weak grin on his face. "Attrition's a great way to make rank.

"Anyway, we were in this hilly area near the mountains. There were a lot of deserted villages around there. It was a free-fire zone. Weren't supposed to be any civilians left in the area. Hell, it was all a free-fire zone up on the DMZ whether the brass said so or not. Screw that 'Don't fire unless you're fired upon first' bullshit. Up there, anything that moved or looked like it might move, we blew it the fuck away."

"There it is," Dan said. "Those rear-echelon desk jockeys down in Saigon could make all the rules they wanted to. We played by our own set of rules up in I CORPS."

"You got that shit straight," Nathan said.

"You were leading a patrol," George said, steering the conversation back on track.

Nathan took the hint. "So, there were these small vills we kept coming across. Some of 'em weren't even on the map. I was trying to keep from panicking. I wasn't exactly the greatest map reader in the world and I was scared shitless. This was Tet, remember. We were finding signs of the NVA everywhere. Almost all of the vills had fighting holes and trenches, fresh ones. And cook fires and trash and shit. The whole 324th NVA Division was supposed to be somewhere in the area, and here we were, a fucking squad walking around in the boonies just asking for it, and with me in charge. It was a shit sandwich waiting to happen. Hell, I wouldn't've felt safe if our whole damn company would've been there. To send a squad out alone was idiotic, but there we were."

He paused for a sip of coffee and cleared his throat. "So, my goal was to keep from fucking up and getting somebody killed. Just keep our eyes and ears open, go from checkpoint to checkpoint and get our young asses back inside our own wire.

"We'd just passed our third checkpoint which was one of the villages on the map. I was pretty sure about our location because there was a blue line just east of the vill and we had visual with a creek in that direction. We were moving up this long slope with rows of dikes running across it like a terrace. Looked like it hadn't been used in years. Then we saw some hooches farther up near the crest of the hill, maybe two hundred meters away. Another vill. I checked the map, but it didn't show. I took another compass reading. We were going the right way, I'm still sure about that, because the hill we were on was there and a bigger hill was off to our right. But according to my map that vill up ahead wasn't supposed to be there."

Nathan swallowed the last of his coffee and began picking at the Styrofoam cup. "I had this black dude named Roberts on point. He'd only been in-country a couple of months but he had his shit together. My best point man was Betz, but I had him and his fire team covering our rear. I figured Roberts could handle the point okay, and I was close enough up front to where I could help out if he needed it."

He set the cup between his legs and gripped the arms of his chair with both hands as if he were in danger of falling to the floor. Sweat darkened the armpits of his shirt. He saw it again, as clear as if it had just happened, putting the folded map back in his trouser pocket and motioning for Roberts to move out. The happy-go-lucky preacher's kid from Ohio who planned to study for the ministry on the GI Bill had flashed a grin and signaled thumbs-up.

"I'd just waved for Roberts to keep going when the gooks opened up." Nathan paused, shook his head and looked away at the wall. "Roberts went flying backwards. I could see the tracers going right through him. They picked him up and flung him back like a rag doll." He feigned a cough to cover his cracking voice. "He landed on his back across a dike about ten meters in front of me, shot all to shit. That gun had done a number on him. His whole chest was laid open, just a big scrambled mess. One side of his head was gone and his brains were oozing out of his skull like it was in slow motion." He swallowed hard, fighting for composure.

"I almost puked. I'd seen gooks blown all to shit, but that never bothered me. I'd seen a lot of dead Marines too, but not like that." Nathan stood and walked over to the window. He stared up into the branches of a tall oak above the roof of the adjoining building. After a moment he turned and leaned against the window sill.

"They had us pinned down behind those dikes. Our gun team managed to move up and started kicking some ass. The rest of the squad was spread out and were pretty much on-line and returning fire. I got on the radio with the Company. The Six told us to hang on, they were sending a reactionary platoon after us and a gun ship was on the way. They told me to pop red smoke in front of our position when I heard the chopper coming. I remember worrying that I wouldn't be able to hear the gun ship when it got there because of all the noise, so I kept looking all over the sky hoping to see it." He looked up and studied the holes in the ceiling tiles for a moment.

"Then I saw Doc Dunn jump up from my left. He crossed the dike we were spread out behind and headed for Roberts. I hollered at him to stop but he either didn't hear me or just ignored me."

The scene reeled through Nathan's memory like a horror movie. His pulse quickened and his knuckles turned white as he gripped the sill.

"I kept screaming for him to get down, that Roberts was already fucking dead, but the crazy bastard just kept going." His voice broke and he tried to swallow. His face showed the strain years of agonizing memories had heaped upon it. He shook his head and stared at the wall behind George.

"Then his head exploded." Again Nathan heard the hollow *thwack!* and watched in horrid disbelief as Doc Dunn's helmet flew back and his head disappeared in a shower of red gore. For an instant the legs kept the body staggering forward, and then they buckled and he pitched forward.

Nathan took a couple of deep breaths and looked at George. "He was laying there fifteen feet away with no head, and his body kept shivering like he was cold."

Nathan limped back to his chair, spent. He sat with hands clasped together. There was nothing else inside him for the moment. He wanted to cry, but like seventeen years earlier, couldn't. He felt empty, hollow and cold, a shell mirroring the anguish the years had failed to erase. Finally, he looked up at George through pained eyes. "I thought this shit was supposed to help. All it's doing for me is ripping my guts out all over again."

George locked eyes with him and nodded. "It's supposed to. I told everyone up front that this wasn't going to be a rap group where we all sit around and bullshit each other with war stories. You can do that on your own time. But to really confront your problems, to finally face things that have eaten you up for years, isn't going to be easy. Sure, it hurts. Sometimes the healing can be as painful as the wounding." He took a drag on his cigarette and let the words sink in.

"You've taken a big step toward that healing today, Nathan. Before, you've talked about Vietnam in a detached sort of way. It's like you've been saying, 'I was there, and this is what I did or saw, but I'm telling you this from a distance because I don't want to get too damn close because I know it will hurt if I do.'

"But today you risked getting close and feeling the pain. You've finally gotten down on eye-level with it again, face-to-face. You've relived a painful experience that's haunted you for years. It's haunted you not only because you saw a couple of your friends get killed, but also because you feel responsible for their deaths." He looked hard at Nathan. "Isn't that right?"

"Yeah, I do," Nathan said, trying to avoid direct eye contact.

"Why?"

"I don't know, I just do. I should've—"

"It wasn't your fault," Vic said. "I don't see anything you did

104

that was wrong or—"

"Whoa there," Dan said. "It seems like we've heard this song before."

Vic looked at him. "What do you mean by that?"

"Like the time you were flying during the bad weather and you couldn't land to pick up those WIAs. Remember how you blamed yourself for that even though you knew you'd probably crash if you tried?"

"Oh yeah," Vic said, almost a whisper.

"I believe what Dan's saying," George said, "and it's a very good point, is that it's a lot easier to solve someone else's problems than it is to work on your own."

"There it is," Dan said.

George turned to Nathan. "You've been blaming yourself because you were in charge of the patrol. But think about it. Where does the responsibility really lie? Roberts was on point, but it could've been anybody. You said yourself that he had his shit together. Chances are it wouldn't have made any difference who was walking point. If it had been you, in all probability you would have been blown apart by that machine gun. But you were the squad leader. It was your job to be back in the column, reading the map, using the radio, making sure everyone else did their job.

"Was it your fault the patrol route carried you into that ambush? Weren't you simply doing your job and following orders? And what about Doc Dunn? Was it your fault he kept going after you told him to get down because Roberts was already dead?" George paused. "He knew the risks. For whatever reason, he kept going.

"So whose fault was it for any of this? Yours, for not disobeying orders and taking another route? Yours, for not walking point yourself even though that's not a patrol leader's job? Yours, for not trying to rescue a man yourself who you knew was already beyond help?"

George let a few seconds lapse. Nathan sat in silence; the

vacant expression on his face reflected the emptiness he felt inside.

"How about it being the brass's fault for ordering the patrol? Or the politicians who got us involved in the war in the first place? Or why not blame God? After all, he sees all and knows all. That's what the Bible says."

George waited a moment. "The truth is it's nobody's fault; not God's, not the politicians, not the officers in the rear sticking pins in a map and playing war like it was some kind of perverse chess game. And it's not your fault, either. You were just doing your job the best way you knew how, just like Vic was doing his that time he couldn't land his chopper. You were both little cogs caught up in a great big machine that unfortunately no one knew quite how to operate properly.

"Have you seen that bumper sticker, the one that says 'Shit Happens'? There's a lot of truth and wisdom in that saying. Things do happen, and often it's bad things happening to good people. Usually it's nobody's fault, it just happens. Your point man died because he walked into an ambush. The corpsman died because he chose to try to save what he probably believed was a wounded Marine. And today Andrew left this group because of circumstances beyond his control. None of the above was anybody's fault. It all simply happened."

George leaned on the desk and locked eyes Nathan. "Do you see now how your reaction to Andrew leaving is a carryover from the way you were conditioned to act by what you experienced in Vietnam? 'My buddy got hit. I was the squad leader, so I must've done something to cause it, or didn't do something to prevent it. Andrew left the group. I'm an active member of the group, so I must've done something to cause him to leave, or failed to do something to prevent him from leaving.' Do you see it?"

Nathan nodded.

"Remember," George said, "you were only nineteen and thrown into an insane situation no one could control. You don't have to be locked into that mindset of guilt any longer. Another lifetime has passed since then. It's time to put things in perspective. It's time to let go of things you had no control over and quit punishing yourself for them."

Nathan slumped in his chair, drained. But there was something else, something he couldn't yet comprehend. Almost imperceptibly, for the first time in many years the burden weighing his soul began to lift.

# CHAPTER FOURTEEN

Tuesday morning Nathan sat in the doctor's office thumbing through an outdated issue of *Sports Afield*. He dreaded this appointment. He'd last seen Dr. Parker in January, and the crotchety old physician was bound to chew him out for the three-month absence. Nathan wished he could go on avoiding the confrontation, but his prescriptions needed renewing and Cyrus Parker was one of the few doctors in town who would accept a veteran's fee-basis card.

"Mr. Henson?"

Nathan was surprised at the unfamiliar voice. That's not Mrs. Givens, he thought. He glanced across the waiting room and focused on a shapely figure in white standing by the swinging doors. No, that most definitely isn't Mrs. Givens.

"Mr. Henson?" the young woman said again in her slightly husky voice. She clutched a file folder to her chest.

Nathan dropped the magazine on the table and limped across the room. Another piece of shrapnel was working its way out of his left foot, but he tried not to let it show. "Room B," she said, standing aside as he passed through the louvered doors. He tried to read her name tag as he walked by but the folder covered it. A hunger stirred inside him and he wished he could trade places with his medical records.

She smiled as he entered the cool, lime-green examination room. "Let's get your weight." He stepped onto the scales, slid the heavier balancing weight in the one hundred-fifty pound slot and slid the smaller balancing weight far to the right. "Shit," he whispered, disgusted with himself when the scales finally balanced out at one ninety-four. A fine damn time to've put on weight.

"Must be these work boots or all the money in my wallet," he said as she leaned in front of him to read the scale. He glanced down. Her hair was like spun gold, pulled back in a French braid and fastened with a tortoise shell barrette. He breathed deeply, inhaling the light scent of honeysuckle.

Nathan stepped from the scales and eyeballed her as she walked to the stainless steel counter where she'd placed his chart. Late twenties or early thirties, he guessed. Tall, with hips that flared from a trim waist. Athletic-looking calves visible beneath the knee-length skirt. His gaze drifted upward, tracing the faint outline of panties and broad strap of bra teasing from beneath the white blouse. He forced his eyes away as she turned.

She motioned to the examination table covered with thin white paper. "Hop up here and let's get your blood pressure."

Nathan sat on the edge of the table, for the first time getting a good look at the woman's front as she stood before him with a blood pressure monitor in hand. HELEN MORRIS, CMA he read from the tag pinned above her left breast. Pretty, he decided, as she wrapped the wide band around his biceps. Not Hollywood-style, but a certain earthy beauty. A bit of a bump midway along her nose; full lips that turned up slightly at the corners giving a hint of a smile. But her eyes were what really grabbed his attention; large and brown with gold flecks. Eyes you could get lost in.

She clasped his forearm to her side with her upper arm and squeezed the bulb to pressurize the band. Nathan's pulse quickened as he felt the side of her breast lightly touch his arm. A carnal charge swept through him, the way it used to when he would 'accidentally' brush against girls in the crowded hallways between classes at school.

Helen listened through the stethoscope. "Hmm." She released the pressure. "Have you been taking your medication regularly?"

"Yeah, every day." He felt uneasy, almost coarse in her presence. He wished he'd dressed better this morning.

"Let's try the other arm," Helen said, removing the cuff and stepping to his other side. She repeated the procedure. This time his arm was positioned lower against her rib cage, away from her breast. "That's better," she said when finished, "but it's still a little high."

She jotted the results in his chart and then felt for a pressure point on Nathan's wrist. No ring, he noted, eyeing her left hand.

She recorded the pulse rate. "Dr. Parker will be with you in a few minutes, Mr. Henson."

"Nathan."

"Excuse me?"

"Call me Nathan. That mister stuff's too formal for me."

She smiled. "Okay, Nathan, the doctor will be right in." She hurried out the door.

A few minutes passed before he heard scuffling footsteps and the door opened.

"Hey, Dr. Parker," he said to a tall thin man with receding gray hair, "how's it going?"

Dr. Parker ignored the greeting and cast a sidelong glance Nathan's way as he lifted the chart from the counter and held it at an angle to catch the light better.

"Where's Mrs. Givens?"

"Retired. And where the hell have you been for three months?" His brows arched as he gazed over the top of wire-rimmed bifocals.

Quickly Nathan mulled over the alibis he'd concocted. None seemed suitable now. "No excuse; I guess I've been in a rut lately."

The doctor grunted. "I've told you before the VA doesn't like it when a patient is hit-and-miss on a prescribed treatment plan. Keep it up and they're liable to cancel your fee-basis card."

Nathan knew Dr. Parker barked loud but rarely bit. He'd

been Nathan's doctor since high school when he'd given free physicals to athletes participating in school sports programs. "Oh hell, Doc, you wouldn't let that happen. You like all that money you make off the VA too much."

Dr. Parker ignored him and scanned the chart. "Blood pressure's acting up, I see. You still drinking all that beer I told you to cut out?"

"No sir," Nathan lied, "just a few now and then." *Your pressure would be up too if that good-looking nurse had just rubbed her boobs all over your arm, you old goat.* "Where'd you get the new nurse?"

Dr. Parker shot Nathan his arched-brow look again. "Miss Morris? She came to work about a month ago right before Celia left. How's the foot doing?"

"Still hurts. Another piece of shrapnel's about to come out."

"Let's have a look."

Nathan removed his left boot and sock. Several purplish dots resembling embedded pencil leads were scattered along the side of his foot below the ankle. "This one here," he said, pointing to a reddened area on the outer edge near the heel.

"Humph." Dr. Parker scrutinized the foot a moment and then looked up. "Like I've said before, you can go to the VA hospital and let them remove what they can, or you can live with it. I don't think it'll do you much good letting them cut on it. There's enough lead in that foot to last a lifetime. It's up to you, though."

"To hell with them quacks," Nathan said, pulling his sock on. "They'd probably cut my leg off above the knee and tell me it was the only way they could get rid of all the shrapnel. Uh-uh, I'm not letting them butchers get hold of me.

"How about some more pain pills while it's working its way out? And I need these other scripts renewed, too." He finished tying the bootlace and handed Dr. Parker the renewal forms.

"You watch these pills with that beer," Dr. Parker said, scratching illegible markings across the renewal slips. "And I want your butt back in this office twice a week to get that pressure checked. We might have to adjust your medication again. And cut down on the beer."

"Yes sir, I will."

Dr. Parker opened the door. "Miss Morris!"

Nathan watched as the she stepped through the doorway. "Yes?"

"Nathan here will be coming in twice a week beginning this Thursday to get his blood pressure monitored. Make sure you keep an accurate record of it and keep me posted."

He turned to Nathan. "I want you back here in two weeks to see me. Two weeks, not two months."

"I'll be here."

"Humph," he grunted and shuffled out of the room to see his next patient.

"Is eight-thirty convenient for you?"

"Yeah, that's fine."

"Good," she said, writing something on his chart. She glanced up. "I'll see you Thursday morning then, Mr. Henson."

"Nathan."

She smiled. "I'll see you Thursday morning, Nathan."

He grinned. "I'll be here." He watched as Helen walked down the hall and into the adjoining room. You can bet your sweet young ass I'll be here.

Vic Guerino trailed the young couple around the car lot. The April afternoon had grown warm and sweat beaded his balding head. For twenty minutes they'd wandered along rows of new Fords, making their way in descending order from the expensive luxury models to where Vic knew from the beginning they would end up.

"The Escort's an ideal choice for a young family just starting out," he said when they finally reached the area where the compacts were parked. "There's plenty of room inside and she's a real gas saver."

They stopped beside a bright red model. "Ooh honey, it's so

cute," the puffy-faced woman said. A recent bout with pregnancy had added several pounds to an already corpulent figure. She caressed the front fender of the car with meaty fingers and turned to her silent husband. "I wanna sit in it," she said, handing the tall rail of a man a drooling bundle wrapped in a yellow blanket.

Vic opened the door for her, hoping the Escort's bucket seat would be wide enough to contain her. After shutting the door he glanced at the fat-cheeked infant with mucous draining from its nose and spittle dribbling down its chin. "Cute kid. What's his name?"

"Natasha," the rail answered in a lackluster voice. "She's a girl."

Vic chuckled. "Sorry; I can never tell the difference when they're that little. I've got one of each at home myself. People were always getting them wrong unless we had them dressed in blue or pink. She's a real cutie, anyway." He stepped downwind and lit a cigar. God, what a homely kid, he was thinking; probably look just like her mother when she grows up.

"Thanks," the thin man said without expression.

"Ooh honey, I love it," the woman squealed. She gripped the steering wheel and whipped it back and forth like a road racer. "Can we take it for a drive?"

"Sure," Vic said. He noted the stock number on the windshield. "Let me run get the keys. Be right back."

When he returned with the keys the rail had managed to fold his stilt-legged frame into the front passenger's seat. The baby squirmed on his lap and blew spit bubbles that trailed down her grimy bib. "A lot more room in there than you'd think, huh?" Vic said, relieved to see an inch or two between the man's head and the headliner as he handed the keys to the woman.

She squealed again and bounced in her seat as the engine fired to life. The starter growled until her husband reached over and forced her fingers off the key.

"We'll be back in a jiff," she said, her face flushed with excitement.

Vic forced a smile. "Take your time." He needed the sale but was glad to be rid of them for the moment. "Give her a good run." He patted the Escort's roof as a leaden foot revved the engine. With a jerk it sped away and bounced heavily over the ignored speed bump near the car lot's entrance.

"Christ, I hope the shocks can take it," he muttered, shaking his head as the compact merged with traffic and disappeared around a corner.

Twenty minutes later Vic saw the red Escort pull into the lot; it almost bottomed out bouncing over the speed bump again. "How do you like her?" he asked, mustering his best salesman's smile as the car lurched to a stop. "Fine automobile, isn't she?" He opened the driver's door and helped the woman struggle from her seat. The suspension seemed to sigh in relief.

"Ooh, we love it," she said as her husband unfolded from the other side with the infant. "Don't we honey?"

"Nice," he muttered, "but I don't think we can afford it."

Vic's hopes faded. He needed this sale badly. He'd figured the eager woman would be an easy mark. "Well, by using the factory rebate as a down payment and financing for sixty months, I'm sure we can get the payments down to around one-fifty. How does that sound?"

The main seemed unimpressed. "Still don't think we can afford it," he said, stepping back until only his head and shoulders were visible behind his wife.

The woman thrust out her lower lip. "You always say that." She turned and took the bubbling baby from her husband and turned to face Vic. "I guess we'll have to wait."

Vic watched as his commission walked back to their rusted-out Dodge. Karen was really going to be pissed if he didn't bring something home this week. He couldn't borrow another dime against future commissions, either. "Hey, wait a minute!" he shouted after them. He fumbled in a shirt pocket for a business card. "Why don't you try our pre-owned lot just down the street?" he said, pointing the way. "I know they can make you a deal you can live with. Ask for Roy and tell him Vic sent you. He'll take good care of you." What the hell, he thought, fifty bucks is better than nothing.

The woman grabbed the card. "Thanks," she said, just as the baby gurgled and spit up curdled milk across her shoulder.

She wiped the mess from her blouse with a stained cloth diaper. "Let's go look at Chevies, honey."

Vic watched the old clunker billow gray smoke until it drove past the used car lot and disappeared. "Fat-ass bitch," he said as he turned to walk back to the office. A familiar *whump-whump-whump* caught his ear. A painful longing, like for a lost love, pricked his heart as he recognized the tiny dot of a helicopter beating its way high across the clear sky.

"Huey," he whispered. He stared at it sullenly and thought of better days.

"Hey, Doc," Nathan said, cradling the phone with his shoulder as he stirred the vegetable soup heating for supper, "what's a CMA?"

"A CMA?"

"Yeah, you know, like a nurse or something."

"Oh. Certified medical assistant, why?"

"Nothing." Nathan wasn't ready yet to reveal his infatuation. "I just read it somewhere and didn't know what it was. You need a ride to the meeting Friday?"

"Yeah. If that ex-wife of mine would lay off for a while I could afford my own wheels. Can you pick me up at the lab around two-thirty?"

"No problem."

"Thanks, bro. I'll make it up for your taxi service as soon as I get back on my feet."

"No sweat. See you Friday."

"It's not cold Mommy, really," shouted a little blonde girl wearing a pink swimsuit as goose bumps prickled her bare skin. "Jump in!"

A slender leg descended ankle-deep into the water. "Brrr."

Helen Morris shivered and quickly withdrew her foot. "Heather," she called to her daughter who was splashing showers of water at the shallow end, "it's still too cold to be swimming."

"Fraidy-cat!"

"It's too cold, honey. Come over here and lie in the sun with me."

The girl's happy face turned into a frown. "You promised."

Helen sighed, defeated. She had promised they would go swimming on her next afternoon off from work. The days were warm lately, and Heather had spent what seemed like hours eagerly watching the apartment complex's maintenance men preparing the pool. She was such a little water bug. Helen glanced at her watch. "Okay then, but only for thirty more minutes. And stay on the shallow side. Don't go beyond the rope."

"Okay, Mommy." Heather resumed her play. She turned in quick circles like a human waterwheel, splashing water skyward and watching it cascade in sparkling drops.

Helen smiled at the six-year-old's antics and lay back on the beach towel. High overhead several gulls wheeled in slow spirals. A few cottony clouds shared their domain. From Helen's portable radio the Eagles sang about making love in the desert.

She lifted her head from the towel and peered through sunglasses down her body and frowned. The chill from the water and the afternoon breeze off the bay caused her nipples to harden. They stood out like darkened peaks atop the mounds of her breasts. She'd been afraid of that. The white one-piece swimsuit that looked so attractive on the model in the Sears catalog left little to the imagination. The thin liner was clearly inadequate. What will it look like when it's wet? she wondered. Still, it'll look great against a tan. Maybe I can sew in another liner from an old suit. She was glad no one else was around the pool area, and that she'd brought a beach cover-up.

"Look Mommy," Heather shouted, "I'm a porpoise."

Helen watched Heather dive beneath the water, kicking furiously and holding a hand above the surface with fingers pressed together like a dorsal fin.

"That's great, honey," she called when Heather surfaced, sputtering and blinking back the water dripping into her eyes. "You look just like Flipper."

Heather grinned and then held her breath and plunged under again.

Helen closed her eyes and willed her muscles to relax. The sun was still high enough to be felt and she imagined herself a sponge soaking in the warm rays against the cool breeze. She was glad the cold weather was ending and that summer beckoned. "Mm," she whispered, picturing herself lounging on warm beach sand with the sound of the surf caressing the shore and the pungent smell of salt air. "It won't be long now."

She found herself thinking about him again, his blonde hair and boyish good looks. I've never kissed anyone with a mustache before, she thought. I bet it tickles. He seems to have a terrific sense of humor, too. I like that. Such sad eyes though, like a scolded puppy. He seems happy enough, but at the same time his eyes make him look sad. Nice eyes, though. I thought they were blue but this morning they looked almost green. Maybe his clothes make them change.

"Quack-quack, quack-quack. Look Mommy, I'm a duck!"

"That's nice honey, ten more minutes."

I wonder if he's married. He wasn't wearing a ring, but lots of men don't wear rings. I guess I could ask Dr. Parker. He'd know, I bet. No girl, not a very good idea; way too forward. I don't want Dr. Parker getting the wrong impression. It might say in his records. Or I could just come right out and ask him.

Helen smiled as she imagined the scene: "Are you married? Just wondering; you see, I happen to be single again and find you very attractive and it's been such a long time since I . . ."

She felt herself blushing at the thought. Get a grip on yourself girl, you can't just blurt out to a man that you're interested. That'll only drive him away or else he'll think you're good for only one thing.

She blushed again and felt anew the warm urge deep inside she'd tried to suppress. *I'll just have to be subtle and let him know somehow that I'm interested. There's plenty of time, twice a week for now at least. That's plenty of time to get him to notice me.*

Helen glanced at her watch. She stood and put on the cover-up and shook the towel into the wind. "It's time to go, honey."

"Aw, do we have to?"

"Come on now. It's getting chilly and I need to start supper. We can swim again this weekend if the weather's nice. I promise."

"Oh, all right." Heather climbed out of the pool and took the towel Helen offered. She dried her face and looked up, beaming. "You look pretty in your new swimsuit, Mommy."

"Thank you, sweetie; you really think so?"

She nodded.

Helen smiled and took her daughter's hand. *I wonder if Nathan would think so?*

Rene Boudreaux lay stoned in his hammock, one arm cradled behind his head. The Coleman lantern hissed from its ceiling hook and painted a pale yellowish swath across the cabin's dirt floor. He inhaled deeply and the tiny coal of ash glowed red. He held the smoke for several seconds and then blew the acrid stream upward where it boiled into the haze hovering above.

Outside the cabin the chirping alto of myriad crickets blended with the croaking bass of bullfrogs as they serenaded the chilly night at Mashburn Lake. The crescent moon hung in the southwestern sky, its profile broken now and then by bats zigzagging after insects over the obsidian water. The tremulous wail of a screech owl shimmered through the darkness, rising and faltering into mournful silence among the shroud of pine and cedar encircling the lake.

He dreaded tomorrow. He was tired; tired of the group with all its bullshit; tired of the area and its redneck cops and judges; tired of the past twenty years. He missed the old days, Brooklyn, his gang.

He took another hit and smiled, remembering . . .

The Cobras had ruled the streets. Angelo, Vinnie, Raoul and the other boys from Bensonhurst. Nobody fucked with them, nobody. Plenty had tried, for sure. It was more than one stiff they had left in the gutter for the rats to feast on and the cops to find.

Like Big Al. Rene's blood raced as he remembered how Big Al and the other Black Knights from Dyker Heights had taunted them and challenged them to a rumble. They swore they would drive the Cobras all the way out of Kings County that night. His head buzzed recalling the moment; his hand stabbing upward in the dark as it had that night when he struck, not air, but the soft flesh of Big Al's throat. The four-inch blade penetrated to the hilt and then ripped upward. Big Al groveled on his knees clutching his throat, trying to stem the flow of blood spilling onto the street. He choked as he tried calling for his mother and God until Angelo—or was it Vinnie?—stuck the .32 behind his ear and squeezed off a round.

That ended Big Al and the Black Knights. After word spread through the streets nobody dared mess with the Cobra's turf again.

Nobody, that is, except the cops. Angelo and Vinnie died on a littered sidewalk when somebody tipped the cops about a liquor store job. And because a cop was nearly wasted during the shootout, Raoul got twenty-to-life for armed robbery and attempted murder. The rest, including Rene, managed to escape.

He'd often wondered who the rat was that set them up. It had to have been somebody from the inside, one of their own; probably Franco. Franco had disappeared shortly after the trial as though he'd vanished into thin air. Yeah, it was Franco, but he'd never been able to prove it.

Then came the grand-theft auto charge. Vinnie's kid brother, Sal, bungled that job but good; strictly amateurish. The kid was stupid and would never learn. But hey, he was Vinnie's kid bro, right? He owed it to Vin to try. Sal had gotten sloppy and they both got busted; juvenile detention for Sal, three-to-five for him.

Or, the judge had offered, four years in the Army.

The military was a drag at first, but then a place called Vietnam heated up. As it turned out, the jungle was a lot like the streets. He'd felt at home there. It was the ultimate rumble, where you were rewarded for killing instead of thrown into prison. And because he was so good at what he did they offered him the LRRPs after six months in-country. Long Range Reconnaissance Patrol. Snoop and poop. Dangerous shit, right down his alley.

There he found a new gang to run with. His team: Pancho, the little cutthroat from El Paso; Ace, former gang leader from the slums of Detroit; and Beaver, the anomaly, the quiet buck-toothed hillbilly from Kentucky and the most bloodthirsty killer of the bunch . . .

Rene felt a slight burning as the roach died against his fingertips. He groped blindly for the plastic bag beneath the hammock. He lit a fresh joint and thought about the lies he'd been forced to tell about his team at the last group. He had to save face for them.

Hey man, the jungle was like the streets and it wasn't nobody's damn business but mine what really happened. What I told the fools at group don't mean nothin. How my bros really died don't mean nothin. Dead is dead. The sky flashed white and thunder rumbled. The wind kicked up and whispered a promise of rain through the forest enveloping Mashburn Lake. A storm would mean isolation for a few days. Rene smiled and hoped it would come.

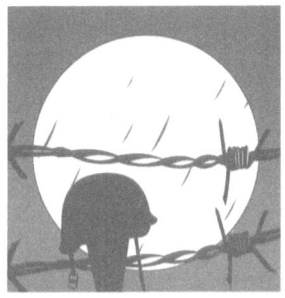

# CHAPTER FIFTEEN

RENE BOUDREAUX GOT his wish. The storm arrived early Friday morning with intermittent thundershowers striking in waves throughout the day. In the meeting room at the Veterans Service Office Vic Guerino sat hunched over and stared out the window.

"Losses," he repeated, searching for words. "You said it can be about anything, huh?"

"Anything at all," George said. "Whatever you feel the war experience took from you."

Vic wrinkled his brow and tried to concentrate. Losses. He and Karen had argued over money again last night. The second time this week, or was it the third? Why couldn't she just let it drop? He was getting damned tired of her throwing it in his face and listening to the same old shit. Sacking out on the sofa was getting old too.

Losses. Their savings were nearly depleted. This morning he'd managed to finagle another two hundred against future commissions but now that pot was empty. There would be no more; his boss had made that clear. What now? Karen would probably swallow his story about making a sale. Flowers and a bottle of wine, that usually did the trick. Hell, she might even be in the mood for a change. How long had it been, a month, six weeks?

"Vic, you still with us?" George said, drumming a pencil on the desktop.

Vic looked up. "Yeah." He paused again. "I don't know; I didn't lose many friends in combat. Nobody really close."

He lit a cigar and leaned forward. "I don't know if this would count or not, but how about purpose or direction in life?"

George laid the pencil down. "Fine, but you'll need to be a little more specific."

"Let me explain." Vic pulled out a handkerchief and mopped his brow. "I joined the Army for the chance to fly. I loved it. Flying is the greatest thing I've ever done. It's all I ever wanted to do since I was a kid." He folded the handkerchief and slipped it back inside his shirt pocket.

"All us pilots knew going in that Vietnam was part of the price. It wasn't all bad either. We had a lot of good times. I guess we had it a lot better than you grunts did," he said, glancing at Nathan and Dan.

Nathan shrugged. "I don't know, what do you think, Doc? Would you've given up your muddy foxhole and cold C-rations for a clean rack, dry hooch, hot chow, cold beer and a Doughnut Dolly for dessert every night?"

Dan and Nathan stared straight-faced at each other for a second. "Naaah!" they said together and laughed.

Vic stared at them, trying not to grin. "You're just fucking jealous."

"Let's let Vic make his point," said George.

Vic scratched behind his ear. "Where was I?"

"The Army gave you the chance to fly; Vietnam wasn't all bad."

"Okay. So after Vietnam and after I got out of the Army there was no question about what I wanted to do. I wanted to keep flying. I worked the oil rigs off Texas and Louisiana for a while. That was okay. The money was good but the hours sucked. We'd work for two weeks on and two weeks off. It got old being on call twenty-four hours a day. We'd get a call at two or three in the morning and have to fly offshore by instruments because some dickhead bigwig wanted to read *The Wall Street Journal* with his breakfast. Okay, maybe I'm exaggerating a little, but there was a lot of petty bullshit."

"Bullshit, like what?" George said, jotting something in his notebook.

Vic thought for a moment, twisting the big class ring he wore on his right hand back and forth. "Well, one time we'd just made a trip out to this rig and back for a crew change. Almost a hundred miles each way. So we get back and shut everything down and go to bed. Twenty minutes later the same rig calls and tells us to come pick up some engineer and take him to this other rig. We'd just flown right by that rig on our way in. Why the hell didn't they have us drop him off when we changed out the crew? Things like that went on all the time."

George looked up from his notes and nodded. "Go ahead."

Vic's cigar had died. He relit it. "After I quit the oilfields I went to work for a private commuter airline out of Miami. Did I mention the Army trained me to fly small airplanes after Vietnam?"

"I don't think so," George said.

"Well they did. "So I wound up flying charters to the Bahamas and the Virgin Islands and other places around the Caribbean. That was a blast." Vic's eyes lit up at the recollection. "I was making some big bucks. Bought a house, drove a 'Vette. I'd gotten married by then. Little Vic was born there. After that I went to work for—"

George held up a hand like a traffic cop. "Hold on a minute. If things were so good in Miami why did you leave?"

Vic rolled his cigar between his thumb and forefinger and thought for a moment. "My boss turned out to be a real asshole. Punk kid kept ordering me around like I was his personal flunky. It was really his old man's business anyway; he just ran it for his dad. He kept telling me I needed to do it 'this way,' or 'that way.' Hell, I could fly circles around that little shit. The asshole was still in high school when I was in Vietnam and here he was telling me what to do and how to fly. I finally got fed up with the bastard one day and told him where he could stuff it."

"Excuse me," Dan said, 'but just what the hell does any of this have to do with losses and Vietnam?" He fumbled for his lighter and lit a Kool. "Not that I'm not enjoying the conversation." His eyes were bloodshot and his voice sounded a bit slurred.

"Yeah," Nathan said, "give us some blood and guts. Tell us how you lost your cherry on Tu Do Street."

George slapped the desktop and glared a Dan and Nathan. "That's enough! If you two want to add to the discussion, fine, but let's cut the jokes."

He locked eyes with Nathan. "There you go again, trying to escape back into that tired old pattern of 'If things get too hot or uncomfortable I'll just make a joke out of it. It can't hurt me then.'"

Nathan looked like he'd been slapped. His face was flushed and he bit his lower lip. He slumped back in his chair and crossed his arms.

George turned his attention to Dan. The change in Dan's speech and the bloodshot eyes hadn't escaped him. "And I think I know where Vic's heading, so let's hear him out."

Vic waited until George signaled to go ahead then continued. "After I left the commuter job I hired on as a civilian flight instructor at Ft. Rucker training candidates to fly helicopters. Man, I was King Shit there." He paused; his thoughts were a world away. "I was pulling down over thirty-five grand a year and those flight school pukes thought I was God. I'd flown in combat for a year and to them that was something special. War was something they could only dream about or wish for, but I'd lived it. They looked up to me because of that."

Vic glanced out the window. The sky had darkened and leaves scudded across the parking lot. "I was tough on my students. They were going to be the best damn pilots the Army had or they were going to wash out." He took a puff and exhaled; he started to speak and then hesitated.

"I guess I was a little too hard on them sometimes. The flight commander called me in one day and said he was getting complaints about me from some of the candidates. He said that being a civilian instructor, it was my job to teach the mechanics of flying, not to jump somebody's ass when they screwed up. Hell, I wasn't that tough on them. I was just trying to do my job, teach them right and maybe save their asses some day. If they thought I was tough they should've been there during 'Nam when I went through flight school. Hell, these guys didn't have it half as bad as we did. The Army's really slacked up a lot since those days. You have to treat people like a bunch of babies now."

"How did you handle it when the flight commander called you down about being too rough?" George said, propping his boots on the desk.

Vic wiped his forehead again. "I don't know. I didn't like it; I really didn't see where I'd been doing anything wrong. The commander was pretty much an asshole anyway, a fucking lifer. He'd been to Vietnam but he'd spent his whole tour flying some bird colonel around. You know the type; a real ass-kisser."

"You haven't answered my question," George said.

Vic's brow wrinkled. "I thought I just did."

"No, you said you didn't like it and then you went off on a tirade about the flight commander. What I asked was how you handled the situation after being told you were coming down too hard on your students."

Thunder rumbled. "Okay, I guess."

"You might try being just a little more specific than, 'Okay, I guess.' "

Vic's face reddened. He puffed hard on the cigar which was now little more than a stub on the plastic tip. Lightning crashed nearby and he flinched. The fluorescent lights dimmed for a few seconds and then hummed noisily as they struggled back to full brightness.

"Okay goddamnit, it pissed me off. I was doing a good job. I was teaching my students what they needed to know if they were going to have a chance to survive in combat. When I was up there," Vic said, pointing up, "sometimes I'd forget myself. Forget where I was. I'd actually be back in 'Nam, at least in my mind. I could see it, smell it and feel it. And I made them experience it, too. I'd get so psyched up sometimes I'd have them believing they were really there, flying a combat mission and going in hot." Vic's mind raced back to Vietnam. He gripped the collective and cyclic; his feet were light on the anti-torque pedals as he played the controls like a well-rehearsed orchestra; and for the moment he was back in the Republic of Vietnam, flying into a hot LZ.

". . . haven't answered my question," George was saying.

"What?" Vic said, snapping back to the present.

George sighed. "I said you still haven't answered my question. You said it pissed you off when the commander said you were being too hard on your students. But how did you handle it? What did you do about it?"

Vic drew hard on the plastic tip, unaware the stub had burned down to nothing and gone out. "I, well, I just went by the book after that. I kept my mouth shut and let the stupid shits fly like they wanted to. I'd nail a candidate if he really fucked up. I didn't want to crash and burn with one of those idiots. But basically I went by the book; made sure their performance charts were up-to-date, kept my nose clean and did my job. I decided if that's what the Army wanted, that's what they'd get. I kept all the other shit bottled up inside. I guess that's when it all started to come apart."

"What 'other shit' are you talking about?"

"You know; all the Vietnam crap."

"You said 'it all started to come apart.' Let's talk about that," George said. "That's where all this is leading isn't it?"

"Yeah, I guess so. It's just that—"

"Go ahead Vic, we're right here with you, bro," Dan said.

George glanced at Dan and frowned.

"Where was I?" Vic said.

George drained the last of his coffee. "You were talking about the Vietnam crap you kept bottled up and how it all started to come apart."

"Yeah." Vic pulled another cigar from his shirt pocket and worked at the cellophane wrapper. "So I started keeping everything inside. I quit riding my students but all this crap was constantly churning in my gut. Only now I had no way of releasing it. Flying had been a way to relieve the pressure. But after I gave up showing them how to really fly a bird there was no way to get rid of all the tension. It just kept building and building." He tore the wrapper from the cigar.

"Somebody in here said at one of our meetings—I think it was Nathan—how Vietnam was on their mind almost all the time and how they thought about it constantly. That's how it was with me. We'd be up there flying and I'd be back in 'Nam. Sometimes the candidate would be talking to me and I wouldn't hear him. He'd have to reach over and tap me on the shoulder to get my attention. Half the time I wouldn't monitor the frequency. Hell, I wasn't there, I was back in 'Nam flying slicks."

He paused to light the cigar. "It wasn't long before I was back in front of that prick flight commander again. Now some of the assholes were complaining that I wasn't paying them enough attention." He held his hands up in frustration. "What the hell did they want? I felt like telling that dickhead desk jockey to shove it, but thirty-five thousand a year is hard to walk away from."

"We're with you, bro," Dan mumbled again.

"Keep going," George said, glancing at Dan. He'd have to deal with him later.

Vic reached over and tapped his cigar on the pedestal ashtray between him and Dan. "I had to really watch myself after that. I had to find a happy medium. Be involved while flying with my students but not over do it. I did okay for a few weeks, but I was having trouble concentrating. If I didn't constantly watch it I'd find myself drifting back to Vietnam. I really had to fight it.

"My stomach was hurting and I had heartburn all the time and I couldn't sleep worth a damn. Some nights I didn't sleep at all. I'd just lie there awake, thinking."

"About Vietnam?" said Nathan.

"Yeah. That and losing the job.

"I finally went to a civilian doctor in town. I couldn't let the flight surgeon find out bout it or that would be my ass. The civilian doctor gave me some pills for my stomach and put me on something for my nerves and to help me sleep."

"You were taking that shit while you were flying?" Nathan said. He sat up and looked Vic in the eye. "Man, no way we would've put up with that in our outfit. If we hit the shit you had to be able to depend on each other. You fuck up in the bush and somebody dies. Uh-uh, never happen."

"Yeah," Vic said, "but I wasn't bombed. I had things under control. At least I thought I did. Anyway, this went on for a few months. The drugs were helping some I guess. I was still thinking about Vietnam on the job sometimes, but I was paying more attention to my students. And I was sleeping better.

"Then I got called in for a physical. The assholes just popped it on us after morning flights one day. They'd never done that before. Naturally they found the meds in my system. I had to go before a board and tell them I was on an antidepressant and sleeping pills."

Vic looked at George and snapped his fingers. "They grounded me, just like that. I lost the job and they suspended my license." He looked as though he were about to cry. "My life's gone to hell ever since. I've just about lost everything. I can't fly anymore," he said, shaking his head. "I can't fucking fly anymore."

Vic walked over to the window and stared out at the rain. He turned to George. "That's what Vietnam took from me. I lost my purpose for living. I may as well have died over there."

"Are you grounded for keeps?" Nathan said.

"No." Vic forced a bitter laugh. "But it amounts to the same thing. It's on my record about the drugs. I'll never be able to fly commercial again, not with that blot. Who's going to hire a drug-crazed Vietnam vet to fly for them? That would be like somebody with a DUI conviction being hired to drive a school bus. It's just not going to happen.

"So here I am, thirty-six years old and my career's already down the shithole. I can't fly and everything else I've tried to do I've screwed-up, too. I can't make a living for my family and my marriage is heading for the rocks."

"I know where you're coming from, bro," Dan said. "I had plans to become a doctor and look at me, a second-rate lab tech. I couldn't keep my mind on my studies at college. I kept thinking about the war and everything we went through over there. It cost me my marriage too, and my son."

Nathan grimaced. "I know a guy who stepped on a mine and got both legs blown off," he said. "Know what he does now? He walks around on artificial legs and you can hardly tell it."

"What's that supposed to mean?" Dan said.

Nathan stared into Dan's bleary eyes. "We just had this conversation a couple of weeks ago, remember? You're trying to blame the war for everything instead of getting off your ass and making the best of what you've got."

Dan's chalky face reddened and he glared at Nathan. "I don't believe it's fair for you to say that. You can't compare—"

"Screw fair!" Nathan said. "Just what is fair in this life? Not a damn thing. You know that guy I was telling you about, the guy with no legs? Back in high school he was a ladies' man and the best dancer you ever saw. He can't dance anymore, at least not the way he used to. So what does he do? Sit in his room feeling sorry for himself and hide for the rest of his life? Not him. You know what that dude does? He loves to fish so he joined the Bass Masters circuit and competes in tournaments all over the country. Runs his own advertising agency, too. He does all that on two artificial legs. He won't ever win another dance contest but he sure as shit ain't laying on his ass feeling sorry for himself and blaming the war for everything."

Dan nudged Vic. "Listen to Mr. Perfect there telling us how screwed up we are. And him the big success story he is."

"Screw you, Doc. I never claimed to be a success story. Vietnam kicked me around too. Almost killed my young ass. But I don't go around moaning and groaning about it. Maybe I'm not as ambitious as I should be. Maybe I'm just a common yard man like you called me. But I pay my own damn bills and I take care of myself. I don't depend on anybody but myself. I am what I am because I choose to be, not because of that fucking war."

George watched the skirmish intently. They were really interacting now, he noted with satisfaction, getting beyond the stage where each supports the other with blind loyalty no matter the cause or justification. Nathan especially was beginning to look within himself for answers. He seemed ready to begin assuming responsibility and to go forward with his life; ready to pay the price.

There would be pitfalls, George knew. The biggest obstacle would be Nathan's reluctance to go on without the others if they chose not to work hard and grow with him. Would he be able to let them go and allow them to bottom out? Or would he revert to ingrained combat behavior and try to save them no matter the cost to himself?

Dan started to respond to Nathan's outburst but George cut him short. "Hold what you've got. Everybody just calm down and cool off." He glanced at his watch. "Let's go ahead and wrap for today. This rain's going to slow me down getting home.

"I want everybody to think over carefully what we talked about. Next week we'll come in fresh and sort it out without all the emotions getting in the way. Any questions?"

Nobody spoke.

"Okay, see you next week."

As they got up to leave, George remembered. "Dan, I need to see you a minute."

# CHAPTER SIXTEEN

NATHAN SLOWED THE van to a crawl and eased over the curb and stopped among the towering pine trees bordering the beach of St. Martin Bay. He turned off the engine, reached into the grocery sack and grabbed one of the six-packs he'd just bought at the Seven-Eleven.

It was nearing high tide. The musty scent of salt and sea hung in the damp air. He walked along the narrow strip of beach and watched the frothy water roll across the sand and lap at the weeds and crabgrass. The heavy rains had ceased but the gray sky continued to drip and thunder grumbled far out over the Gulf of Mexico. Dark tattered clouds scudded low across the choppy bay. The gloomy discordant weather mirrored his mood. He twisted a can of beer from the plastic ring and popped it open and drank. He needed to think, to cut through the fog of confusion muddling his mind.

After the meeting Dan had refused a ride home. Now Nathan wondered why he'd confronted Dan the way he had. Was he getting too close? He'd done just fine without friends for a long time and then Doc showed up. Could that be it?

A jellyfish lay stranded at the edge of the grass. Nathan wedged the toe of his boot under the clear gelatinous mass and flipped it back into the foamy water. Several yards ahead a small flock of sandpipers darted back and forth, pecking tiny morsels from the wet sand at the beach's edge. They kept a cautious interval from him, scurrying ahead when he drew too close.

He saw a rat scamper into a thick stand of brush ahead and thought of the terrain along the desolate road between Con Thien and Cam Lo and noted what an ideal location this would make for an ambush. He checked the treetops for snipers and the trunks for claymores.

A pair of laughing gulls flew by, taunting back and forth with their chortling call. He forced his mind back to Dan and how he seemed to be wasting his life feeling sorry for himself and blaming the war for everything instead of taking control. It's the damn pills, Nathan thought, he's killing himself with that shit.

Suddenly Nathan looked at the beer he was holding and thought about all the beer he drank daily. Who the hell was he to judge? On the other hand he always managed to get up and function instead of laying around all day, vegetating.

He watched a Least Tern hovering a few yards from shore; its arched wings beat rapidly like the rotors of a tiny helicopter. Then it dove and hit the water with barely a splash. Rising victoriously the tern flew away with a silver minnow dangling from its beak.

Maybe Dan's right. Maybe it *is* the war, a cancer eating us up, destroying our drive, our ambition, our reason for living. Hell, maybe that's it; we're not really living at all, just existing.

The wind gusted. Nathan shivered and goose bumps prickled his arms. Distant lightning zigzagged through the dark clouds over the gulf and it began to rain harder. He wished he'd worn his windbreaker.

Maybe he saw too much of himself in Dan and didn't like what he saw. He's got his pills, Nathan thought, and I've got my beer. Shit, I don't know, it's just so damn confusing sometimes.

A hazy orange glow gilded the horizon as the sinking sun

struggled through the gloom. It lingered for a brief moment and then, like a great gray eyelid, a bank of clouds closed over it.

The rain continued falling into the night. It dripped from the roof striking Clarence's upended metal bowl with a steady hollow *plink-plink-plink*. Nathan sat at the kitchen table drinking a beer. *The Dirty Dozen* was on TBS but he'd seen it several times. He had planned to watch the Braves play the Mets but the game was in a rain delay.

He opened another beer and stared blankly through the screen door. Lights were still on in Mrs. Ard's kitchen. Now and then shadows appeared behind the drawn curtains. Probably baking, he decided.

Through the beer-induced numbness he felt a deep bitter loneliness. He needed to talk but Dan obviously was pissed at him and he was tired of listening to Vic's lying answering machine. He thought about calling George but knew he was too drunk to pull it off. Even Clarence had deserted him. Probably curled up in front of Mrs. Ard's stove, he thought. He wished he had something warm to curl up to.

He found himself dialing the number again. He hadn't consciously thought about it, he was suddenly just doing it. The phone rang once, twice—

"Hello," a voice answered, a woman's voice, beautiful, almost musical. "Hello?"

Nathan hung up, his heart pounding. It had been Laura this time, not Tom or one of the kids. He slumped in the chair and drained his beer. He opened another and chugged half of it down.

Why did he keep torturing himself? What could he possibly hope to gain? It's over; for seventeen fucking years it's been over! He pounded the table with the ball of his fist and knocked over an empty can. It rolled off the table. He kicked it and sent it flying into the cabinet beneath the sink.

Why couldn't he just let go and get on with his miserable life? Why was she always on his mind? Hadn't he done everything possible to avoid her? Then why? Had she woven some magic web years ago from which he'd never escape?

Emptiness gutted him. "Laura," he whispered. He tilted the can and drank like it was water, trying to wash the taste of her name from his mouth.

It didn't work. It was still there like it had been during the terrible months of the war. *Laura.* The name he'd whispered to himself every night before drifting off into restless sleep because in war there was no promise of tomorrow. The name he'd repeated over and over when bullets began to fly, wanting it to be his last utterance should he die. *Laura,* his hope, his desire, his salvation.

*Laura.* Destroyer of his hopes and dreams that May afternoon long ago which began so full of promise and expectations.

*Laura.* Bitter, bitter memory.

*Laura.* Bittersweet memory.

# CHAPTER SEVENTEEN

TUESDAY MORNING HELEN Morris greeted Nathan with a warm smile. "Good morning, Nathan. How are you?"

He tried to return the smile, not quite sure he managed. How was he? Wonderful, considering the two-day hangover. Let's see, my head feels like somebody nailed me with a sledge-hammer. I don't know whether I need to shit or puke or both. All my friends are pissed at me. Hell, never felt better. "Still alive. You?"

"Great," she said. "It's such a pretty day after all the rain this weekend. Isn't that the way it usually goes, though? Nice weather all week while we have to work and can't enjoy it and then it rains all weekend."

I'd like to enjoy you for a weekend, he thought. "Yeah, that's the way it usually works out."

He sat on the examining table and pushed up his right shirt sleeve. He'd noticed she tended to support his arm higher from that side. "So the rain messed up your weekend?" he said as she adjusted the cuff around his biceps. He felt her breast brush his arm and fought the urge to press against it.

Helen nodded. "I promised my daughter I'd take her swimming. I was hoping it might be warm enough for the beach."

His heart sank. So there it is, he thought, she's married.

He'd been foolish to think that someone so attractive might still be available.

Helen pumped the bulb. The cuff tightened around Nathan's arm and she listened through the stethoscope. He envied the man who shared her bed.

"High again," she said, the Velcro ripping as she loosened the cuff. "One-sixty over ninety-three. You haven't been skipping your medication have you?"

"No, Mother. I've been a good little boy; haven't missed a day."

Helen laughed. "I'm sorry; I suppose I deserved that. Sometimes I catch myself talking to patients like I do to Heather. Motherly instinct, I guess." She took his wrist and began counting his pulse.

"No sweat, I was just joking," Nathan said. "I've got a weird sense of humor. Half the time people don't realize I'm joking around." He gazed at Helen's eyes as they followed the second hand of her watch. He wanted to reach out and pull her body close and crush those beautiful lips against his. *Shit; no wonder my blood pressure's up*, he thought.

Helen jotted the numbers in his chart and then looked up and smiled. "I like a sense of humor. There's too much dreariness in the world as it is." She glanced at her watch. "Can you stay for a few minutes? I'd like to check your pressure again after you've been sitting still for a while."

"Sure."

"Great. You sit here and relax. I'll be back in a few minutes."

His eyes consumed her as she walked out the door and disappeared down the hall. *Man, what an ass. And those legs; I bet she could wrap 'em around me twice.*

He glanced around the room trying to occupy his mind. A framed smiley-face hung on the opposite wall with *Have a Happy Day Grandpa!* stitched in crude needlepoint. The adjoining wall held charts with lateral and frontal views of the internal human body. Nathan studied them and imagined how his own guts must have looked after being scrambled by the NVA rocket. He located the spleen under the left rib cage. Don't have to worry about that anymore.

The massive coils of intestines caught his eye. He thought back to that night in March when he and Betz had gone hand-to-hand with the NVA. Seventeen years had passed and yet the memory was so vivid it seemed like yesterday. He could still feel the flesh giving way to his KA-BAR, and the hot sticky mass spilling out across his arms and down his front; the sickening overpowering stench of shit and blood like the stink of a gutted deer, only worse, much worse.

"Let's try again and see how we do," Helen said, startling him.

The right arm again; nestled in that wonderful haven. It felt safe and comforting and he wished he could lay his head there cradled to her bosom and feel her breath against his cheek and her heartbeat soothing his soul.

"That's better. One-forty-seven over eighty. Still a little high, but better."

"Does that mean I'm gonna live?" He straightened his sleeve and his fingers lingered over the area her breast had touched.

She was writing in his chart again. Looking up, she smiled. "For now, anyway."

"How old is your daughter?" he said, surprising himself. He didn't want to leave.

Helen set the chart on the counter and leaned her back against it, facing him. "She turned six a couple of months ago, February twenty-second. She was born on George Washington's birthday."

"Really? That's my old man's birthday too. Or was; he's dead now."

Her smile faded . "Oh, I'm sorry. I didn't mean to—"

He waved her off. "That was a long time ago. So, is Heather as pretty as her mother?"

Helen's cheeks flushed. "She doesn't look much like me

except for being a blonde. She's very pretty but I guess all mothers say that about their children. Heather gets her looks from her daddy's side of the family. She's the spitting image of my ex-husband's sister."

Nathan didn't hear the rest. It was drowned out by the words racing through his mind: ex-husband, ex-husband. "Oh, then you're not married?"

She shook her head. "I've been divorced almost three years now. Heather and I moved here from Montgomery a few months ago. My parents settled here a couple of years ago after Dad retired from the Air Force."

"Was your father ever in Vietnam?" Nathan was beginning to feel comfortable and didn't want the conversation to end.

"Yes, twice I believe. My dad was a fighter pilot."

"No sh—" He barely managed to catch himself. "Really? I was there with the Marines back in '67 and '68."

"You were there?" Helen looked surprised. "You don't seem old enough to—"

"Yeah, I'm thirty-six."

"I'm sorry. Of course you're old enough. It's just that my dad was there, and he's so much older. I sometimes forget that it was people our age doing most of the fighting in that awful place."

"Our age? My age, you mean. What are you, twenty-five maybe?"

Helen beamed. "Thank you. I'll take that as a compliment." She picked up his chart and thumbed through his records. "I don't see a thing about it in here."

"What're you looking for?"

She smiled and the tip of her tongue showed between glistening white teeth. "I'm trying to find where it says you need glasses. I'll be thirty-one in a few weeks."

"Well you sure don't look it. You must come from good stock."

"My parents will be glad to hear that. Dad would probably enjoy talking with you about Vietnam sometime."

"What did he fly? Was it Phantoms or do you know? Man, those Phantom drivers were something else. They saved our young butts more than once."

"I'm really not sure. I believe—"

"Miss Morris!" Dr. Parker bellowed from another room.

Helen rolled her eyes and smiled. "I've got to go. See you Thursday?"

"I'll be here."

She hurried past him and then hesitated in the doorway and turned. "Nathan?"

"Yeah?"

"I really enjoyed talking with you."

He grinned. "Me too; see you Thursday."

Nathan took a deep breath and dialed the number. It rang once and then picked up.

"Hello?"

"Helen?"

"Yes?"

"It's Nathan . . . Henson."

"Hi! This is a surprise. How did you get my number?"

"From the receptionist. I told her you needed some information from me and the office would probably be closed by the time I got it."

"Information? I don't re—"

"No, I just thought I'd call and see how you're doing." He felt awkward and began to wish he hadn't worked up the courage to dial her number.

She giggled. "I'm just fine. You could've asked me, you know."

"About what?"

"My phone number. I don't bite."

Nathan forced a laugh. "That's good to know." He wrapped the phone cord around his finger. "I'm a little nervous calling you. I haven't had much practice lately and you don't really know me or anything." He grimaced, detesting his awkwardness.

"You seem harmless enough. I'm glad you called"

Nathan wondered what to say next. In the background he heard muffled voices. "How's Heather?

"Fine. She's in the living room watching Andy Griffith."

Nathan uncoiled the cord from his finger. "Listen, would you like to go out sometime? Maybe to a movie or dinner or something?" There, he'd done it. So what if she rejected him? There was always the Silver Saddle to fall back on.

"That sounds like fun. When?"

He nearly dropped the receiver. "Great. What's a good day for you? How about Friday?"

"Friday's fine. I'll get my parents to watch Heather. They love having her over. What time?"

His pulse raced. What time? He couldn't remember the last time he'd had a real date. Bars didn't get going until nine or ten. "Is seven okay, or eight?"

"Seven's good."

"Okay, I'll pick you up at seven."

"Nathan?"

"Yeah?"

She giggled again. "Don't you want to know where I live?"

There was a brief silence while he mentally kicked himself. "Yeah, that might help."

"We live in the Seawall Apartments on the west end of Bayview Drive where it meets Bedford Avenue. Do you know where that is?"

"Yeah, right on the bay. We're practically neighbors. You ever go walking along the beach there?"

"We've taken a few short walks. It's been so cold though."

"I used to jog there before they built the apartments. Have you been to the old seawall?"

"No, we usually go toward town."

"We'll have to go to the seawall one day. I used to fish there and it's a great place to snorkel, too. About a mile past the seawall there's this place called Morgan's Cove. They say pirates buried treasure there. It's beautiful."

"Sounds wonderful. I love the outdoors."

"Me too. I'd go nuts if I had to stay cooped up all the time. Okay then, I'll pick you up Friday at seven."

"Nathan?"

"Yeah?"

"You need my apartment number."

"Yeah, that would help too."

"It's B-29, the second building on Waterfront Drive. Upstairs."

"B-29. Got it. That's easy to remember; like the World War Two bomber."

"I didn't know that."

"Well shame on you, your father being career Air Force."

"Please don't tell Dad I didn't know what a B-29 was. He'd never forgive me."

Nathan laughed. "I won't. That was a little before your time anyway." He glanced at his watch. "I better go. See you Friday."

"All right." Helen's voice lowered to little more than a whisper. "I'm glad you asked me out. I'm looking forward to it."

"Yeah, me too. See you then."

"Bye-bye. And don't forget your appointment Thursday morning."

"I won't, Mother."

Nathan hung up the phone and grabbed a beer from the refrigerator. He opened it and switched on the TV to catch the early local news. He felt relieved and excited. A real date. A real date with Helen.

An automobile dealership was hawking the Super Spring Sale to end all spring sales. Nathan watched idly for a moment and then an idea struck him. He picked up the phone and dialed Vic's number.

Emma Matthews rapped lightly on her son's bedroom door.

"Come in."

She eased the door open and stepped into the room. "Are you feeling better, dear?"

Dan lay stretched upon the bed, a paperback novel in one hand and a cigarette in the other. A reading lamp mounted on the headboard provided the only light in the dim room. His pallid face was haggard in the bulb's glare. "My head still hurts like a bitch," he said, placing the cigarette between his lips while he turned a page.

Mrs. Matthews winced. "You shouldn't be smoking in bed, dear. Maybe if you stopped reading and tried to get some rest your headache would—"

"There's lots of things I shouldn't be doing," he snapped, "and my head's going to hurt whether I read or not."

"I'm sorry. Can I fix you something to eat? You might feel better with something warm in your stomach."

"I'm not hungry. I don't want to eat. I don't want to sleep. I just want to be left alone. Did you call Rick like I asked?"

"Yes. He sounded upset that you—"

"That fat tub of shit better get off my case."

"Daniel, your language!" She didn't care to hear such things in her house, especially from her son's mouth. She'd taught him better than that.

"I'm sorry; it's just that I've felt so lousy the past few days. Did you tell him I'd try to be back by Friday?" Friday was payday. Friday he would see Brenda Lewis again. Friday he'd be okay if it would ever get here.

"Yes, I told him you have the flu like you said. I don't like lying."

"It's not lying, Mother. I am sick. It's just better if Rick thinks I have the flu instead of trying to explain about these headaches. He might not understand that. You're not really lying."

"I suppose it's all right then. Oh, I almost forgot." She pulled an envelope from her apron pocket and handed it to Dan. "This came today."

Dan glanced at the envelope and frowned. It was from the Clerk of the Circuit Court of St. Martin County. He laid it on the night stand. "I'll look at it later. I think I'll try to get some sleep now. Wake me for supper, okay?"

Emma took the cigarette from her son's fingers and snuffed it out in the ashtray. She brushed the hair from his forehead and patted his pale cheek. "I will, dear. You rest now. Call me if you need anything."

As soon as she closed the door Dan bolted upright on the edge of the bed. He lit another cigarette and tore open the envelope and scanned the letter. "That son-of-a-bitch," he muttered, flinging the letter into a dark corner. "That no good son-of-a-bitch!"

A formal complaint for non-payment of child support had been filed against him by Mr. and Mrs. John Waldrop. The court mandate said he had thirty days to make full restitution or further legal action would be taken.

Dan rummaged through the cluttered drawer of the night stand and unscrewed the top of a prescription bottle. It was empty. He tried another with the same results and slammed the drawer shut.

That bitch of an ex-wife! He'd explained to her over the phone hadn't he? There was no reason why she couldn't give him a little more time. It was that son-of-a-bitch she was married to. He knew what they were after; he was on to their game.

Dan lay back on the bed. He took a deep drag and blew smoke into the gray shadows of the room. Yeah, I know what this is all about, he thought. They want the only thing I have left in this fucked-up world—my son.

Nathan drove into the parking lot of Fred Cummings' Ford dealership. Last night after talking to Helen he'd decided he needed a new vehicle. He'd been driving the same Volkswagen van for fifteen years and it was time for a change.

But with the morning came the doubts and a hundred reasons

why last night's carefully thought out decision was just so much folly. The old VW had served him well and it still ran good and got decent gas mileage. The clutch was beginning to slip a little and it tended to burn up generators and voltage regulators for some reason he hadn't been able to figure out, but the engine was practically new with only fifteen thousand miles since he had it overhauled.

It wasn't because of Helen he was doing this, he tried to convince himself. Hell, it would be crazy to buy a new vehicle just to impress a date. That wasn't the reason at all. He really did need a new vehicle and it was best to trade in the old van while it was still worth something.

He parked and saw Vic Guerino walking out of the showroom. "Hey," he called, climbing out of the van. "Bet you thought I wouldn't show up, huh? I guess you and Karen will be flying to Hawaii as soon as you get the commission you're gonna make off me."

Vic grinned as they shook hands. "I know how tight you ex-grunts are. I might be able to take the family out to McDonald's."

"And rich too, don't forget that. Us dumb-ass ground-pounders didn't have much opportunity to spend our hundred and sixty-eight dollars a month up on the DMZ. No fancy bars and loose women to spend it on like you winged warriors had."

"Bitch, bitch, bitch," Vic fired back. "Let's see, last night you said you wanted to look at Continentals, wasn't it?"

"Yeah, right. Only you former officers and gentlemen can afford pussy mobiles like that. Trucks, a-hole."

Vic snapped his fingers. "Trucks, of course; the vehicle of choice for rednecks, cowboys and grunts."

"Up yours, flyboy."

It was a beauty. An F-150 Fleetside, forest green trimmed with gold pin striping; Marine Corps colors. That was what first caught Nathan's eye. And when he checked out the interior he was sold. The plush full bench seat and padded dash with full instrumentation looked more suited for a sports car. And Nathan couldn't get over having carpets in a pickup truck.

The V-8 engine purred as he cruised through the business district that in recent years had sprouted strip malls along 23$^{rd}$ Street like unchecked weeds. It was a pleasant change from the hollow roar of the old VW's straining four-cylinder.

Nathan bumped the turn signal down and checked his rearview and side mirrors. He goosed the gas pedal and pulled into the left lane ahead of a Southern Bell utility truck, admiring the unfamiliar power. It was everything he could imagine wanting in a truck. The eight-foot bed could carry whatever he needed for his business. He'd have a bed liner installed soon to prevent it from getting scratched up. The automatic transmission was a welcomed relief from working a clutch pedal with his aching left foot.

He slowed and turned onto Jenkins Avenue. He traveled north a few blocks and drove into the Jenkins Medical Complex where Dr. Parker's office was located. He circled the building twice but resisted the urge to park and show Helen his new toy. Bad idea, he decided. She might think I'm showing off.

Nathan couldn't get her off his mind, not that he wanted to. He smiled and ran his hand over the soft material of the bench seat. Friday night she'd be sitting right there. And with the automatic transmission he'd be able to put his arm around her instead of constantly shifting gears.

He was surprised to find his arm resting along the top of the seat back. Christ on a crutch, he was acting like a giddy teenager getting ready for his first date. He grinned. So what? It felt good for a change

.

# CHAPTER EIGHTEEN

"MY, MY, AREN'T we something," Sarah Potter said as Nathan entered the Veterans Service Office. "What's with the new truck? A rich uncle die, or did you rob a bank?"

He grinned. "Like I always say, if you got it, flaunt it. George here yet?"

Sarah finished rolling a VA form into her typewriter and attacked it with rapid-fire strokes. "He's with a client. You're early; where's your sidekick?"

"Dan? I called him at work. Said he didn't need a ride. I think he's pissed off at me. You seen him lately?"

Sarah shook her head and kept typing. "I talked to his mother yesterday. She said he's been sick." She stopped typing and looked up. "Just between you and me, I think the boy's drugging again. He looks like a refugee from a concentration camp. It's the worst he's looked in the three years I've known him."

Nathan frowned. He wanted to talk about his concern for Dan but that might be betraying the group's confidentiality. "Maybe he'll show up. His didn't say anything about missing group."

Sarah shrugged and returned to her typing. Nathan walked to the lounge and poured a cup of coffee. He took a sip and grimaced. It reminded him of the coal tar Betz used to make in Vietnam from the C-ration coffee packets. He dumped the coffee into the sink as George walked in.

"This coffee still good?" George asked, reaching for the pot.

"Yeah, if you like burnt motor oil. I think we better make another pot."

George sniffed the decanter. "Ugh." He emptied and rinsed it and filled it with fresh water. "How was your week?" he said, spooning grounds into a clean paper filter.

"Pretty good. In fact, real good. Best I've had in a long time."

George glanced at him. "That's a surprise after the way things went down last week."

"Yeah, well I did have a shitty weekend but then things picked up."

The old coffee maker began moaning, its "oohs" and "aahs" sounding like a couple embroiled in the throes of passion. Nathan snickered. "Christ, I get all excited when I listen to that porno coffee maker."

George grinned. "You've noticed it too, huh? I'll bet it hasn't been cleaned in years." He glanced at his watch. "I need to make a couple of calls before we get started. I'll just be a few minutes."

"No sweat. I'll wait here and listen to Mr. Coffee getting off."

George returned as the coffee maker uttered a final passionate sigh. Nathan filled two Styrofoam cups and handed one to George. "Where is everybody?" he said as they walked down the hallway to the meeting room.

"We're it for today. Vic called before I left Tallahassee. Two salesmen are out sick so his boss asked him to work until closing. Rene called yesterday and said his truck wouldn't start. He's trying to find somebody to haul it out of the woods and fix it. Dan's mother called this morning and said he's got the flu. So I thought we'd do a little one on one today if you're up to it."

Nathan started to tell George that he'd talked to Dan at work a couple of hours ago but decided to let it drop. "Fine with me," he said, taking a chair. The coffee burned his palate as he sipped it. "Man, a bunch of shit happened this week."

George propped his boots on the edge of the desk and lit a cigarette. "I thought you said you had a good week."

"I did. It's mostly good shit I'm talking about."

George's eyebrows arched. "Why do you suppose you do that?"

"Do what?"

"Refer to everything as 'shit.' "

"I didn't know I did."

"Well, you do. You're always saying, 'good shit, bad shit, all that shit, it don't mean shit.' "

Nathan thought about it for a few seconds. "Yeah, I guess I do. I don't mean anything by it. Maybe it's just a holdover from my Marine Corps days. We were a bunch of foul mouths back then."

"Back then?" George smiled. "Unless my ears deceive me you still are. I'm not singling you out; a lot of vets tend to revert back to speech patterns they used in the military when they get around other vets in this sort of environment. I'm not saying it's all bad, either. In a way it helps you get back into character so you can deal with issues more honestly. I'm just curious about your use of the word 'shit.' You seem to use that word more than most vets I've been around."

Nathan fidgeted and blew on the steaming coffee. "I don't know, I guess it's just a bad habit."

George leaned toward the desk and flicked the ash from his cigarette. He took another drag. "Maybe," he said, exhaling, "but I'd be willing to bet it's more than that."

"Like what?"

"I think it's a statement you're making about life. You said there's 'good shit' and 'bad shit.' If you look at life in general as 'shit,' you protect yourself from having to feel too strongly one way or another about things."

"I'm not sure I get it."

"Here's my theory," George said. He took his feet off the desk and sat up straight. "You use it as a protective device like a shield. If something bad happens in your life you throw up the shield, 'it don't mean shit,' so now you don't have to hurt so much. If something good happens it's still just so much 'shit,' only now it's 'good shit.' But it's still just 'shit' so you don't get too excited about it or attached to it. That way, if something happens to change it from 'good shit' to 'bad shit' you've kept yourself shielded from being hurt too deeply. For you it's a defense, a survival mechanism."

Nathan thought about it a moment and decided what George said made sense. "Yeah, I guess so. You think I got that shit from Vietnam?"

At first Nathan didn't realize he'd used the word, and then it dawned on him. He slapped his forehead lightly with an open palm.

They laughed and George said, "A lot of it probably did develop from Vietnam, and trying to cope with the world after you got back. Your sense of humor, too. I see that a lot in vets who experienced heavy combat. That gallows humor helped to keep you from going crazy over there."

Nathan tapped his temple with a finger. "A lot of people might argue that it didn't work."

George smiled. "Anyway, you might want to keep track of when you use the word. It could help you to key in on your emotions.

"I'll give it a try."

"Okay, enough on that. Let's talk about the 'good shit' that happened this week."

Nathan took a sip of coffee and a deep breath. "It's no big deal. I met this girl and bought a new truck."

George tapped a pencil on the desktop. "Sounds like a pretty big deal to me. Let's hear it."

"Okay. I had a lousy weekend. That crap with Doc at group really got me down. I guess I was a little hard on him, huh?"

George shrugged. "Not really. I think you were making some fairly clear observations that Dan isn't ready to deal with yet." He rocked back and forth. "Does it bother you?"

"What? You mean him being pissed at me?"

George nodded.

"Yeah, it bothers me. I don't like having hard feelings between us."

"Why?"

"Because . . . I just don't. We're supposed to take care of each other aren't we?"

"Not to the point of being his nursemaid."

"What's that supposed to mean?"

George crushed out the cigarette and leaned back. "You've been chauffeuring Dan around since day one. You've gotten him out of the house and encouraged him to do things with you and Vic like partying and barbeques. And then when you speak up in group and confront him with the truth he gets pissed at you and starts pouting. And you feel bad. Why? Because Dan gets mad when you tell him the truth instead of just being his yes boy."

"So?"

"So?"

"So, what am I supposed to do?"

"You tell me."

Nathan thought for a moment. "Doc's my friend. We went through a lot of the same shit. It's almost like we were in the 'Nam together, you know? But sometimes it seems like he wants to wallow around in self pity; like he wants the world to pat him on the back and say 'poor baby' or some crap like that. I don't know. I'm not sure what I mean." He looked up at George. "You know what I'm trying to say?"

"I think I do. But you can't control other people's behavior. It's hard enough to control your own. Be Dan's friend but don't get down on yourself when he doesn't react the way you think he should. Besides, Dan's hiding from himself right now."

Nathan wasn't sure what George meant but decided not to ask. "Back to the weekend. I started drinking Friday night. Figured if I stayed drunk enough I wouldn't think about all the crap with Doc. By Sunday I'd had it; I felt like crap the whole day." He forced a smile. "I haven't been that wasted in a long time. I stayed home Monday just trying to survive."

"Sounds to me like you were trying to punish yourself for what happened at group," George said. "The old guilt trip again, remember? We spent a whole session on that a few weeks ago. You leading the patrol that was ambushed?"

"I don't know, maybe. Whatever I was trying to do I sure did it right, big time."

George lit another Marlboro and snapped his lighter shut. "Self-medicating with alcohol is another escape mechanism you tend to use. 'If I get drunk enough I won't have to feel or remember.' That's something we can work on later. Go ahead and tell me about the good stuff."

Nathan spent the next several minutes telling George about meeting Helen and how they'd struck up a conversation in Dr. Parker's office and how he'd finally worked up the courage to call and ask her out. He felt embarrassed and tried to act like it was a small matter but couldn't hide his exuberance.

"I guess this is weird, huh? Getting all worked-up just because I asked some girl to go out."

"I don't think it's weird at all," George said. "When's the big date?"

Nathan grinned. "Tonight."

"Good. I'm glad to see it happen. From what little I know about your track record since Vietnam, you haven't exactly been setting the world on fire in the social graces category. Meeting someone you care about is a good step whether it goes any further or not."

"I hope so." Nathan was pleased by George's approval. "I really like her. I mean, this isn't like picking up some broad for sex. Not that I wouldn't like to—"

Nathan caught himself. "It's different with her. I can't explain it, she's just different."

George got up and opened the window to let in some fresh

air. "I think I know what you mean. Before, it was just sex, just another physical act, like eating or sleeping with no emotional involvement. You weren't putting yourself in a position of risk and setting yourself up to possibly get hurt. But with Helen you feel something more, and the key word here is feel. You're willing to get involved and to chance taking that risk. And that's good. It tells me you're making some progress and that you're beginning to take control of your life."

Nathan gazed out the window and watched a red-bellied woodpecker working its way up the trunk of a big oak that shaded the far end of the parking lot. He looked back at George. "I don't know if it's a risk or not, but it feels right. I think she's worth it. I can't explain it but I'm starting to feel like I'm alive again." He tapped his chest. "Maybe there's something in here worth saving after all. Guess I'll find out tonight."

# CHAPTER NINETEEN

NATHAN WAS STEPPING out of the shower when he heard knocking on his front door. He grabbed a towel and glanced at his watch laying on the toilet tank. Ten after six. There it was again, more a pounding than a knock.

He wrapped the towel around his waist and hurried to the front door wondering if Mrs. Ard needed help. Using the door as a shield, he opened it and saw Vic Guerino.

"What's going on, man? George said you had to work tonight."

"I come to party with my fuckin' grunt buddies."

Vic was red-eyed and weaving like a sailor on the deck of a yawing ship. He clutched a half-empty bottle of Wild Turkey in one hand and an unlit cigar in the other. "Jesus H. Christ," said Nathan, "you're wasted. Come on in."

Vic stumbled over the doorstep and into the living room. Nathan grabbed an arm to keep him from falling.

"Nope, fuck work; I come to party with my buddies." He looked around the room with bleary eyes. "Where's Dan?"

Nathan winced at Vic's foul breath. "Probably in his rack wasted on pills."

Vic lifted the bottle and downed a swig. "Well go call 'im and tell 'im to get his sorry ass over here right now 'cause we gotta party. We got some celebratin' to do."

"Looks to me like you've already celebrated enough for all of us," Nathan said. "I can't party; I've got a hot date tonight. Sit down and let me throw some clothes on and I'll drive you home. No way I'm letting you drive like this. Karen's gonna kill your young ass."

Vic slumped onto the worn green sofa and clanged the bottle of bourbon on the coffee table. The cigar slipped from his fingers onto the floor. He made a clumsy attempt to pick it up and nearly fell out of his seat. His mood changed like someone had thrown a switch. He looked up at Nathan with wet eyes.

"She already did."

"What?"

"I can't go home; don't have a home anymore," he said, staring across the room and shaking his head. "I don't have nothin' anymore."

"You're not making sense, man. What're you talking about?"

Vic's demeanor flip-flopped. Looking up, he grinned. "Nothin'. Don't matter anyhow, I come to party. Let's go get Dan."

"Christ," Nathan said, "you show up drunk on your ass all teary-eyed, and you're telling me nothing's wrong? Give me a break. I told you I've got a date and Dan's probably passed out in his room." Suddenly he remembered the time. "Damn, I'm supposed to be there in a half hour."

Vic slugged down another drink and then burst into choking sobs. "I can't believe it, just can't fuckin' believe it." He bent over with his arms resting on his thighs and his hands clasped so tight his fingers turned white. The ceiling fan light reflected off his scalp.

Nathan tightened the towel around his waist and sat beside Vic and rested a hand on his back. "Tell me what happened?"

Vic shook his head and his voice was wrenched with pain. "Can't believe it, just can't fuckin' believe it."

"Believe what, for Christ sake?"

Vic turned and looked at Nathan. His face was whiskey-flushed. Tears streamed down his cheeks and saliva oozed from a corner of his mouth and matted his beard. His breath came in rapid gasps. "Sh-she did it to me."

"You talking about Karen? What did she do?" Nathan hadn't seen anyone this upset since Vietnam. The way Vic struggled for breath Nathan was concerned he might be having a heart attack.

Vic nodded and tried to speak but his voice broke.

"Come on man, calm down." Nathan gently pushed Vic back until he rested against the sofa. "Take some deep breaths and relax."

Gradually Vic's breathing grew less labored and he stopped crying. He wiped his wet cheeks with the backs of his hands. Nathan picked up the cigar and placed it between Vic's lips. Vic fumbled in a pocket for his lighter and lit the cigar and then rested his head on the sofa back and blew a stream of smoke toward the dappled ceiling. After a long silence he leaned forward and thumped a bit of ash into an empty beer can sitting on the coffee table. Again he shook his head and then spoke clearly, as though the bitter tears had purged the alcohol from his tongue.

"I couldn't make the meeting this afternoon. My boss asked me to work till closing. A couple of guys are out sick."

"Yeah, George said you called him about that."

Vic picked up the bottle of Wild Turkey and stared at the label. "Could I have a glass? I need a drink. Bring one for yourself, too."

Nathan didn't question why Vic suddenly wanted a glass after downing most of the bourbon straight from the bottle. He went to the kitchen and found a clean glass and handed it to Vic.

"You don't want any?" Vic said, pouring until the glass was a third full.

"Not now. I told you I've got a date. I can't show up with that shit on my breath."

"A date? With who?"

"Just some broad I met the other day. Now what's going on;

what's got you so messed up?"

Vic's hand shook as he brought the cigar to his lips for another draw. "Like I said, my boss asked me to work till closing. It was hot today so at lunch instead of eating out I decided to go home to clean up and put on a fresh shirt. You know how I sweat.

"Anyway, when I got home there was a Centurion Real Estate car parked in the driveway. I thought that was odd since Karen's only been working there a couple of months and doesn't have a company car yet. I figured she must be using somebody's or maybe she finally got her own because she's been doing real good at work. So I thought I'd sneak in and surprise her."

Vic rested the cigar on the beer can and drained his glass and winced at the burning whisky. "I surprised her all right. I thought she'd be in the kitchen having lunch but she wasn't, so I checked the patio." He poured a refill. "Sometimes we eat outside, but when she wasn't there either I figured she'd be in the bathroom. I started down the hall and then I heard this noise. I didn't know what it was at first." He picked up the cigar and traced the burning tip around the lid of the beer can.

"It's funny. I guess I've heard that sound a thousand times but it didn't register. By the time I got to the bathroom I realized it was coming from our bedroom, so I eased on down the hall. It was Karen . . . moaning."

Vic paused and forced a laugh. He gulped Wild Turkey and pounded the glass on the table. "What a fool, what a gullible fucking fool." He looked at Nathan through pained eyes. "I thought she was sick, can you believe it? I thought she'd come home from work and was lying in bed moaning because she was sick."

Vic hung his head and sighed. He picked up the glass and his hands shook so much the bourbon nearly sloshed out. He managed to set it down. "I opened the door and there she was. There *they* were." He turned his head away as though ashamed. "She was on top of this guy screwing his brains out. They were going at it so hard they didn't even know I was there for a minute. She was riding him like a bucking bronco, moaning and groaning about how good it felt. The sorry bastard was lying there with his eyes closed with both his hands squeezing her tits and she was humping the shit out of him right in my own bed."

Vic shook and tears welled again. He tried to drink but the whiskey stuck in his throat. He coughed violently and his face turned a deeper red. Suddenly he leaned over and vomited the awful mixture of emotions and Wild Turkey onto the floor.

Nathan was dumbstruck. He remembered the cookout at Vic's house and the signals he thought he'd detected from Karen. It was true then, she *had* been coming on to him. That bitch, that fucking bitch! He put an arm around Vic's heaving shoulders and supported his head with the other hand as Vic retched.

Helen picked up on the second ring.

"It's me, Nathan."

"Hi, Me," she said. "You're late; it's five past seven."

"I know." He hesitated, trying to think of how to tell her.

"I was kidding. Heather's at Mom and Dad's. They're taking her to the beach tomorrow if the weather cooperates."

"That's nice. Listen, I don't think I can make it tonight." He squirmed in the tortuous silence that followed.

"Oh. Why?"

"You remember the counseling group I told you about?"

"Yes."

"One of the guys showed up about an hour ago looped out of his mind. There's some serious trouble with his wife. He's in pretty bad shape and I'm afraid to leave him here by himself." Nathan braced, expecting to be lambasted.

"I'm sorry. Of course you shouldn't leave him alone."

"You understand then? I swear I'm not making this up."

"I'd tell you if I thought you were."

Nathan sighed. "Man, does that makes me feel better. I was really looking forward to tonight but I can't desert him. He might do something crazy."

"It's okay and I do understand. How is he?"

Nathan glanced through the doorway into the living room. "A little better. He's sleeping on the sofa."

"Good, that's probably what he needs most right now."

"Yeah. Anyway, I'm sorry about all this. I've been waiting all week for tonight."

"Quit apologizing please," she said. "These things happen. Why don't you come over tomorrow, if your friend is better, that is. It'll have to be during the day, though. I'm picking Heather up tomorrow night at eight-thirty."

"Yeah, that'd be good. Even if we just sit and talk awhile. Or we could go for a walk or a drive or something. Tell you what, I'll call you in the morning, okay?"

"Okay."

"Good. Listen, I better go check on Vic; sounds like he's starting to stir."

"All right. Goodnight."

Nathan hung up, remembering and savoring the sound of Helen's voice. Vic gurgled and leaned over the edge of the sofa and vomited again. Then, mumbling incoherently, he drifted back into a restless stupor.

"Shit." Nathan unrolled a wad of paper towels and spread them over the putrid puddles. "I should be with Helen right now, but no, here I am cleaning up puke and babysitting this asshole."

He took what was left of the Wild Turkey into the kitchen and poured himself a drink. Clarence meowed and clawed at the screen door. Nathan let him in and poured the dregs of a warm beer into his bowl. Clarence lapped it up, purring his appreciation.

Nathan sat at the table and sipped the bourbon. Down the block a dog was barking. A mockingbird began serenading the rising moon. Nathan swallowed the warm whiskey and stared through the screen door into the darkness. It would be another long and lonely night.

# CHAPTER TWENTY

THEY WALKED WEST along the shore of St. Martin Bay to the old crumbling seawall. Stoic pelicans perched on boulders jutting into the bay. At the far end a great blue heron stood like a statue on a section of submerged rubble waiting in ambush for an unsuspecting fish or crab. Gulls and terns flew low over the bay in search of an easy meal. The noonday sun was warm and the mild southern breeze carried the fragrance of sea and a hint of early summer.

Nathan took Helen's hand and helped her over and around the maze of broken concrete and boulders strewn about the beach. He realized it was the first time he'd touched her. Always before it had been her touching him and then only when checking his blood pressure or pulse. Her hand felt soft and delicate in his calloused grip.

"Let's take a break and sit here a while," he said. "It's still another mile or so to the cove."

He led her to a huge flat boulder that extended into the water. Small waves lapped against the seawall. A school of pinfish pecked hungrily at barnacles clinging to the rocks and others darted after silvery minnows flitting among the sunken debris. Helen sat on the edge of the rock dangling her feet over the side. Nathan set the wicker picnic basket and small cooler down and sat beside her.

"It's beautiful," Helen said. She drew her bare legs up and hugged them and rested her chin on her knees. Her gaze focused on the pass and the green waters of the gulf beyond where whitecaps danced on the horizon. "You're lucky to have grown up here. We moved around so much while I was growing up that it never felt like any place was really home. This is so nice."

Nathan watched her and smiled. She was so pretty sitting there with the endless sea for a backdrop and the wind tousling her hair. He wished he were an artist so he could capture the moment on canvas and keep it forever. Memories could be so untrustworthy.

"This is one of my favorite spots. I used to fish right out there where that big bird's standing," he said, pointing to the heron, "and me and my friends used to snorkel all along these rocks."

Helen sighed. "Mm, the sun feels so good. I was beginning to think winter would never end." She turned to Nathan and flashed her easy smile. "I'm glad we decided to do this." She leaned back on her elbows and stretched out her legs. She tilted her face to the sun with her eyes closed and her hair draped across the rock like cascading honey.

Nathan devoured her with his eyes; the slim neck and bare shoulders, the slight bulge of breast visible from the side of the sleeveless blouse, her flat stomach and toned legs. He resisted the urge to lean over and kiss the beautiful mouth with its slightly parted lips. No, he thought, take it slow; let her get to know you better. He hoped she'd still like him then, though he had his doubts.

Nathan grew hot under the sun's glare. He reached into the cooler for a can of Budweiser. Helen stirred when he popped the tab. "How about a beer, Sleeping Beauty?" he said as she yawned and stretched.

"Oh goodness," Helen said, stifling another yawn. "I was so relaxed I nearly fell asleep. Yes thanks, I'd like one."

Nathan fished in the cooler. "Bored already I see." He

opened a can and handed it to her. "Our first date; we're together for less than an hour and you're already falling asleep. Just call me Mr. Excitement."

"Oh, you're terrible," she said and shoved him playfully on the shoulder.

Her touch sent a charge through him.

"You want to get rough, huh? How'd you like to go for a swim?"

"You wouldn't dare."

He grabbed Helen's arm and pulled her up as he stood and slipped an arm around her back. Then he scooped her legs out from under her. Before she realized what was happening Nathan was cradling her like a baby.

"Put me down, help!" Laughing and kicking, Helen twisted against his grasp as he feigned tossing her into the bay. She dropped the beer and clung to his shirt with her freed hand. The can clattered across the rock and spewed foam as it rolled. The strength of her grip surprised him.

"I'm taking you with me if I go!" She worked her left arm free and held Nathan in a hammerlock with her warm breath panting against his face.

"Okay, a truce!" he said, stepping back from the boulder's edge and easing her down. "I'll spare you this time."

"Spare me, ha!" Her eyes flashed and a big smile spread across her flushed face. "You just didn't want to get wet."

"Okay, we'll call it a draw."

"That's better." Helen straightened her shorts and blouse. She spied the spilled beer. "Now see what you've done—wasted my whole beer and I didn't even drink a drop."

Nathan retrieved the empty can and placed it in the cooler and handed her another. He tapped his can against hers. "To the victors go the spoils," he said, and they laughed together.

They strolled hand-in-hand along the narrow beach toward Morgan's Cove. Nathan carried the picnic basket by a strap slung over his left shoulder and held the cooler in that hand. They'd removed their shoes and Nathan carried them strung together around his neck. The squeaky warm sand felt wonderful beneath their bare feet. Occasionally Helen broke away to examine a shell or piece of driftwood that caught her eye. She slipped the keepers into a plastic shopping bag.

"Tell me about yourself," Nathan said as she dropped his hand and waded ankle-deep to examine the shell of a horseshoe crab. "I want to know everything about you."

"Everything?" She smiled coyly, carrying the spiny shell by its long pointed tail. Suddenly she dropped it and shook her hand. "Ooh, it stinks." She frowned and swished her hands in the water.

Nathan laughed. "Yeah, but think how pretty it'll look hanging on your living room wall. You'll be the talk of the whole apartment building."

Her sparkling eyes burned through him. "You really are terrible, Nathan Henson." She wiped her damp hands across his shirt, the up-turned corners of her mouth betraying false anger. "Now," she said as she picked up her scavenging bag and found his hand again, "what was it you wanted to know about me?"

"Oh, the last thirty-one years will do for starters," he said and pointed to a flight of pelicans sailing inches above the water's surface.

"Aren't they beautiful?" Helen said.

"Yeah. Okay, back to the subject. What've you been doing all my life?"

Helen sighed. "There's really not much to tell. I remember it being very dark and warm inside my mother's womb and then suddenly this mean man wearing a mask was holding me by the feet and started spanking me."

Nathan stopped and stared at her. Helen was smiling with her lips slightly parted and the tip of her tongue showing between white teeth. "Now who's being terrible?" Before he realized what he was doing he freed his hand and lightly swatted her backside.

"Ouch!" She rubbed the spot and pouted. "You men are all alike. First the doctor spanks me and now you."

Nathan grinned. "Sorry, I shouldn't have done that. Want me to kiss it and make it better?"

"Huh? Oh, you!" She chased him then, swinging playfully as he retreated. Nathan dropped the cooler and basket on the sand and darted to-and-fro along the shore staying just out of reach. Helen sprang quickly and cut off his escape and backed him into the water. Suddenly she lunged forward and attacked.

Nathan laughed and fended off the blows she hammered lightly about his chest and shoulders. "Okay, I give up, I surrender!" He managed to grab her wrists and pull her against him in a boxer's clench.

They stood there a few seconds catching their breath and laughing together in the chilly knee-deep water. Then the laughter stopped as their eyes met, their faces close and their hearts beating fast. They trembled as their lips touched, softly at first, and then growing in intensity as he pulled her even closer. She snaked a hand around the back of his neck and crushed her mouth against his.

"Whew," Nathan said when the kiss finally ended. He laughed and his breath came in short gasps. He shook his head. "Wow."

Helen smiled up at him. "What?" She laid her face against his chest and clung to him.

His heart pounded. "Man, I feel like I'm sixteen again."

Helen didn't say anything and pressed her face tighter against him. Nathan looked down and ran his fingers through her hair, wishing it could be this way forever.

"Come on," he said after a moment. He took Helen's hand and led her to the beach. "We've got to get to Morgan's Cove. I'm starving."

Far into the night Nathan lay awake unable to sleep. He turned onto his back again. Soft gray shadows slipped through the curtains above his bed and inched silently along the ceiling and opposite wall. It would be daylight soon.

The drone of Vic's snoring came from the living room, constant and irritating as a dripping faucet. Maybe that was why Nathan hadn't slept, or maybe it was because he'd gone to bed sober for the first Saturday night in years. No, that wasn't it. He knew the real reason. Helen. He was afraid if he slept he might wake up and find the day had all been a dream.

He sighed wearily and turned onto his side and pulled the covers tighter about his shoulders. He hugged the extra pillow the way he'd hugged Helen as they stood clinging in the water. But it wasn't a dream; it was real, the whole wonderful day was real. . .

After a leisurely walk getting to know one another and collecting shells and interesting driftwood they had finally arrived at Morgan's Cove, a pristine inlet of white sandy beaches with high bluffs topped by sprawling oaks and towering pines.

Nathan led the way up the serpentine trail to the top of the bluff. "This is just about my favorite spot in the whole world," he said, stopping for a moment to point out the view below. "When we were kids we used to play here all the time. A friend of mine had this leaky old rowboat and we'd pretend we were pirates hunting for buried treasure or Marines storming the beach at Iwo Jima."

They reached the top of the bluff and walked inland a ways to a huge live oak whose moss-draped branches seemed to stretch out forever. "This was our favorite camping spot," Nathan said. "See that old rope there?" He pointed to the frayed remains of a rope still knotted around a stout branch. "We'd swing off that branch and pretend we were buccaneers swinging from the rigging of our pirate ship. And at night we'd sit around a campfire and scare each other half to death with ghost stories."

Nathan cleaned debris from a spot in the shade of the oak and spread the vinyl tablecloth. They feasted on fried chicken, cole slaw, baked beans and rolls he'd bought that morning. Afterward they sat side by side and sipped beer and enjoyed the commanding view of St. Martin Bay. Sunlight danced on the blue water and colorful sailboats tacked into the brisk afternoon breeze. Gulls and terns shared the sky with billowy white clouds and distant gray thunderheads. The sun beamed its warmth and the wind serenaded them with whispered song through shimmering pine boughs. And there, surrounded by the few pleasant memories of his past, Helen told Nathan about her life.

"There's really not much to tell," she'd said again.

She was born in Germany where her parents met when Henry Meyers was stationed there as a young lieutenant fresh out of Officers Candidate School. A typical career military family, they had resided in Japan, the Philippines, Hawaii, England and several bases throughout the United States.

The frequent transfers and subsequent moves were difficult for the Meyers and their two daughters. No sooner had friendships taken root than orders would arrive making it necessary to relocate. But to the young military family staying together was a priority, and sacrifices were made to that end whenever possible.

Helen attended three different high schools, two during her senior year alone. She graduated from Lee High in Montgomery with the class of '71 and then earned a degree in business at a local junior college. After college she landed a good job with Sears working in the credit department as an assistant manager. It was there she met Carl Morris, a part-time employee in menswear and a college junior with aspirations of becoming an attorney. Nathan frowned when Helen mentioned this, but she didn't seem to notice.

She and Carl dated frequently for a couple of years. Gradually the relationship grew serious and they were married in June 1976. The first two years were happy enough, though Carl seemed more intent on having a good time rather than applying himself to his studies and their future. Coming from a well-to-do family, he seemed to think nothing of living off his parents' money which they dispensed generously to their son and his young wife.

Things began to turn sour shortly after Helen discovered she was pregnant. Carl left her alone with greater frequency, spending more and more time with "the boys." Eventually he quit his job with Sears. That left only her salary and the money from the Morrises. Carl's lack of responsibility upset her and she worried constantly knowing she would have to leave her job soon to care for the baby. But none of that seemed to bother her husband.

Soon after Heather's birth Helen learned from a mutual friend that Carl had been unfaithful. Some of "the boys" turned out to be old girlfriends from high school and college. Helen was devastated and didn't know what to do or where to turn for help. Her parents were living in California near Edwards Air Force Base. Her younger sister, Gretchen, was a struggling newlywed living in Fort Bragg, North Carolina with her husband, an Army second lieutenant. Helen's few close friends from school had moved away.

For Heather's sake she decided the best thing to do was try and work things out with Carl. And she had tried very hard. For more than two years she put up with the empty promises, the lies and deceit. Finally, she'd had enough.

She left Carl and filed for divorce and moved with Heather into a modest efficiency apartment. She found a trustworthy sitter in the building and returned to school for her certified medical assistant's degree. Working part time at Sears, she supported Heather and herself with the small salary plus child support payments faithfully paid by Carl's parents to keep their son out of trouble.

And then about six months ago when she learned her parents would be retiring to Bay City, she made plans to join them as soon as she could work out the details.

"So, here we are," Helen said, sighing and looking relieved to have her story out.

Nathan was touched by her honesty and his feelings for Helen grew stronger. He realized she had experienced her share of pain and disappointment in life, too.

He put his arm around Helen and hugged her. They shared another gentle kiss, one born more from care and understanding than passion. For a long time they sat in silence content in the security they felt in each other's arms. They watched the sun sink low as it painted the sugary bluffs of Hurricane Island across the pass with golden rays. They listened as the sea breeze grew weary and sighed its last breath. Night sounds began to play from the growing shadows. Together they witnessed the beautiful day draw to an end and felt the flickering promise of something new and wonderful warming within. . . .

Nathan listened as Vic got up and padded down the hall into the bathroom. He heard the noisy splashing as Vic emptied his bladder and the swirling roar of the flushing toilet.

He thought again of Vic walking into his bedroom and finding Karen with another man. Vic's pain and anguish were just beginning. Nathan felt for him and remembered that just last weekend he himself had been so drunk, so utterly empty and sick with loneliness.

A week; could one short week span the huge chasm between the despair of so many years and the joy and aliveness he'd found in Helen? Was such a transformation possible?

"Helen," he whispered. He hugged the pillow to his chest and tried to sleep.

# CHAPTER TWENTY-ONE

THE PHONE WAS ringing when Nathan returned home Wednesday evening from a landscaping job. He unlocked the door and raced to the kitchen thinking it might be Helen.

"Nathan my man, how ya doin'?"

"Rene?" It was the first time he'd spoken to Boudreaux outside the group. "What's going on? We missed you the last couple of weeks."

"Yeah man, well you know how it is. That monsoon washed out my road ya see, and then last week my truck broke down."

"You get it fixed yet?" Nathan hoped Rene didn't want help hauling his truck out of the woods. He pictured his new pickup churning through chassis-deep mud and getting scratched to hell by bushes and overhanging branches.

"This dude that runs a garage down the highway from my road towed it to his shop. The thing is man, the dude needs his bread before I can get my truck outta his shop and I'm broke till my VA check gets here on the first. I was wondering if you could spot me a few bucks till next week."

A caution flag waved through Nathan's mind. Rene's uncharacteristic friendliness made him uneasy. He started to say he didn't have the money and then a twinge of guilt hit him. Things were going so good lately with Helen and the new truck

and the landscaping jobs. Maybe Rene was really making an effort
to do better. He'd seemed sincere enough when he said he needed
the group, and without his truck he'd have to miss again Friday.

"How much you need?"

"It's a little over two-fifty," Rene said, "but I could really use
three hundred. I need a new headlight and an oil change. Hey bro,
I'll pay you back. The first is Wednesday. I can pay you back
then."

"Damn, what'd you do, blow your engine?"

"No man, my starter was wasted. The U-joints were shot
too, and I needed a new tie rod and a lot of other little shit. The
dude dug my eyes out, okay, but what could I do? I had to let him
do the work, otherwise I'd still be stuck out in the boonies, ya
know? Hey bro, you're the only one I could turn to. Can you help
me out?"

Three hundred dollars was a lot of money, especially at the
end of the month, but he'd get paid tomorrow for the Davenport
job, and hell, Rene *was* a fellow vet.

"Okay, no sweat, but I've got to get it out of the bank. I've
got a doctor appointment in the morning at eight-thirty and
should be finished by nine. Can you meet me at Bay Commercial
Bank, the one on Harris Avenue? You know where that is?"

"Yeah man, next to McDonald's, right?"

"Yeah. Can you be there at ten?"

"No problem bro, there's a dude out this way that works at
the mill. I can ride in with him and hitch back out."

"Okay, I'll meet you at the bank in the morning at ten
sharp."

"My man, I really appreciate this. Ten it is. Thanks again,
bro."


George Browne returned to the room and closed the door behind
him. He frowned and propped his feet on the desk and opened a
fresh pack of Marlboros. Nathan, Vic and Dan sat before him in a
loose semicircle. Rene Boudreaux was absent.

"Two weeks ago we were discussing losses," George said. "I believe Vic had just finished and things started to get a little heated. I hope everyone's had a chance to sort things out so we can move on without this becoming a shouting match." He brushed some lint from the leg of his trousers. "Dan, it's your parade."

Dan Matthews straightened his drug-worn body and coughed. "First off I'd like to apologize for the way I acted at the last meeting. I've been having a lot of problems with my back lately and I overdid it with the muscle relaxer I was taking. George and I discussed it after the meeting." He glanced at George who nodded back. "I'm sorry and hope you'll accept my apology." He turned to face Nathan. "Especially for what I said to you. I was way out of line. It won't happen again."

Nathan reached over and gripped Dan's shoulder. "No sweat Doc."

Dan took a drink of Sprite and rolled the can back and forth between his hands. "I've tried to think about what I was going to say in group today but I'm still not sure. Losses; we've all lost so much." He paused a moment; his brow was wrinkled and he seemed to be deep in thought. "I suppose I'd have to say it was the people I tried to save but couldn't that's affected me the most."

He set the can on the floor and tapped the last cigarette from his pack of Kools. He dug in his pants pocked for his lighter and lit up. "I know it's unreasonable to believe I could save everyone who was hit, but there were times I know I could've done more." His eyes seemed to cloud over as memories crossed the years.

"Being a corpsman it was my responsibility to take care of the sick or wounded first. Everything else was secondary. I don't mind saying that I was good at what I did. When somebody called 'Corpsman up,' they could count on me being there ASAP. That's the way it was in the 'Nam. I took care of my Marines and they took care of me. It was a special relationship, something most people never experience."

"There it is," Nathan said.

Dan sighed. "Then one night . . ." He lowered his head and tore at the cellophane wrapper of the cigarette pack. He looked up with wet eyes and tried again. "One night I——" His voice broke.

"Relax, take your time," George said.

"Back to back," said Nathan.

Vic sat quietly; he was too wrapped up in his own recent troubles to offer Dan any encouragement.

Dan took several deep breaths. That seemed to help but his voice trembled when he spoke again. "We'd just come back in from a three or four day op. We were bushed and everybody was dragging ass. We'd taken several casualties and morale was pretty low. To make matters worse, it had been raining constantly for a week. Our base camp was a quagmire. Instead of being able to sack out and relax everybody had to bail a couple of feet of water out of their bunkers. I was wet and cold and miserable."

He paused to drag smoke deep into his lungs and exhaled. "I'd had just about all I could take at that point. One of our corpsmen was on R and R, and another had been killed on the op. I was the only doc left in the platoon right then." He seemed more composed now and his voice gaining surety as he forced the words out.

"When I saw all that water in our bunker I said 'Fuck it, I can't deal with this right now.' I used my poncho to rig a lean-to along the back wall of the bunker. Then I waded in the bunker and found a few beers I'd saved up and crawled under my lean-to. I dug some pills out of my Unit-1 and proceeded to get bombed as fast as I could. I didn't have to pull radio watch and it would be morning before I'd have to hold sick call, so why not, I thought."

Dan took a deep breath and leaned back and stared at the ceiling. "Sometime during the night we took incoming from mortars. I didn't even hear it and slept right through the whole thing. It was the beer and the pills I guess." He blinked back tears and the empty cigarette pack crumpled in his fist.

"One of the bunkers on the perimeter collapsed. There were

four Marines inside." His face contorted with pain.

"It was pitch black and there was a lot of confusion. We'd taken a couple of casualties from the incoming and then somebody noticed the bunker. People were yelling 'corpsman up!' trying to get help for the wounded and organize a rescue party to dig out the bunker. They also had to make sure the lines stayed manned in case the NVA tried a ground assault.

"But while all this was happening I never heard a damn thing because I was still passed out." He coughed and sniffled and wiped his eyes. "Finally somebody found me. This Marine was running toward the collapsed bunker to help when he stumbled over the lean-to. He lit his Zippo and saw it was me and started shaking me and asking if I was okay. I asked him what had happened and he told me about the bunker. There was some blood and he thought I'd been knocked unconscious by a mortar round.

"By then my head was beginning to clear a little and I could hear all the commotion. I grabbed my bag and followed him to the bunker. They'd managed to dig three of the guys out by the time I got there and . . ." Dan's throat constricted and he couldn't finish the sentence. He buried his face in his hands for a moment before looking up.

"Somebody was saying, 'Doc, where were you? We thought you were in there,' meaning the bunker. Then the Marine who'd stumbled over me told them I'd been knocked out by a blast. There was blood running down my face from a small gash in my forehead where he'd kicked me when he tripped.

"I found my flashlight and started examining the Marines they'd pulled out. There was nothing I could do; they were all dead. This one grunt started screaming that one of them had to be alive because he'd just talked to him a few minutes before. So I checked him again." Dan shook his head, picked up the Sprite and took a drink. "They were dead, all of them."

He stared into space with a look of resignation. "And it was my fault," he said, barely a whisper.

Silence filled the room.

"Fuck it, Doc," Nathan said after a long pause, "there wasn't a damn thing you could've done; they bought it, that's all. A round hit and the bunker caved in and they got wasted. There it is."

Dan looked at him. "It's not that simple. I checked them again at daylight while I was filling out the tags. Two of them might've made it if I'd been there sooner. I could've trached them, one for sure. His windpipe was damaged but he was alive when they pulled him out. If only I'd been there instead of . . ."

Tears filled Dan's eyes again. "It's my fault goddamnit, they needed me and I wasn't there for them. I was lying out there in the mud passed out from the booze and pills. I let them die, don't you see that? I fucking let them die!" He leaned over and buried his face in hands.

After a moment Dan got up and walked to the window. He stared out for a few seconds and then turned. "You want to hear something funny? I got a purple heart out of the deal. I fuck up and pass out and get kicked in the head and awarded my second purple heart for letting those Marines die."

Nathan sat in silence, his face pinched.

"You shouldn't blame yourself," Vic said, his own eyes clouding with tears. "It's not your fault."

George took his feet off the desk and sat up. "I believe we need to look at this for what it is. You two are trying to save Dan from his feelings of guilt and blame. But telling him it's not his fault isn't going to be much help. That's like putting a Band-Aid over a bullet hole and telling the person who's been shot he should feel better because he can't see the entrance wound, as if it'll go away if he'll just ignore it.

"But what about the damage the bullet causes inside when it hits bone and tumbles, ripping apart tendons and muscles and veins? Is all that supposed to just go away because the visible hole has been covered? That's what you two are trying to do for Dan. It's unpleasant to see someone suffering, so, 'Let's just bandage it up and we'll all feel better.'" He paused to let the words sink in.

"I'm sorry, but it doesn't work that way." George tossed his lighter to Vic who had unwrapped a cigar. "Dan has a terrible wound inside and he's had a bandage over it for a lot of years trying to hide it and hoping it would heal on its own someday. It hasn't happened yet, has it Dan?"

Dan stared blankly at George, his eyes red against his pasty face. "No."

"But finally the bandage has come off," George said. "Dan reached down and ripped it away and gave us a good look at that old festering wound. And by doing that he's admitting to this group and himself that he's hurting, that he needs help and that he wants to be healed."

George turned to Nathan. "Do you see now why telling him, 'It's okay, it's not your fault, it just happened,' isn't going to help? In Dan's mind, it *is* his fault. He screwed up by not being there when those Marines needed him. Maybe he could've helped them and maybe not, but in his own mind he could have. And that's what Dan needs to deal with, that's what he has to face up to. That's what he has to quit running and hiding from."

"That's exactly what I've been doing all these years, running and hiding," Dan said, his voice steadier now. "I know I let those guys down when they needed me most and it cost me my self respect."

He locked eyes with George. "How do I get that back? What can I do to make myself feel that life is worth living?"

George drained the last of his coffee. "It won't be easy. It's going to take commitment and hard work. Chances are you'll never completely get over it, but you can reach a point where you learn to live with it. It doesn't have to dominate your life forever.

"It's like dealing with a physical handicap. You learn to adjust and to make certain changes in life to accommodate it because you'll never fully be the way you were before it happened. It's never easy but it can be done. The guy Nathan told us about earlier, the one who lost both legs, is a good example. He could've chosen to be bitter and to hide and shut himself off from life. He'd been Fred Astaire, but without his legs he couldn't dance like before, could he? But with a lot of hard work he could learn to walk again and make the best of what he had left.

"It's the same with you, Dan, and with all of us. Life is out there waiting to be grabbed by the horns if you've got the guts and determination to work hard and do what's got to be done to make it happen."

Rene Boudreaux secured the tarp over the few belongings packed in the bed of his battered pickup. He walked back into the cabin and checked again to make sure he'd loaded everything he would need for the trip. Satisfied, he turned and walked out, pausing for a final look at Mashburn Lake.

A solitary Wood Duck called and circled above the far end of the lake and then descended, its wings back-beating rapidly as it landed among the shadows creeping over the darkening waters. Here and there bream popped the surface as they fed along the grassy edges. The orange ball of sun was sinking below the silhouetted trees. It was time to leave.

Rene slid behind the wheel and turned the key. He smiled at the smooth hum of the well-tuned engine. He was pleased the way things were working out. He'd planned well and carried it out perfectly. He'd be halfway across the country before the checks for the truck repairs and supplies bounced on Monday. The three hundred dollars in cash he'd bummed from Nathan would be enough to get him where he was going if he watched it. And should the money run out, there was the stash of marijuana hidden in the springs of the worn truck seat.

He laughed as he pictured the fuming judge issuing a warrant for his arrest for violation of parole. Screw all the redneck bastards; they can't touch me now.

He eased the truck down the rutted road toward the highway and freedom. He glanced in the rearview mirror for a final glimpse of the lake but it was gone, swallowed by the woods. It was a beautiful place and he would miss it.

His thoughts drifted to his team and the many hours they'd spent communing there. He missed his bros. Then he brightened, knowing they would follow him. They always did.

# CHAPTER TWENTY-TWO

TONGUES OF FLAME flared from the charcoal and licked the hamburgers sizzling on the grill. Nathan muttered a curse and doused the burgers with beer. It was Friday evening and he was depressed. Yesterday Dr. Parker had told him the bi-weekly checkups would no longer be necessary. A change in medication had his blood pressure under control and monthly visits would suffice.

At first he'd nearly panicked at the news, thinking he'd only see Helen once a month. Then he remembered the wonderful day they'd spent together the previous weekend and realized how ridiculous the thought was. Their relationship was no longer tied to his doctor appointments. That realization made him feel warm inside. After so many years of bitter loneliness life again held a glimmer hope, and so he'd called Helen Thursday night full of high expectations of a weekend together.

"I'd like to but I can't," she'd said when he asked her out. "Heather and I are going to Montgomery with my parents for the weekend. I've got things in storage I need to bring back and Heather's spending some time with her dad and his parents."

"Oh. When are you leaving?"

"Right after work tomorrow. We should be back late Sunday."

The thought of Helen seeing the man she once loved, the man to whom she'd freely given herself and whose child she bore, filled Nathan with jealously and a dark rage. Images of Laura and Tom Carter flashed through his mind and betrayal riddled him like machine gun fire. Somehow the past had reared its ugly head and become muddled with the present, leaving the future mired in doubt.

Nathan worked the spatula beneath a burger and flipped it over. Steam hissed and rose as grease dripped onto the hot coals. Evening shadows lay heavy across the yard. Near the bird feeder Clarence waited in ambush in the tangled honeysuckle choking the sagging fence. Vic slouched in a lawn chair nearby, cigar dangling in one hand and a beer in the other.

Nathan finished turning the burgers and glanced at Vic. He'd been this way all week. His marriage was ruined and he'd lost his job. It seemed his very spirit was crushed. He went through the motions like a robot. Each morning he left the house to supposedly look for work, and every evening he returned around supper time. "No luck today," he'd say, all bleary-eyed and toting a couple of six-packs or a liquor bottle. Twice Nathan had spotted Vic's car parked in front of bars in the middle of the day but kept quiet about it. He didn't want to take Vic's pride from him, too.

Nathan tilted his head back and drained his beer. He opened another. The alcohol was kicking in. What's the use, he thought, who am I trying to kid? He was a fool to think things would be different with Helen than they were with any other woman. He'd been burned once, and once was plenty enough.

He looked at Vic sitting and staring into emptiness with vacant eyes and thought again of how Vic had walked into his own home and found his wife in their bed with another man. That bitch. Little wonder Vic was wasted.

And what about Doc? Nathan thought, the beer giving him permission to see things in a no-nonsense way. Dan's ex-wife had done him in, too. Some other man had his wife and his kid and now they were hounding him for his money. Shit; no damn wonder Doc's screwed-up. Hell, we're all screwed-up when you think about it.

First the war and then the women. How did he know that Helen didn't still have the hots for her ex-husband? Maybe that's the real reason she went to Montgomery instead of staying home and going out with him. Hell, for all he knew she might be humping his brains out right this very minute. Women were all alike; impossible to understand and not to be trusted. She didn't give a damn about him; if she did she wouldn't have gone up there to see her ex, would she?

Nathan crumpled the empty beer can and hurled it as far as he could toward the overgrown fence separating his and Mrs. Ard's backyards. It landed a foot beyond where Clarence lay dozing in futile ambush. A yellow flash shot through the twilight across the yard.

"Hey flyboy, you ready to eat?" Nathan said, giving the burgers a final turn. "This shit's about done."

Vic glanced up from his chair. "I'm not hungry." The tip of his cigar glowed fiery red as he took another puff. "You go ahead."

Nathan stared at the pathetic figure slumped in the chair and then back at the burgers sizzling above the hot coals. He had a mellow buzz from the beer and hated to ruin it with food.

"Fuck it, I ain't hungry either. Here you go Clarence, have at it," he said, and tossed the burgers one by one toward the big yellow cat.

Nathan was in the kitchen watching *Sixty Minutes* when the phone rang. Vic lay sprawled across the sofa sleeping off the day's drinking. The ringing broke the rhythm of his snoring. He rolled onto his side and buried his face in a pillow. The snoring resumed.

Nathan picked up the receiver and grunted "Yeah," ready to do battle with a telemarketer or wrong number.

"Hi! How was your weekend?"

"Helen? You're back already?"

"Yes, about an hour ago. I'm pooped. We just finished carry

a ton of boxes upstairs. I sure missed you."

"Me, too."

In the background Nathan heard the hollow sound of voices and people milling about. A door slammed shut. "Heather be careful," a woman called in the distance.

"Where do you want these?" a deep voice nearer the phone asked.

"In the kitchen," Helen said. "I'm sorry Nathan, things are still a little hectic around here. You should see this mess; no, I take that back, you shouldn't see it. It's going to take forever to get this place straightened out. I'm glad I have tomorrow off."

Nathan perked up. Maybe they could—he frowned, remembering he'd promised Mrs. Blackwell that he would start her flower beds first thing Monday morning.

"Dr. Parker's in Atlanta for a convention. He won't be back until Wednesday so I've got the next two days off. That'll give me time to get this mess put away."

"If you need any help I could—"

"I'll be right there," she said, her voice muffled.

"Sorry about that," Helen said. "We're going to the Pizza Hut for dinner in a few minutes. Why don't you join us?"

For a moment Nathan was tempted to say yes. He longed to see her but he and Vic had polished off nearly a case of beer and he still felt the effects. Besides, he wasn't in the mood to meet her parents right then.

"I better not. I already ate, and Vic's still here. Thanks for asking though."

"Tell Vic he's invited, too. My parents are dying to meet you. I told them all about you."

"Thanks for that. Your father probably wants to shoot me on sight."

"Tell him to get his butt over here and let's go get some pizza," the deep voice said.

Helen giggled. "Dad says to—"

"I heard him loud and clear. I better pass. Maybe next time."

"Well darn. Hey, why don't you come for dinner tomorrow night? Mom and Dad really want to meet you and it'll give you and Heather a chance to get to know each other. She's asked a million questions about you."

Nathan hesitated. "I don't know. I'm not very good at meeting people."

"You've got to meet them sooner or later. They're not going to bite you, you know. Now say you'll be here because I won't take no for an answer."

"Okay, I'll be there. What time, and should I bring a blindfold or will your dad provide one?"

"Oh, you're awful. We'll plan on eating around six-thirty, but you can come over earlier if you'd like."

"Sounds good. What can I bring?"

"Just yourself. Oh, you might want to bring along a bodyguard in case Dad doesn't approve of you," she said, and giggled. "Seriously, you're welcome to bring Vic if you'd like."

"I don't think he'll feel up to it, but thanks for offering. I better hang up so you can go eat. See you tomorrow."

"All right; bye-bye."

"Helen?"

"Yes?"

"Thanks for the invite."

"You're very welcome. Um, Nathan?"

"Yeah?"

"Sweet dreams."

For a while after the conversation he felt terrible and guilt showered him like a monsoon. He chastised himself for the terrible things he'd thought about Helen. He'd been too quick to condemn her without cause and to cast her among the convenient targets for all the painful, confusing years. It was survival, the law of combat—shoot first and walk away because the dead have no court of appeal. So when his wary mind had fabricated the scenes of betrayal he hadn't hesitated to attack their budding relationship, to blow it away with callousness.

In an instant Helen's call had changed all that. She'd missed him and called soon after she'd gotten home. She wasn't like all the rest; she really *did* care. When he'd heard her voice the feelings of guilt and remorse stung him. Then he remembered something George had said:

"It's not the feelings themselves that matter; feelings can change minute to minute. It's what you do with the feelings and how you channel them that count."

And so Nathan did something totally out of character. He decided to forgive himself and believe he was worth whatever struggle it might take to achieve some measure of happiness in this world. He'd already wasted too many years in the bog of despair. He might not win but he wouldn't go down without a fight, even if the enemy was himself.

Nathan arrived at Helen's apartment at five-thirty Monday evening. He'd been upbeat all day, thinking she must really be interested in him if she wanted him to meet her family.

When Helen answered the doorbell and saw Nathan standing there grinning with his arms laden with gifts, she laughed. "Hi. I see you just brought yourself like I said."

"Hi, back," he said, his eyes feasting on her. She wore a dark blue gym suit and white sandals. Her hair was swept back and tied in a loose ponytail. "These flowers are for you, and these are for your mother," he said, handing her the two bouquets and freeing a hand. "The stuffed panda's for Heather. I figured she'd like that more than flowers." He handed the panda to Helen. It towered above her head, covering her face. "The wine is for supper." He carefully placed the bottle of Chardonnay in the palm of her free hand. "And I got your father a six-pack of Beck's beer. It's imported from Germany so I hope he likes it. Aren't you going to invite me in?"

For several seconds Helen stood giggling with her face buried against the panda's belly and her hands clutching the flowers and wine. "Please, come in," she finally managed. She backed through the doorway into the living room. Cardboard boxes were stacked high against one wall. Nathan took the panda and tossed it onto the sofa and helped Helen set the other items on a nearby coffee table. She reached up and cupped his face and kissed him. "Glad you're here." Then turning, she called, "Heather, come here hon, there's someone I'd like you to meet."

Heather Morris skipped into the room wearing jeans and a red pullover shirt. Her braided blonde hair hung midway down her back. "Hi," she said without a hint of shyness, and extended a small hand as Helen introduced them.

Though Nathan had never been around children much he was immediately drawn to Heather. There was something about this precocious six-year-old that tugged at his heart, and despite what Helen had said, there was a strong resemblance between mother and daughter.

Heather beamed when Nathan gave her the panda. "Thank you." He bent over as she reached up to hug his neck. Then she bounded back to her room with panda filling her arms.

"That was sweet of you," Helen said.

He grinned. "Hey, I'm a sweet guy."

They carried the flowers, wine and beer into the kitchen. Helen put the wine and beer in the refrigerator and searched a cabinet and found a matching pair of crystal vases. She filled them with water and carefully arranged a bouquet in each. She placed one on the dining table as a centerpiece. The other she put on the island counter top which separated the kitchen from the dining room.

"They're so pretty," she said, admiring the arrangements. "Mom may just have to leave hers here." She turned and kissed him lightly on the lips. "It's been a long time since anyone's given me flowers. Thank you."

"Glad you like 'em," Nathan said, pleased with himself for the idea. He sniffed and glanced at the stove. "Mm, something smells good. What're we having?"

"Marinated baked chicken, scalloped potatoes and green

beans. The chicken is Mom's recipe. I hope you'll like it."

"If it tastes half as good as it smells you got nothing to worry about."

Helen spent a few minutes checking on the various dishes. "Would you open the wine, please? There's an opener thingy in that top drawer."

Nathan found the corkscrew and took the bottle from the refrigerator. He worked the pointed end into the cork and carefully pushed the handles down and removed it.

Helen took two stemmed glasses from a cabinet and poured the wine. "Dinner won't be ready for an hour. Let's sit outside for a while."

Nathan opened the sliding glass door and followed her onto the patio overlooking the bay. A round redwood picnic table and matching bench seats occupied one side. At the other end were a padded chaise lounge and chair. A Weber barbeque grill stood against the apartment wall, centered between rose bushes in clay pots. The three open sides were fenced by a waist-high wrought iron rail.

The sun was sinking below the horizon and the golden ribbon it cast danced across the dark water. To the right the old seawall was barely visible in the shadows. Far out on the bay tiny red and green running lights bordered the indistinct outline of a shrimp boat heading for its nightly run.

They sat at the table enjoying the view and sipping wine and making small talk. Then Helen asked abruptly, "Why haven't you ever married?"

The frank question caught Nathan off guard. He started to laugh it off with the pat answer he'd used before when others had asked, but then decided Helen deserved better. She'd opened herself to him that afternoon at Morgan's Cove and she was entitled to a legitimate answer.

"I thought I would be once, a long time ago," he said, his gaze slipping past Helen into the dusk beyond. Lights from a few boats and the buoy markers guiding their path along the channel dotted the darkness. "There was this girl back in high school. We were sort of an item for a couple of years, but it didn't work out." And then he told Helen about those carefree days, and Laura. . . .

Nathan met Laura Johnson the second semester of his sophomore year. Her father, a civilian engineer employed by the government, had transferred from Memphis, Tennessee to Randall Air Force Base outside Bay City. On her first day at the new school she sat at the desk beside Nathan in geometry. He was smitten with the green-eyed, auburn-haired beauty at first sight.

Nathan cut classes the rest of the day to show Laura around school. He escorted her to the door of each of her classrooms and waited patiently like an obedient dog to guide her to the next. During lunch they chatted and got to know a little more about each other. He invited her to the baseball game that afternoon to watch the Hurricanes battle the Redford High Tigers. She sat in the bleachers behind the backstop and watched as Nathan slapped two doubles and drove in three runs in the five-to-one victory over their cross-town rivals. Tom Carter was the winning pitcher, yielding only three hits to the Tiger batters.

After the game Nathan introduced Laura to Tom, his best friend and battery mate, and that weekend they enjoyed the first of what proved to be many double dates. Within a month Nathan asked her to go steady and for the next two-and-a-half-years they were inseparable.

Graduation approached. Tom accepted a full football scholarship to Florida State. Nathan had an offer from the local junior college to play baseball, but something else was stirring inside him. In a faraway land almost no one had heard of, America was at war. Nathan became obsessed with Vietnam; he devoured every newspaper and magazine article he could find on the war and watched the nightly news devoutly. Sleeping became difficult as he was torn between his dream of someday playing major league baseball and this sudden attraction to war and patriotic duty.

Finally he spilled his guts to Tom.

"Are you out of your mind?" Tom said. "A year or two at the juco and you're a cinch to get an offer from FSU. Coach Jerrell's already told you that. Don't be a fool."

For weeks Nathan agonized over the situation, and then one day he made his decision; the only one he could live with—the Few, the Proud, the Marines. Baseball could wait. His country needed him.

When he told Laura, she'd cried, unable to understand his attraction to the Marines and war. After a while the tears stopped and she promised to wait for him.

Briefly he recounted for Helen his tour in Vietnam, sparing most of the painful and horrific details. He did mention how he'd been wounded and hospitalized for several months. And then he told her about that warm May afternoon with birds singing sweetly in the high branches of a great live oak and squirrels chasing playfully across the green lawn. A day filled with the promise of renewal, but ending in betrayal with his hopes and dreams and future shattered. . . .

"I haven't had anything to do with either one of them since," Nathan said, surprised at how quickly and easily the words had come. He'd said much more than he intended but felt relieved, as though he'd belched up some foul malady that had sickened him for years.

Helen reached over and took his hand in hers. "You must have loved them both very much to have been so hurt by what they did."

"Yeah, I reckon. Who knows if it's really possible to love anybody at that age? Maybe a person doesn't know enough about life yet to qualify for love."

Nathan placed his other hand over hers. "I'll tell you this much, though. My buddies in Vietnam, they loved me. And I loved them. We depended on each other and took care of each other and never let each other down. *That* was love."

He glanced out over the bay. "I haven't seen anything back here in the World that even comes close to what we had over there. I thought I had that with Laura. But after what she and Tom did it just didn't seem worth the effort or the risk." He looked into Helen's eyes. "Until I met you. When I saw you in Dr. Parker's office that morning I knew there was something."

They leaned toward each other with hands clasped as their lips met in a lingering kiss. The chiming doorbell broke the magic.

Helen giggled. "Mom and Dad are here," she mumbled, her lips still touching Nathan's.

"Tell 'em to go away," he said, his mouth searching hers.

"Mm . . . mm, come on," she said, breaking contact and leading him by the hand into the kitchen. She surveyed his face in the light and playfully brushed a corner of his mouth with her fingertips. "Lipstick." She winked. "We don't want Dad thinking you're taking advantage of his little girl."

"Thanks; you're a real confidence booster."

She laughed. "Relax, I'm only teasing. My parents are very nice people; you'll like them, I promise."

The doorbell chimed again.

She smiled and pulled him toward the living room. "Now come on or they really will think something's going on."

"Dum de dum dum," Nathan said, mimicking the theme from *Dragnet*.

Nathan and Helen sat nestled in a corner of the plush sofa. The glare from the television and a small nightlight in the hallway provided the only illumination in the apartment. Johnny Carson was at his best; the Great Carnac was divining questions that had been hermetically sealed in a mayonnaise jar and kept on Funk and Wagnall's front porch all day.

The evening had gone much more smoothly than Nathan had imagined it would. Hank Meyers was a likable man in his early fifties, slight of build with sharp features and reddish hair brushed with gray along the temples. A hearty sense of humor belied his hard look and imposing voice. His strong handshake and resounding laugh quickly allayed Nathan's uneasiness.

Bridget Meyers matched her husband's height of five feet, nine inches. Still an attractive blonde at fifty, she shared Hank's quick wit while retaining a warm gracious manner. Her voice barely hinted at her German ancestry and held the same husky quality as Helen's. A quick glance told Nathan where Helen inherited her good looks and figure.

Dinner was pleasant; the food was delicious and the conversation varied. The Meyers were a jovial couple and their love and concern for their daughter and granddaughter was evident. Hank carried the conversation and never once left Nathan feeling like he was on the hot seat. They talked about Vietnam, the one common ground besides Helen the two men shared.

"I flew F-4s out of Bien Hoa on my first tour," Hank said. He sat ramrod-straight and his voice was strong and proud. "We provided close air support for the troops in III CORPS and IV CORPS. We also flew sorties over Cambodia and Laos along the Ho Chi Minh Trail. Those were great days," he said, his eyes shining. He seemed pleased his daughter was seeing someone who could appreciate the difficult job they had accomplished in Vietnam.

"The sorry bastards made me a desk jockey my second tour," he said, frowning as he cut a piece of chicken. "I hardly ever got a chance to fly." He took a bite and waved his fork in the air. "There's just nothing like sitting in the cockpit of a Phantom and making a treetop-level run. No sir, nothing like it at all."

The subject turned to politics and Nathan agreed with Hank's assessment of how ". . . the bleeding-heart, chickenshit left-wingers are undermining this country and everything it stands for, just like they did during the war."

Soon a second bottle of wine was gone and they started on the Beck's.

"You think this is good," said Hank after enjoying a healthy swig from his bottle, "you ought to taste it fresh from the tap.

There's two things those Germans know how to make—good beer and beautiful women."

"There it is!" Nathan said as he lifted his bottle in a toast. The gesture drew a good laugh from everyone.

After dinner Nathan and Hank were enjoying another beer and the cool night air on the patio while the women cleared the table and loaded the dishwasher. The inevitable subject Nathan had been dreading all night finally came up. Hank unzipped a leather tobacco pouch and pulled his pipe from a sweater pocket. "Helen tells me you're in business for yourself."

Nathan's stomach churned. There was nothing wrong with what he did for a living but he didn't want to tell Helen's father he was a common yard man. "Yes sir, I'm in landscaping. I'm not getting rich yet, but with my VA check I do okay." It was mostly true. He'd been concentrating more on landscaping lately rather than routine lawn maintenance.

"Hmm, that's right, you were wounded," Hank said, his pipe bobbing up and down as he lit it. "Helen mentioned that. What happened, if you don't mind my asking?"

Nathan took a quick gulp of beer and chose his words carefully. "We were assaulting a fortified village in the Cua Viet River area just north of Dong Ha," he said, the words rushing out. "The NVA had us outnumbered and pinned down outside the vill. We were zeroed-in by their artillery and rockets and mortars. The gooks had several 12.7 millimeter machinegun emplacements, too. Those things were bad news.

"I took some shrapnel from a rocket through here," Nathan said, touching his left rib cage. "It was the third time I'd been hit that day. I was wounded in both legs and feet, too." He gave a half-hearted laugh. "The NVA sure did a number on me. I guess it just wasn't my day."

Nathan was uneasy now but managed to continue. "I spent about six months in the hospital in Japan and Pensacola. After my discharge the VA awarded me ninety percent." He quickly downed the last of his beer. "I get along pretty good. I've got my aches and pains like everybody else, but I can do about anything I want to physically."

Hank drew on his pipe and gave a slow nod of his head. "Well, it's good to see you came out of it with your head on straight," he said. "That war screwed up so many good young men." Then he added, "You Marines take a lot of ribbing from the other services, but you boys did a hell of a job over there. Damn fine fighters. I remember one time up near——"

"Are you two going to stay out here talking all night?" Helen said, smiling as she stepped through the doorway. "I'd like some time with him too, Dad."

"Watch out for her," Hank said as they walked back into the apartment, "she's just like her mother; nag, nag, nag, all the time."

"Oh Dad," Helen said as she lightly slapped his shoulder, "you're awful."

"So?" Helen said. She smiled, her head resting on Nathan's shoulder.

"So, what?"

"So, what do you think of my parents?" The Meyers had left a half hour earlier after tucking Heather into bed.

"They're nice. Your father's a real kick. I haven't done this since high school but I think it went okay."

"What do you mean?"

Nathan shrugged. "You know, meeting parents, socializing, that kind of stuff."

Helen pushed away from him and sat up. "You're not telling me you haven't dated in almost twenty years, are you?"

"There it is. Not a real date anyway, where I picked up a girl at her house and met her parents."

"Come on, I can't believe that."

"It's true. You're looking at Mr. Anti-social here. After that mess with Laura and Tom I sort of withdrew from everything. Since then my so-called dating life has been hitting on somebody at a bar. I know that doesn't sound very nice. It's not, but it's the truth and you might as well know about it now." There it is, he thought, I blew it.

Helen turned from him and stared at the television for a moment. Nathan tried to read her face but it was expressionless. His spirits sank.

Helen faced him again and smiled. She ran her hand along his shoulder until it rested on the back of his neck and snuggled against him. His breath quickened as he felt the supple mound of her breast press against his side. "I guess that makes me special then, doesn't it?" she whispered. "After all these years, after that awful time, I'm the first."

"Yeah, you're special. You don't know how spe—"

The words were lost as Helen pulled Nathan's face down to meet hers. The soft lips parted and hungrily sought his.

# CHAPTER TWENTY-THREE

THE FOLLOWING FRIDAY the group's discussion topic was "worst days" in Vietnam. George urged Dan to go first.

"It happened on May 22, 1968 near the village of Loc Sanh," Dan said.

Outside the open window nesting English sparrows chattered noisily under the eaves of the building. A warm early May breeze filtered into the room and helped thin the clouds of tobacco smoke.

Dan's hands shook as he took a drag on his Kool. "We left Alpha-Three before daylight on a company-size sweep. The scoop was there was an NVA force operating from one of the nearby vills." He forced a quick humorless laugh. "S-2 suspected it was a company but it turned out to be a reinforced regiment."

His thin cheeks collapsed as he drew on the cigarette. He leaned forward and rubbed his palms together as though trying to generate warmth. "We had a K-9 team walking point. The dog kept alerting—this was maybe an hour after daylight—and the handler kept passing the word back to the CO that there was a lot of sign and that we'd better slow down and check it out.

"We had a new CO, a Captain Hertz. 'Hurry-till-it-Hertz' is what we called the bastard. He'd only had the company for a couple of weeks and already knew it all. Nobody could tell him anything, not even the staff NCOs. We figured it was only a matter of time before he got us into a big-time shit sandwich."

Dan fidgeted in the chair and reached in his pocket for his lighter. Realizing he already had a lit cigarette, he began snapping the lid open and shut.

"Captain Hertz said to keep pushing because we had to reach our objective by mid-morning. I suppose he was hell-bent on getting to the village and kicking the gooks asses by noon to impress the brass back at Battalion and Regiment.

"Hertz had never been with a line unit before. He'd been a REMF before taking over the company, supply I think. Usually a CO would have some bush experience as a platoon leader before getting his own company but there was a shortage of qualified platoon leaders after Tet."

Dan paused to pinch off the burning end of his cigarette and place the butt back inside the pack. "It amazes me how brilliant the brass could be at times. Hertz was one stupid son-of-a-bitch to think it would go like clockwork. Like S-2 was omniscient and all we had to do was mosey up to the vill and get on line and blow the gooks away, one-two-three. What a SNAFU."

"Why didn't the platoon leaders step in and set the dumbass straight?" Nathan said. "Be damned if I would've diddy-bopped past all that sign without checking it out."

Dan glanced at Nathan. "All three platoon leaders were green, too. We had one KIA and one WIA the previous month, and the third had just rotated home, so we were stuck with a whole new crop of officers. None of them had any combat experience. And the LT's were too intimidated by gung ho Hertz to pay attention to any of the enlisted salts. The whole thing was one big fuckup waiting to happen."

"Okay, we've established that your command group was lacking experience," George said. "And while that probably had a lot to do with the way things went down that day let's not lose our focus. We don't want to get sidetracked by pointing fingers at who was responsible. Let's concentrate on the specific events that made this your worst day in Vietnam."

"Bullshit!" said Nathan. "If the captain or his ass-kissing platoon leaders would've had something besides shit for brains they wouldn't have gotten their asses waxed in the first place. Then maybe Doc wouldn't be as screwed up over it as he is." He stood and limped to the window trying to get a breath of fresh air. Damn, how he hated that choking tobacco smoke! Then he turned to face George. "You're always taking the fucking brass's side and letting us grunts hang out to dry."

"That's not the point," George said, remaining calm. "The fact is it doesn't matter who caused it. It happened, period. Blaming the CO or platoon leaders isn't going to help Dan. If you come down with the flu does it do any good to know where you picked up the germ? No. What matters is treating the symptoms and making yourself feel better and getting well. We're not here to point fingers. That's not going to help anybody."

George sat up straight and locked eyes with Nathan. "It's not a question of who caused it or why it happened. What matters is *what*. What happened that particular day to make it Dan's worst day in-country? How did he react? How did he deal with it? Has he dealt with it?"

George tossed his pack of Marlboros to Vic who was out of cigars. "That's what we're after here," he said. "You're trying to save Dan from himself again for the umpteenth time. You figure if you can convince him that the officers or intelligence were to blame, then it won't eat at him so much." He paused and reached for his coffee cup. "It doesn't work that way."

Nathan's brow wrinkled as he thought over George's words and recalled a similar discussion during a previous meeting. "Maybe you're right. I need to look before I leap in with my big mouth.

"Okay, go ahead and tell us how you stepped in the shit and got your ass kicked, Doc. I won't try to save you again."

Nathan grabbed the bottom of the window and opened it as far as it would go. "Damn, it's smoky in here. You assholes are going to give me lung cancer yet." Gazing outside at the beautiful day he thought of Helen and briefly forgot the collective years of misery inside the room.

Dan flicked his lighter open and shut. "All of a sudden there was gunfire up front. Our point squad had spotted some NVA sitting around a cook fire. They opened fire and took off after them when the gooks broke and ran. The CO got all excited and radioed for the entire lead platoon to pursue."

He hesitated a few seconds and took a deep breath. "That's when the hammer came down. Our guys ran straight into the killing zone of a U-shaped ambush and the gooks opened up and just annihilated them. Nearly the whole damn platoon went down."

Dan rubbed his hands together; his face was pinched with the emotions he was dredging up. "I was back with second platoon. We could hear them over the radio screaming for help. You could hear gook voices on the radio, too. The NVA were either using the same frequency or had already captured one of ours. The platoon was about a hundred meters ahead. We knew they were in a world of hurt from the amount of gunfire and the radio chatter." He shut his eyes for a second, trying to squelch the horror of that day. "They were neck-deep in shit."

Dan leaned back and sucked in a breath and shivered. Turning his face away, he stared at the far wall and tried to regain composure. "Then second platoon started double-timing ahead," he said, his voice low and quavering. "We got close enough to make visual contact with the survivors of first platoon. They were huddled behind some pitiful little dikes. I could see them lying there and looking back at us. You could see the fear in their eyes and you could almost smell it. Somebody was screaming for a corpsman so I moved forward. I didn't think about what I was getting into, I just took off running.

"By this time second platoon was pinned down too, but we had better cover. My best friend, Doc Emerson, was somewhere with first platoon and I knew he needed help. They were almost wiped out and there was no way he could handle all the casualties by himself, if he was still alive.

"I don't recall hearing the rounds as I ran but the NVA must've been firing like crazy at any visible target." Dan's face flushed as he relived the scene. "My only thoughts were that Emerson and those Marines needed my help and I had to get to them. It seemed to take forever but I finally made it to where Emerson was working on some wounded behind a burial mound at the edge of a small cemetery. Tracers were crisscrossing from every direction and explosions going off everywhere. It's almost impossible to describe; one big continuous crescendo."

Dan relit the Kool he'd saved. He drew in the smoke, held it for several seconds and exhaled. "When I got to Emerson, he looked at me and smiled like we were sitting in a park feeding pigeons. He said, 'Well bud, it looks like we stepped in the deep doo-doo this time, huh?' His voice was steady, like he was talking about the weather. Then he nodded toward a little rise of ground just beyond the next dike and said, 'Hilton and Foster are over there.' Just matter-of-factly, like people say 'Have a nice day' or whatever. And all the while he kept working on this Marine with a sucking chest wound. I couldn't believe how calm he was. I can't explain it but he seemed different that day, like he knew he'd been dealt a lousy hand of cards and had to play them. No discards. It was almost as if he was resigned to whatever fate was about to dish out."

Dan crumpled the empty cigarette pack in his fist and tossed it at a round garbage can a few feet away. It banked off the wall and into the can.

"Three points, Doc!" Nathan said, trying to relieve the tension.

Dan didn't seem to hear. He was bent over and shaking as though an icy wind blew through him. For several seconds he remained silent. And then looking up at George, he said, "I told Emerson, 'I'll go get them,' and just as I said it, he . . ." Dan's voice choked and his eyes filled with tears. "Just as I said it his face exploded all over me."

He sniffed as tears streamed down his sallow face. "A piece of Emerson's jaw hit me in the face. I must've had my mouth open because I got sick and spit up blood and pieces of flesh." He buried his face in his hands and his thin body shook.

Nathan walked over and draped an arm around Dan's neck. "Christ Doc, that's some awful shit." It was all the comfort he could muster. Dan's pain was stirring painful memories of his own.

Vic leaned across the empty chair between him and Dan and placed a meaty hand on Dan's knee and squeezed tightly. Vic was crying. He tried to speak but gave up and wiped his eyes with his handkerchief.

The show of support seemed to help. Dan brushed at his cheeks and sat upright. Coughing to clear his throat, he said, "Emerson had just gotten back from R and R in Hawaii with his wife. She was expecting a baby in a couple of months."

He almost broke again, but steadied himself. "One look and I knew he was gone. He never felt a thing; alive one second and dead the next. At least that's good.

"Then I snapped out of it and remembered the men Emerson had pointed out to me. Hilton was a close friend, and Foster was a new guy. I scrambled for the next dike, crawled over it and around a little rise. I found Foster first," Dan said, breathing deeply. "He was dead, shot through the head. He had a shoulder wound too so he was probably alive when Emerson saw him go down.

"I saw Hilton a few feet away and crawled over to him. He was lying on his stomach and groaning with his face pressed into the ground. It took some effort to roll him over because he was a big guy and I had to stay prone. He'd taken a round through the throat. He was choking and struggling for air. I tried talking to him but he was out of it. His eyes were rolled back but I thought I might be able to save him if I could get him back and maybe trache him."

Dan got up and walked to the window. He stared out with

vacant eyes. After a moment he turned and leaned against the wall next to the window. "Hilton was at least six-two and two hundred pounds. The NVA had us pinned down. The only thing I could do was roll him over on top of me and try to crawl him back. So that's what I did."

Dan pushed away from the wall and paced slowly back and forth across the room. He seemed calmer now, almost resigned.

"It seemed like it took hours. Rounds were hitting all around us. Then I felt something like a sledgehammer pound Hilton's body and a pain below my left shoulder. I thought I'd torn a muscle in my back."

Dan stopped pacing. He reached for George's pack of Marlboros on the desk. Lighting up, he returned to his chair. "I finally managed to get him back far enough where some other Marines ran up and dragged us back to cover. I was bushed. I must've crawled at least seventy-five meters with him.

"I caught my breath and checked Hilton but he was dead. He'd taken two rounds in the back straight through the lungs.

"Then somebody told me I was hit. My back was all bloody. I thought it was from Hilton but this Marine said I had a hole in my flak jacket. We got the flak jacket off and he checked me over. There was an entrance wound just below my left shoulder blade. The bullet had gone through Hilton and through my flak jacket and lodged in my back."

Dan paused a moment and then laughed bitterly. "I tried to save Hilton but he wound up saving me."

He sat there smoking and staring at the floor. A hush fell over the room. Finally, George spoke. "What did you feel?"

"Tired. Exhausted. My back hurt."

"What else?"

Dan looked George squarely in the eye. "I felt like shit. Half the goddamned company was wiped out and two of my best friends were dead. I felt like day old dog shit."

George reached for his cup and leaned back. "Anything else?"

Dan frowned. "Such as?"

George shrugged. "Guilt, maybe?"

"Guilt for what?"

"For surviving when so many others didn't."

Dan thought for a moment. "Of course I felt some guilt. They were dead and I was still alive. Emerson had a wife and a baby he'd never get to see. Hilton took rounds that were meant for me. Why wouldn't I feel guilty?"

"And whose fault was that?"

"Whose fault for what, George? I don't feel like playing guessing games."

George rocked back in his chair and clasped his hands behind his head. "Whose fault was it that Hilton was dead? And Emerson, and half your company? And whose fault was it that you and the other survivors were alive."

"I don't know. Nobody's. The NVA, maybe. Or our country for sending us there. How the hell should I know?"

"Do you blame them for dying?"

"What kind of question is that? "How the hell can I blame them for dying? It wasn't their fault. They were the bravest people I ever knew and they'd do anything for you. They never let me or anyone else down. How the hell can I blame them for dying? How can you even ask such a fucking question?"

George remained unfazed. "The others in your company, the ones who made it out alive that day; do you blame them for living? Or Nathan, or Vic?"

"Of course not," Dan said. "That's absurd. Why should anyone be blamed for surviving what we went through?"

George leaned forward and rested his elbows on the desktop. His eyes burned into Dan's. "Then why blame yourself? Why continue to harbor guilt and blame for something you didn't cause, something you had absolutely no control over?"

"Are you better than anybody else?" George said. "Is that it, do you think you're better than anybody else who went through the same shit? Is that why you deserve to carry the blame and guilt around after all these years? Are you some sort of martyr?"

"Fuck you!" Dan said. Tears rolled down his anguished face. "No, I'm not better." He buried his face in his palms and sobbed.

George moved from behind the desk and sat beside Dan. He wrapped his arms around Dan and hugged him tightly. "Let it out, Dan," he said quietly. "You've carried it for too long already. Let it go, just let it go."

During the break Sarah Potter walked into the lounge where Nathan and the others were standing around drinking coffee and talking.

"Got a message for you," she said and handed Nathan a yellow slip of paper. She winked. "She said for you to call her when you got the chance." Then in her best Mae West imitation, Sarah said, "Sounds like a real hot number, lover boy."

Nathan reddened and glanced at the note. Helen's name and number were all that Sarah had scribbled down. Wonder what she'd be calling me here for? he thought. Hope nothing's wrong. He looked up. "Hey, it's business, that's all."

"Uh huh, sure," Sarah said, clucking her tongue and poking him playfully in the ribs as she turned and left the room.

"I'll be back in a minute," Nathan said to George. He found an empty office, dialed 9 for an outside line and then Helen's number.

She answered on the first ring.

"What's up?" said Nathan. "Anything wrong?"

"I just wanted to hear your voice," Helen said.

Nathan thought she sounded tense. "What's the matter?"

"Nothing really, we just need to talk. Can you come by after group or do you have to go back to work?"

"I can come right now if you need me. I can tell something's bothering you."

"Don't worry, it's not that important. We'll talk when you get here. When will your meeting be over?"

He glanced at his watch. It was almost four. "Should be finished by five. You want me to pick up something for supper on the way?"

"No, I'm making a casserole. I'll see you in a little while, then. Bye-bye."

"Wait! You sure you're okay?"

"Yes, I'm fine. Quit worrying. I'll see you when you get here."

"Okay," he said, unconvinced, "see you then."

# CHAPTER TWENTY-FOUR

"VIC, YOU FEEL up to talking?" George asked when the group reconvened after the break.

"I guess so," Vic said half-heartedly. He looked haggard. He'd lost weight and there were bags under his eyes from worry and lack of sleep. His usually neat beard was shaggy from days of neglect.

"I guess my worst day was the second time I was shot down," he said, tearing the wrapper from a pack of Swisher Sweets he'd just bought at a nearby convenience store. He wet one with his lips and lit it. "I believe I mentioned before that I was shot down twice my first week in-country." He looked around for confirmation. Nathan and Dan nodded.

"I got shot down on my very first combat assault. We flew into a hot LZ and—"

"You've already told us about that day," George said. "Remember, first actions? We're concentrating on worst days now."

"Oh, okay. Anyway, it happened again five days later. Yeah, five days, because six would've made it a week exactly and I remember it was twice within the same week so—"

"You're starting to wander, Vic," George said. "Focus on the details."

Vic held up his hands. "I'm sorry guys. Things have been a

little fucked-up lately. Okay, so it was on another insertion. We were close to the front of the flight going into the LZ. I was still flying as J.J.'s co-pilot."

He shifted in his seat and sweat broke out on his forehead. "So we're flying into this LZ and the chopper ahead of us is just starting to flare, and we're slowing and getting ready to touch down."

He squirmed and shifted again and scratched at the whiskers growing below the usual trim line on his neck. "There was high elephant grass all around the LZ. We were putting down in a small clearing in the middle. All of a sudden I heard these loud pops. I remember hoping our engine was backfiring but I knew better. Then tracers started flying everywhere and *bam-bam!*" Vic pounded his fist into an open palm. "We were taking rounds, like somebody slamming the bird with a hammer.

"I was thinking, Oh shit, not again, and then the ship ahead of us exploded right in our faces. It was all flame and black smoke." Sweat covered his balding head and his hand trembled as he tugged at a long thread from a buttonhole of his shirt.

"The grunts in back were screaming for us to land the fucking chopper so they could get out. A couple of 'em jumped or fell out but we were still too high. The freq was going crazy; everybody was talking at once except for us. We didn't have time to talk. Hell, we didn't even have time to think. This was all happening fast but at the same time it was like we were in slow motion. It was weird. I don't know if I can explain it."

Dan took a swig from the can of Coke he'd bought during the break. "I've had that experience before," he said. "When I first got back from 'Nam I wrecked a couple of cars. It's like you said, it's like floating through time and seeing everything in detail and recording it in your mind. But at the same time it's happening so fast you can't do anything about it because it's all over in a flash."

"Yeah, that's it," Vic said. "Weird. Anyway, people were yelling, 'Grenades!' and 'Booby-traps!' I don't remember if it was over the radio or somebody inside the bird; maybe both. I looked out my window and there was this pole hidden in the elephant grass. I can still picture it like it was yesterday. I'm looking right at it just a few feet away at eye-level. There was a tube attached horizontally to the pole with the open end facing me. Then I saw a grenade falling out of the tube in slow motion and the spoon flying off." Vic's eyes seemed to follow the memory as it replayed in his mind.

"The dinks had set up poles along both sides of the LZ. They put grenades in the tubes and strung thin wires attached to 'em across the clearing. The pins were already pulled so when we came in our rotor wash blew the wire down and out they came— *boom!*" Vic pounded his fist again. "Very simple and very effective.

"The next thing I know we're starting to spin. This is where the slow motion shit really got heavy. We're turning and I look out of my window toward the back of the bird. I can see our tail rotor's been blown off. Uh-oh, I'm thinking, that's our ass. We're going down; there's no way we can fly without that rotor. And then I see that damn blade spinning like a big boomerang coming right at me. I closed my eyes and tried to duck, as if that would've done any good," he said. "It was just a reflex. I was strapped in and sitting there like a dead duck waiting for this six-foot flying machete to cut me in half."

Sweat dripped from Vic's face. He mopped it with his handkerchief. His cigar had died. He relit it. "We spun so fast that it missed the cockpit but it hit the fuselage dead center, like this," he said, turning his hand palm down and striking it behind the wrist with a karate chop.

"That damn rotor nearly cut us in half. It took out our hydraulics, the transmission, everything. It sounded like we'd flown into a steel wall. Then we dropped like a rock."

Vic's hands shook and the color drained from his face. He started to speak but his voice cracked. Taking a deep breath, he tried again. "The worst part . . ." He stopped and coughed. "The worst part was what it did to those poor fuckers back there," he said, motioning over his shoulder with his head as if he were sitting in the cockpit of a helicopter again. "Instant hamburger." He lowered his eyes and shook his head. "It killed our door gunner and a few grunts. Our crew chief and a couple of other grunts made it out, but the rest looked like they'd been run through a meat grinder."

He swallowed hard and stared at the cigar. "After that, nothing much is clear. I don't remember the crash. I don't even know how I got out of the chopper. The next thing I know I'm sitting on this log at the edge of the LZ. Enough troops had been landed by then to form a small perimeter and there was a hot firefight going on. They were waiting for a gunship team to work the area before the other choppers tried to land. Anyway, I'm sitting on this log and I keep thinking, I don't believe this shit. One week in-country and I've been shot down twice!

"Right then I made up my mind that there was no way in hell I was ever getting out of Vietnam alive, so I just said fuck it. Somebody, I think it was our crew chief, kept yelling for me to get off the log or I was gonna get fucking dinged. I remember looking over at him and saying, 'Fuck it, it don't mean nothing, just fuck it.' "

Vic looked up and sighed. "It was a lot easier from then on. I just resigned myself to the fact that I was going to die sooner or later, so why worry? I'm not saying I wasn't ever scared again. I was. But from then on it was a lot easier to handle just going through the motions."

"Hmm, interesting," George said after a moment.

"What is?" said Vic.

"The method you chose, subconsciously I'm sure, to handle Vietnam," George said. "When we were discussing losses and you mentioned not losing many friends during your tour. The loss you focused on was more of an intangible type. But what you told us today blows the idea you didn't lose people right out of the water. You were shot down twice within a week. Your door gunner and several grunts on your chopper were killed."

George paused a moment for a sip of coffee. "It seems to me

you chose early on to detach yourself from the personal side of the war experience. You said, 'Fuck it,' and went through the motions from there on out. You functioned more as a machine, an extension of your helicopter if you will, than as a human being with feelings and emotions.

"It's not that unusual," he continued after jotting down something in his notes. "A lot of people deal with combat stress that way. But it's usually a long drawn out process before it finally comes to that. It's interesting you were able to detach yourself after only one week in-country."

George waited for a response but Vic remained silent. Given Vic's current state of mind, George decided not to press the issue any further for the time being. He checked his watch. "We need to wrap. That was some good work today. I think we accomplished quite a bit and maybe got rid of some excess baggage.

"Remember this because it's an important point. Talking about these things is like airing out your feet when you have a bad case of jungle rot. The more you expose them to the sun and fresh air, the better they'll get. It may take a while but at least they can begin to heal and feel better.

"That's where we're at now. Taking the boots off and peeling off the socks and exposing the festered feet. We've made a start but there's a hell of a long road still ahead. It's up to each of you just how far you're willing to go and how hard you're willing to work. What each of you gets out of this process depends on what you're willing to put into it."

He tapped a Marlboro from his pack and lit it. "There's something I need to tell you as a group before we wrap. I decided to hold it for the end so we wouldn't get off on something that had nothing to do with our topic." George hesitated, and for once looked unsure of himself. Taking another drag, he continued. "Rene has flown the coop. He wrote several hundred dollars worth of bad checks around town and took off."

Nathan's mouth went dry. Great, he thought, first Helen's

call and now this. A cartoon image of his three hundred-dollar bills flying away on wings flashed through his mind. For a moment he considered mentioning the ill-advised loan, but decided against it.

"Where'd he go? Why would he just sky out like that?" Nathan said, mentally kicking himself for the misplaced trust.

"Nobody knows," George said. "I got a call from Judge Wilkes this week. I need to explain something about Rene before this goes any further."

George told them about Boudreaux's run-in with the law for petty theft and how Judge Brandon Wilkes had offered him the choice of jail or counseling with the Vet Center program.

"Judge Wilkes is an old World War Two vet," George said, "and he wanted to give Rene a chance to straighten himself out. I agreed. Rene burned us and I accept full responsibility for what happened. I just wanted you to have the whole story; you deserve that. I couldn't tell you about his background before because of client-counselor confidentiality. But I wanted to get it all out on the table now and see how you feel about it."

"I'll kick the bastard's ass if I ever see him again," Vic said. "I never liked the asshole anyway."

George looked at Nathan.

He shrugged. "Shit happens." The taste of lost money was bitter on his tongue. He was anxious to get out of there and see Helen. "No big deal. Don't sweat it."

"Dan?"

"I don't see where the group will be losing much with him gone," Dan said. "It's not like when Andrew left. I think we're better off."

George pursed his lips and nodded. "Okay then, case closed.

"Anything else? Questions?"

Nobody spoke.

"Okay, see you next week."

# CHAPTER TWENTY-FIVE

IT WAS FIVE-FIFTEEN by the time Nathan arrived at Helen's apartment. Ignoring his aching foot, he took the stairs two at a time. Helen opened the door before he could ring the doorbell.

"Hi." She smiled and hugged him.

Nathan heard a slight sniffle. He held her close for a moment and then pushed away to arms' length and looked into her eyes. "You've been crying. What's wrong?"

"Come on in and I'll tell you about it." She took his hand and led him into the kitchen. Nathan sat on a stool by the island while Helen took two cans of Budweiser from the refrigerator. She handed one to Nathan and sat facing him.

She opened her beer and took a sip. "Carl called me at work today.

"So he's in town?" Nathan was confused. He didn't like the idea of Helen's ex-husband calling her, but Carl was Heather's father. It didn't seem like anything to get upset over.

"No, he's in Montgomery." For a moment she was quiet, and then she turned and looked him in the eye. "He's thinking about moving here to be closer to Heather and me."

"What?" The word almost stuck in Nathan's throat. He took a healthy swig of beer. "What for? Why all the sudden interest?" He searched her eyes. "You told me he doesn't even pay his own child support." He took another drink.

"I don't know," Helen said. She stared past Nathan. "He says he's changed and that he wants his daughter back. He told me he's done a lot of growing up the past several months and he realizes now what's really important in life." She took another sip and dabbed her eyes with a paper napkin. "He wants us to try to make it as a family again."

Nathan was stunned. The walls seemed to close in around him. He felt pinned down and helpless. The rounds were flying again and he couldn't move. *No Doc, no!* He was about to lose someone close again and there was nothing he could do.

"Are you okay?"

"Huh? Yeah, I was just thinking about . . . where's Heather?" In his mind Helen and Heather were in danger. He felt the urge to throw himself over them to shield and protect them. The brief flashback had been so vivid. He didn't know if he could stand to lose anyone again.

"She's with Mom and Dad for the weekend."

"I could use another beer," Nathan said, draining the can as he walked to the refrigerator. "Let's go sit outside."

They moved to the patio and sat side-by-side at the picnic table. The evening air was warm and rain threatened. Ominous gray clouds hung low over the bay, turning the water to ink. The open space and salt air helped calm him. "What're you going to do?" Nathan said after they'd sat quietly for a moment.

"I don't know." Helen cupped her chin in hand, her elbow resting on the table. "I'm so confused right now." She stared across the bay into the dusk and tapped the beer can with her fingernails.

Nathan felt as though a bayonet had been shoved through his ribs. 'I don't know' wasn't what he'd wanted or expected to hear. Was she about to twist the blade? "Are you two getting back together? Do you still love him?"

Helen tore her eyes from the gloom and looked as if she'd been slapped. "No! Oh, is that what you were thinking?" She moved closer and wrapped her arms around his neck and hugged him. She kissed his cheek and sniffled. "No, I'd never go back to him. That's been over for a long, long time. I still have feelings for him but not in that way. He's Heather's father. I guess that's what I meant by, oh, I'm just messing this all up. I'm just afraid he might try to cause trouble for us."

She removed her arms from around his neck and looped her left arm around his right and rested her head against his shoulder. "What I mean is, it would be nice for Heather to have more time with her father. She misses him and Carl adores her. I have to give him that much credit, even if he hasn't grown up yet."

"Adores her? Bullcrap. He lets his parents pay his child support to keep his sorry butt out of jail. So much for adoring her."

Helen sighed. "I guess you're right. But we could never be a family again anyway. I wouldn't want Heather getting the idea that that's even a possibility, because it isn't."

"Did you tell him that?"

"Yes."

"What'd he say?"

"He asked me how I knew things wouldn't work out for us unless I gave it a chance. He said we owed it to Heather to try again."

"You don't owe him shit!" Nathan said. "Excuse my French."

Helen laughed. "I told him that, too. Not with those exact words, but he got the message."

Nathan was beginning to feel a little better about the situation. "What did you tell him?"

Helen took sip of beer and rested her head on his shoulder again. She tightened her grip around his arm and snuggled closer. "I told him that Heather and I have been on our own for over three years and that we have a life of our own now and are doing very well for ourselves, thank you very much. I said he was welcome to visit her, but only in the company of his parents like the court ruled. Believe me, he didn't like hearing that at all."

Nathan snickered; he was pleased Helen had stood up to her ex and not given in. "What'd he say then?"

"That I wasn't being fair and that I was only thinking about myself, not Heather or him. He said he'd done a lot of growing up and that he really had changed and that we could be a family again if I'd give him the chance to prove himself." She paused to catch her breath.

"So I reminded him about all the chances he'd had while we were married, and how he'd lied and cheated on me. And if he was so concerned about Heather and me, then why were his parents the ones paying child support instead of him? I said as far as I was concerned he was out of my life forever, and that . . ." She paused again and stared into Nathan's eyes.

"I told him about you, Nathan. About us. I said there was no chance for him and I ever getting back together because I'm in love with you. I know I shouldn't have dragged you into this, but I couldn't help it. I just blurted it out without thinking."

Nathan's jaw dropped. He wasn't sure he should trust his ears. She loved him, that's what she'd said, right? He'd hoped it might happen someday, but it seemed so futile, so far-fetched to dream she ever would. He felt dumbstruck but finally managed to get the words out. "You told him you love me?"

Helen giggled. "Yes Mr. Nathan Henson, I love you." She touched a finger to her lips and pressed it to his.

"Christ," he muttered, still not fully trusting his senses, "really?"

"Yes, really."

"Christ," he repeated. "I love you too; I have ever since that second day in Dr. Parker's office when we talked."

"Oh," she said, feigning hurt. "Then it wasn't love at first sight for you?"

Nathan grinned. "Sorry, no. You'll have to settle for love at second sight."

She laughed and pinched his arm. "You're terrible."

Then she was in his arms again, returning his kiss. Lips

211

opened and tongues explored the wet warmth of each other's mouth. Nathan's hand drifted to her side; his thumb lightly traced the curve of her breast and then moved to cup its fullness. Helen shivered under his touch, unresisting.

Nathan broke away. "Man."

Helen's eyes searched his. "What's the matter," she whispered.

"Nothing, I just don't want to lose control. Not tonight. It wouldn't be right."

"What do you mean?"

"I don't want you thinking that just because I said I love you I . . ." He stopped and looked out over the dark bay at the storm clouds rolling in as he searched for the right words. "I don't want to cheapen what we have. I want to make love with you more than anything, but I wouldn't feel right about it, not right now. You mean so much more to me than that."

Helen was silent for a moment, and then she kissed him on the cheek. "That's sweet. I believe that's the sweetest thing I've ever heard." And then feigning a gasp she pinched his arm again. "What makes you think I'd even consider such a thing, anyway?" she said, fighting back a smile. "You're awful."

For a long time they sat holding each other and staring across the bay at the lights dotting the far shore. The sky grew black and the wind rose in swirling gusts. Streaks of lightning danced across the southern horizon. Thunder clapped and a few scattered raindrops dotted the patio.

"So, what do you think Carl will do?" Nathan said after a while.

"I don't know. I'm afraid he might try to make trouble for us some way if he moves here. He can be difficult. Or he could be bluffing about the whole thing. I just don't know."

"Well don't worry about it," Nathan said. "Whatever happens, we'll face it together."

Suddenly the sky opened. Rain fell in sheets over the bay and moved swiftly inland.

"We better go in," Nathan said, "we're fixing to get our butts soaked."

Helen clung to him and sighed. "Let it rain; it's a beautiful night."

# CHAPTER TWENTY-SIX

VIC WASN'T THERE when Nathan returned home shortly
after eleven that night. He opened a beer and switched on the TV
in the kitchen. A rerun of *The Rockford Files* was just beginning
when the phone rang. Thinking it was Helen, he grabbed the
receiver.

"Nathan?"

He didn't recognize the voice. "Speaking."

"This is Karen Guerino. Vic's wife."

"Oh. He's not here right now," Nathan said as he watched an
attractive blonde client make a pass at Jim Rockford.

"I know. I'm at the hospital with Vic."

"Hospital? What's wrong? Is he all right?"

"I'm not sure. They're running tests. He might've had a
heart attack. Can you come to the hospital? He's been asking for
you."

Heart attack? Hell, he's only thirty-six. "Yeah. Yeah, I'll be
there in a few minutes. What room's he in?"

"I don't know yet. They took him for tests. Just come to the
emergency room. If I'm not there, ask at the desk."

Nathan's mind was racing; too much was happening. "I'm on
my way."

Nathan scanned the waiting area of Bay City Memorial's

emergency room. Karen wasn't there.

"I need to know what room Vic Guerino's in," he said to the young woman behind the information desk. "He came in tonight, might've had a heart attack or something."

"Guerino, Guerino," she mumbled, eyeing the computer monitor on the desk.

"It's spelled with a G," Nathan said, growing impatient.

"Guerino, ah, here we are. Victor Guerino. Room 314."

"Thanks." Nathan rushed through the swinging doors leading to the hallway and elevators. Taking the elevator to the third floor, he stopped at an intersection of hallways next to the nurses' station. He checked the overhead signs for directions.

"Can I help you?" asked a middle-aged nurse sitting behind the counter.

"No thanks, I found it." He continued down the corridor toward room 314.

"Nathan!" The voice came from a waiting room on the right. Karen Guerino stepped into the hallway to greet him and touched his shoulder. "Thanks for coming." She led him inside to a blue vinyl sofa.

"They told me he was in 314. Can we go in yet?"

Karen shook her head. "I talked to the doctor a few minutes ago. Vic's in the room but they're not finished hooking everything up. It'll be a few minutes."

Nathan sat on the edge of the sofa. He cracked his knuckles and was almost afraid to ask. "How's he doing? Was it his heart?"

"No, thank God. The doctor believes he had a severe anxiety attack but they want to keep him overnight just to be on the safe side."

"Man, that's good to hear." Nathan relaxed a little and leaned back against the sofa. "What happened?"

"He scared me to death," Karen said. "When I got home from work this evening he was sitting in the driveway in his car." An elderly couple walked in and sat across the room. Karen lowered her voice. "I don't know exactly how much Vic's told you about our problems. We haven't been getting along for a long time now and I've, uh, gotten involved with someone else."

Nathan bit his tongue. "Vic just said you were separated and he thought you were seeing somebody." He struggled to push the image of Karen straddling her lover in Vic's own bed from his mind.

She stared at the floor as though ashamed. "It's not entirely my fault; I want you to know that. Anyway, when Kendra and I drove up Vic got out of his car. He said he wanted to see the kids and just visit for a while.

"He watched TV and talked with the kids in the den for a few minutes while I started supper and then he came into the kitchen." She paused as two women entered the room and exchanged quiet greetings and hugs with the older couple.

"He started talking about how much he missed the kids and me and missed us all being together. He said he didn't care what had happened between us, he just wanted his family back." She fumbled in her purse for a tissue and wiped her eyes.

"I told him I was sorry and that I still cared for him, but things just weren't the same anymore and it just wouldn't work." She looked at Nathan, her face pinched.

"Then Vic started begging. He kept saying how much he loved me and how he knew I still loved him. He was crying like a baby. God, it hurt so much to see him carrying on like a little child begging to get his way.

"I told him again that we were different people now and that it wouldn't work out." She paused, turned her head and blew her nose into the tissue.

"Then Vic turned pale and started gasping for breath. I thought maybe he was just hyperventilating. But he had this scared look on his face and then he grabbed his chest."

Tears rolled from her eyes. She took a moment to compose herself. "I asked him what was wrong but he didn't answer. He stumbled across the kitchen and leaned against the wall and then sagged down to the floor. He was white as a ghost and still gasping like he couldn't catch his breath.

"It almost scared me to death. I was sure it was his heart because my father died from a heart attack and it was almost exactly how my mother had described it.

"I dialed 911. The kids ran in and saw their daddy lying on the floor and started crying and screaming."

She took several deep breaths. "It was just awful for them to see him like that. I sent little Vic next door for our neighbor. I told her what was happening and asked her to watch the kids. A few minutes later the paramedics arrived. They worked on Vic a couple of minutes and then we left in the ambulance. I called you when we got here."

Karen's makeup was smeared from the tears still dripping down her cheeks. "Vic just has to be all right," she said, still crying. "If anything happens to him I'll never forgive myself."

Nathan sat there doing and saying nothing. Part of him wanted to reach out and comfort Karen, but another part felt like strangling her.

"Mrs. Guerino?" They both turned at the voice. A smiling young nurse stood in the doorway.

Karen stood. "Yes?"

"You can see your husband for a few minutes now. He's still groggy from the medication we've given him so don't be alarmed if he doesn't seem quite himself."

"Can I go in?" Nathan asked.

"Are you family?"

"Please," Karen said, "he's a close friend. My husband was asking for him earlier."

"Sure, but only for a few minutes. He needs his rest."

The blood pressure and pulse rate readouts flashed red in the dimly lit room. A heart monitor emitted a slow steady beep as the wavy green line danced left to right across the screen. Vic lay on the bed between crisp sheets. Intravenous tubes trailed from both arms and a forked oxygen tube extended from his nostrils. Thin wires from electrodes attached to his chest snaked alongside the bed to the cardiac monitor.

He stirred as Karen and Nathan eased into the room and stood beside the bed.

"Hi, honey," Vic said, barely above a whisper. He lifted an arm a few inches off the bed and smiled. "You're here."

Karen moved closer and returning the smile. "Yes, I'm here. Don't try to move, just rest. The doctor says you're going to be fine."

Vic noticed Nathan. "Hey, you dumb-ass grunt. What're you doing here?"

"Just checking on you, flyboy. Karen told me you were up here laying on your ass. Trying to skate again as usual I see."

"Yeah, glad you could come." The medication was doing its job. His voice was weak and he could barely keep his eyes open.

When Karen stepped to the foot of the bed to adjust the light blanket that had slid to one side, Vic's eyes grew wide and he struggled to sit upright. "Don't leave, honey. Please stay with me, don't leave." He sounded pitiful, like a scared child seeking comfort from his mother. It turned Nathan's stomach.

"I'm right here," Karen said as she moved beside Vic and stroked his brow. "I won't leave you. Try to sleep now; I'm not going anywhere. I'll be right here when you wake up."

It was all Nathan could stand. His stomach churned. He thought of Helen and tried to imagine how he would react if he caught her in his bed riding some sweating stud. No way would he want her back. This wasn't love Vic was expressing, it was weakness.

He gripped Vic's shoulder and gave it a light squeeze. "Hey, I've got to go. I'll check on you tomorrow to see if you're still kicking." He turned and nodded to Karen and then hurried out of the room.

Jesus H. Christ, he thought as he hurried down the corridor, how could he want that bitch back after what she's done? Where's his fucking pride?

# CHAPTER TWENTY-SEVEN

NATHAN SQUIRMED WHILE the others waited for him to begin the account of his worst day in Vietnam. He felt uneasy, exposed, as if a sniper were taking aim, zeroing in, slowly squeezing the trigger. "I don't know if I can do this," he said after a long silence.

"We're here to work," said George.

An idea struck Nathan. "I guess my worst day was when Roberts and Doc Dunn were killed on that patrol. I already talked about that so I guess we can move on to something else."

George stared through him. "Okay; I'll accept that, but I would've sworn you were struggling with something else a minute ago." He leaned back in the chair and sipped his coffee. "Well?"

Nathan wavered and his right leg kept pumping. He shifted from one uncomfortable position to another. He glanced at Dan and Vic, hoping to find support for his avoidance. There was none. Dan sat stoically and stared at nothing in particular. Vic grinned and puffed contentedly on a cigar. He was in high spirits after moving back in with Karen following his release from the hospital. They were going to try and work things out, he'd announced at the beginning of group.

"Earth to Nathan," George said.

Nathan's eyes darted back to George as conflicting thoughts

ran through his mind. What should he do? The day Doc Dunn and Roberts bought it *was* bad. But Betz; Christ, poor Betz. Should he tell them? Would they understand? Would Betz understand? Or would sharing the awful truth somehow be a betrayal of his memory?

"Shit," Nathan muttered and glanced out the window. The May afternoon was clear and warm. The scent of wisteria drifted in from a nearby yard and mingled with the acrid stench of tobacco smoke. Nathan got up and walked to the window and opened it as wide as it would go. A pigeon wandered across the parking lot pecking at grit; its iridescent neck glittered in the sunlight. Nathan watched the bird for a moment and then went back to his chair.

"I've never told anybody about this before. Not the way it really happened."

All eyes were riveted on him.

He took a deep breath and held it a moment before remembering to exhale. "I think I mentioned Betz before. Doc, I know I told you about him."

Dan nodded.

"Well," Nathan shifted and leaned forward and stared down at the floor, "he didn't die the way I told you he did."

"Betz?" George said. "Isn't he the guy you said was your best point man? You had him walking rear security the day your patrol was ambushed?"

"Yeah, that's him. We arrived in-country about the same time. We went through a lot of shit together and got to be real tight." His voice trailed off and there was a long pause.

"What about Betz?" said George.

Nathan took another breath and stretched out his legs and folded his arms across his chest. He glanced up at the ceiling. "I don't know if I should talk about it. Don't seem right."

George sat up and tapped a Marlboro from his pack. "We've been at this now for what, eight or ten weeks? You've made a lot of progress. This isn't the time to back off. Everyone in this room has earned your trust just like you've earned theirs. Something is eating at you that you've never talked about. Whatever it is, you've carried it around for seventeen years."

George paused. When Nathan didn't respond, he said, "You'll never have a better opportunity to unload it than you have right now. You're among friends and you can tell us anything. Nobody here is going to judge you for what you say, and you know whatever is said will stay inside these walls."

"Yeah grunt, we're your buddies; you can trust us," Vic said. "Hell, I'd even land with zero ceiling for your sorry ass."

"Back to back, bro," Dan said.

Nathan let out a deep breath. "Okay. We'd been in the Cua Viet area for about a month. Months before the NVA had moved across the DMZ and built fortified positions in most of the villages in the sector. Every day was like World War Two. We'd move out across hundreds of meters of open ground and then the gooks would open up with arty from across the Z and hit us with mortars and RPG's and weapons from the vills. Once we started across the open ground here was nothing we could do but keep charging toward their positions. You couldn't just lay there in the open and do nothing with all that incoming. Hell, if we were going to die we might as well die trying to get to the gooks and kill 'em in their trenches.

"After so many days of that shit you got, I don't know, maybe punch drunk's a good word for it. You were so damn tired you didn't know if you were coming or going. And we lost so many people, Christ."

He paused and sat up straighter. Awful as it was, the words were coming easier now. "It all became one big blur like a never-ending nightmare. A lot of it still isn't clear to me. It's like bits and pieces of a puzzle, or little snatches of memory. Like snapshots flashing in my mind with no real order to any of it. It was like seeing things through a dense fog."

There was another pause while Nathan finished the coffee he'd been nursing. He began tearing off little pieces of the

Styrofoam cup and rolling them into balls between his fingers and dropping them in the bottom of the cup.

"Then one night in the middle of March the NVA hit us big time. We'd been fighting for this vill all day and finally took it late in the afternoon. We had just enough time to dig-in before dark. We found this dead gook near our hole that had been napalmed." Nathan's eyes lit up at the memory. It was 1968 again and he was nineteen.

He laughed. "That gook was one genuine crispy critter. We named him Charcoal Charlie. Me and Betz strung him up on a pole standing a few yards behind our fighting hole. Then we started hollering at the gooks in the next vill where they'd di-di'd after we overran 'em. We gave 'em the finger and dared 'em to use old Charlie as an aiming stake. Not that they could really hear us; they were too far away, but I guess it helped us blow off some steam. I know all this sounds crazy, but hell, I guess we were crazy."

His smile faded. "Wasn't so funny later that night when the incoming started. They hit us a couple of hours before daylight. We didn't have any wire to slow 'em up, just our claymores which didn't do much good. There were too many of 'em; must've been a couple of hundred or more. Christ, the bastards had brass balls. They came running in right on top of us behind their arty and wound up overrunning us. Wasn't a damn thing we could do; there were just too many of 'em."

Nathan got up and tossed the mutilated cup into the trash can. He sat back down and crossed his legs and rubbed his aching left foot. He took a breath.

"Our CO wound up calling our own arty on top of our position." He shook his head. "Nothing else we could've done. Next morning dead gooks were everywhere. Man, we'd really stacked 'em up. Me and Betz had a couple of 'em in our fighting hole. The bastards just jumped in on top of us and we wasted 'em right there in our hole.

"Our platoon was pretty much wiped out. Me and Betz made

it, and Gabby and Walker and a couple of new guys. That's all from our squad, but we made out better than the rest of the platoon. Most of our guys were either dead or wounded. I don't think we had more'n maybe fifteen people left in the whole damn platoon, and most of them were FNGs. How those new guys survived I'll never know.

"Our lieutenant and platoon sergeant were KIA and so were the other two squad leaders. The skipper put me in charge of the platoon since I was senior, so for a couple of days I was temporary platoon leader. Can you believe that shit? I'd just made corporal a couple of weeks before and now I was the platoon leader."

Nathan stood to stretch his legs and stared out the window again. A pair of mourning doves had joined the pigeon. One ruffled its feathers and bobbed its head back and forth at the other in a mating ritual. Nathan leaned against the sill and cracked his knuckles.

"Next few days we laid around doing nothing. I guess the higher-ups figured we wouldn't be worth shit till we got some rest. Then the word came down for us to start running listening posts and ambushes. I took half the guys with me the first night and left Betz with the others to guard our sector. We didn't see or hear anything which suited the shit out of me. The next night Betz was supposed to take his guys out."

Nathan was silent for a few seconds. He blinked rapidly as if trying to hold back tears but his eyes were dry. He swallowed hard. "Me and Betz were sitting around our hole chowing down just before dark. Gabby came walking up with one of the new guys in his team. His name was Terrell, I think. He'd been in-country about a month but I don't know how he'd lasted that long. He just about went ape-shit whenever we made contact.

"Anyway, Gabby comes up and says Terrell is refusing to go on the ambush, so I said, 'What's your fucking problem, Terrell?'

"And he says, 'I'm not going on the ambush. There's no reason for it. We're just asking to get killed if we go out there.' I guess when we got overrun that night it was all the guy could take."

Nathan coughed and glanced up at the ceiling and then down at the floor. "So Betz looks up at Terrell and calls him a chickenshit son-of-a-bitch. Tells him he ain't no fucking better than anybody else and he'd better get his shit together or he'd kick his ass all over I CORPS.

"Then Terrell looks down at Betz and he's got this wild crazy-eyed expression on his face. Tells Betz he'd better leave him the fuck alone or he'll blow his ass away."

Nathan shook his head; his brow was furrowed and his chin quivered. "So Betz says, 'You gutless motherfucker, you ain't got the balls to blow anybody away.'"

Nathan pressed his palms against his eyes for a moment and then looked past George at the wall beyond. "So Terrell chambers a round and lowers his M-16 and blows Betz away right through the fucking heart. Just blew his shit away right before my eyes; it happened so quick I couldn't do a fucking thing about it."

Stunned silence fell over the room. Agonizing seconds passed and Dan broke the awful vacuum. "You told me Betz was killed while you were assaulting a vill, remember? You said he was taking out a gun position. Why did you lie about how he died?"

Nathan looked at Dan through pained eyes. "I don't know. It wasn't all a lie. He really did take out that gook gun like I told you. He was the bravest bastard I ever knew."

"It's still a lie," Dan said. "Why lie about how he died? Didn't you trust me enough to tell me the truth?"

"Fuck it," Nathan said, "what difference does it make? Dead is dead goddamnit."

"He did it for Betz," George said, stepping in before the situation grew too heated. "And himself."

Dan looked at George. "How's that?"

"It's simple. Nathan and Betz were tight. You know the kind of relationship I mean, closer than brothers, the combat thing. They had shared so much, seen so much, been through so much together and then *bam!*—Betz is dead just like that," he said, snapping his fingers.

"Nathan couldn't handle it; it was simply too much for him. After everything they'd survived together Betz was suddenly dead at the hands of one of their fellow Marines. And not even by accident. It was a deliberate act, manslaughter at best. I'm not saying the guy's mind wasn't screwed up because I'm sure it must have been, but he still deliberately chambered the round, pointed the weapon and pulled the trigger.

"So, Nathan's mind registered an overload. It was too much for him to handle on top of all the combat stress he'd already experienced. Killing the enemy or being killed by the enemy was bad enough. But this didn't compute. It was insane and so he shut down emotionally. Betz was his best buddy and he couldn't allow him to die in such a senseless, unbelievable manner.

"So Nathan decided to give his friend's death some meaning, some dignity as it were. He decided to tell anyone who asked that Betz had died a hero while taking out an enemy machine gun. That made a lot more sense than trying to explain the way it really happened, and I'd be willing to bet that after a while Nathan himself began believing the story he made up about Betz.

He glanced Nathan's way. "Am I right?"

"Yeah, sometimes I do. If I don't think too hard about it I just go ahead and let him die knocking out that machine gun. It helps some, gives it some meaning like you said."

"And since Betz died a hero," George said, "Nathan doesn't have to face the awful horror of seeing him gunned down by a fellow grunt. It's much easier to face life that way, isn't it, Nathan?"

Nathan didn't answer.

"It's much easier to pretend it never happened. Betz died a glorious death on the field of honor, a death that wasn't in vain." George paused. "But it doesn't always work, does it?"

There was still no response.

"No, it doesn't always work," George said. "You let your guard down ever so slightly and then reality starts to creep in on you. And you remember. You remember sitting there with Betz, so tired and worn out with no hope in sight; and up ahead was just more combat, more killing, more suffering. And then you give the order. Betz has to lead an ambush. One of your men doesn't want to go. Words are exchanged; just idle threats, nothing you probably haven't heard dozens of times before. But suddenly, before you can even comprehend what's happening, Terrell chambers the round and points the rifle and pulls the trigger and—"

"Stop it," Nathan said, "goddamnit, just fucking stop it!" He buried his face in his hands; he wanted to cry, wanted to force the tears out so badly but they refused to come. Finally, he looked up. "I know how he died," he mumbled. "I don't have to be reminded. I know how he fucking died." He limped back to his chair and sat down. He was spent.

George leaned across the desktop. "It doesn't matter how he died," he said quietly. "You said it yourself, dead is dead. And just what is dignity, anyway? Is it more dignified to die in bed of old age than as a young soldier on the battlefield? I can't see how it is. The human body is still going to evacuate at death. And when it comes right down to it, does it really matter if Betz was killed by an NVA machine gunner or his own man? The bottom line is he's dead. Nothing can change that, ever. How isn't important.

"What *is* important was his life; how Betz lived his short life and how it affected others. From what you've told us Betz was a hell of a good Marine. He certainly influenced you. You've never been able to forget him nor should you want to.

"His memory is something to hold on to, but let your memories of him focus on the way he lived and not on how he died. We're all going to die; there's nothing much special about that. But the way a person lives *is* special. Not everyone lives in such a way as to have a deep impact on other people. Betz seems to have done that for you."

He locked eyes with Nathan. "Take that thought with you and hold on to it. Remember Betz for the way he lived. Remember him for his life."

## CHAPTER TWENTY-EIGHT

"HAPPY BIRTHDAY!" NATHAN said when Helen opened her apartment door. He brought his hands from behind his back and handed her a dozen long-stemmed red roses and a small gift-wrapped box.

Helen smiled and cradled the roses to her breasts. "They're beautiful." She pressed her face into the red blossoms and then gave him a quick kiss. "Thank you. Come on in while I put these in something."

Nathan followed her into the kitchen and watched as she found a large vase and arranged the roses and greenery. She looked especially pretty tonight with her honey-blonde hair flowing across her shoulders as she moved about the kitchen. He admired how the floral print dress clung to her trim waist and flared at the hips and wondered again how he'd gotten so lucky.

"How about some wine while I open my present?"

Nathan checked his watch. "Yeah, our reservations aren't until seven."

Helen poured Chablis into stemmed glasses and sat beside Nathan at the island. She toyed with the blue velvet box, stroking the gold ribbon. "Now whatever could this be?" She smiled with her lips slightly parted and tip of her tongue showing between front teeth.

"It's not much so don't get your hopes up too high."

She worked the ribbon from the box and lifted the top. "Oh, it's beautiful," she said, admiring the gold bracelet engraved with tropical birds and flowering vines.

"Hope you like it. I thought it was pretty."

Helen slipped the bracelet around her wrist and fastened the clasp. "I love it. I love you." She put her arms around his neck and kissed him.

"Whew," he said when the embrace ended, "I should've bought you a diamond ring. No telling what I might've got then."

She slapped him playfully on the arm. "You're terrible."

Nathan and Helen sat in a secluded corner booth at the High Seas restaurant sipping wine and talking quietly while awaiting their order. A large chandelier fashioned from a ship's wheel provided subdued lighting. Candles from several glass-encased portholes along the planked walls cast a subtle glow. Hand-blown glass balls, once used as net floats by Asian fishermen, hung in macramé fishnets from exposed ceiling beams. Centerpieces fashioned from driftwood and seashells adorned each table.

Nathan was enjoying Helen's company but still felt a little uncomfortable. He wasn't used to such fancy surroundings but he'd wanted to do something special to celebrate her birthday.

"I'll never be able to finish the seafood platter you ordered for me," she said, sipping the Chardonnay the waiter had suggested to complement their dinner. "You're trying to make me fat."

Nathan grinned and pointed his salad fork at her. "You're forgetting that I've seen you eat before. Besides, if there's anything left over, which I doubt, I'll take it home in a doggie bag for Clarence."

"Clarence? Who's Clarence?"

"My cat. Well, my landlady's cat really, but he hangs out with me most of the time."

"Poor kitty; he must be totally depraved by now."

"That's funny, ha ha. Clarence does like his beer, though."

228

"You're awful, corrupting a poor innocent kitty like that."

Just then a match flared a few tables away. Mesmerized, Nathan stared as a young woman leaned forward with a cigarette between pursed lips and accepted a light from the man seated opposite her. The restaurant began to fade. . . .

Corporal Nathan Henson crouched behind the foxhole where three grungy Marines hunkered, the tips of three cigarettes glowing in the inkwell of the fighting hole. A yellow flame drifted away from one of the red coals, flared briefly and died.

"Betz, you crazy fucker," Nathan whispered to the shadowy figure who'd blown out the match, "don't you know three-on-a-match is bad luck? And you're the third. That's your ass; you're gonna get zapped for sure now."

A scoffing laugh came from the blackness of the hole. "Never happen, Nate my man, never happen. I am the Invincible One. Fucking gooks'll never get my young ass. You know I don't buy that superstition bullshit anyway."

"Yeah, well keep your ears open and your eyeballs peeled," Nathan said. "Gooks're snooping and pooping all over the place out there tonight. And don't let these newbies fall asleep on you." Then he crawled away to check on the next position. . . .

"Nathan? *Nathan?*"

"Huh?" He jerked back to the present and was surprised and relieved to be back inside the High Seas with Helen.

"You didn't hear a word I was saying. Is anything wrong?"

"No, I was just thinking about something."

"What?" she asked as her eyes searched his.

He stared blankly at her and pictured Dan lighting cigarettes for the two women and himself that night at the Silver Saddle. Three-on-a-match.

"Hello, anybody home in there?"

"Nothing important," Nathan said just as the waitress arrived with platters piled high with seafood. He watched as she placed the various dishes in front of them, grateful for the interruption that took his mind off the disquieting flashback.

"Mm, this is delicious," Helen said as she speared another broiled scallop with her fork. She watched as Nathan thoughtlessly picked at the stuffed crab on his plate. "Are you feeling okay? You've barely touched your food and you've hardly said a word all night." When there was no answer, she offered a smile. "Clarence got your tongue?"

Nathan glanced up and realized he'd been ignoring her. He'd been unable to shake the foreboding thoughts about Dan and the match incident. The last thing he wanted to do was spoil Helen's birthday. He forced a smile. "I'm sorry. I was just deciding what to eat first. It all looks so good." He popped a fried shrimp in his mouth. "Mm, ol' Clarence is gonna be mad when I show up empty-handed."

For several minutes they talked and enjoyed their dinner and each other's company. Then Helen leaned forward and whispered, "Those people over there—don't turn your head—they keep looking at us. Do you know them?" She motioned with her eyes toward a couple sitting at a table across the restaurant.

Nathan waited a moment and then nonchalantly shifted in his seat and glanced out the corner of his eye. "Shit!" he muttered and quickly averted his eyes. He grew cold all over; his pulse raced and his temples throbbed.

Helen stared wide-eyed at him. "What is it?"

Nathan's mind raced in circles. He was a cornered animal and the walls were closing in. "Come on, we've got to go." He pulled three twenties from his wallet and tossed them on the table and stood. "Let's go."

"But why? What about our food? Aren't we going to—"

"Now!" he said, and then turned and hurried for the exit.

Helen caught up to him in the parking lot. "Nathan, Nathan stop!" She grabbed his arm. He kept walking. She tugged harder. "Stop! What in the world is going on?"

He jerked away and whirled to face her. "I had to get out,"

he said. Sweat beaded across his brow. "That was Tom Carter and Laura in there."

Helen searched his eyes. "So?"

"So?" he said, mimicking her. "So I don't want to see 'em, that's what."

"Why? Are you afraid of them?"

"Hell no! Afraid of that chickenshit coward? You've got to be kidding."

They walked in silence to his truck. He unlocked the door and held it open. Helen slid past the steering wheel all the way over to the passenger door.

"Then why?" she said when he'd climbed in and slammed the door shut.

"Why what?" He was tired of the subject.

Helen looked at him. Her face was framed in the soft light of an overhead street lamp. Her lips quivered and she blinked at the tears in her eyes. "Why did you run away and leave me sitting there?" A tear traced down her cheek. "Why do you let them bother you? Are you ashamed of me, of us?"

"Oh, Christ on a crutch. No I'm not ashamed of you; how can you even ask such a stupid question? You're the only decent thing that's ever happened to me. I don't know why I acted like that. I just did, that's all."

She turned away and said nothing. The strained seconds seemed interminable.

"Look, I'm sorry, okay? It's your birthday. It's still early; we can go someplace else. Where would you like to go?"

Nathan sat with his hands on the steering wheel waiting for Helen's response. When she didn't answer he tried again. "Come on, where would you like to go?"

"Just take me home, please," she said, staring out the window into the darkness.

# CHAPTER TWENTY-NINE

"JESUS H. CHRIST, flyboy." Nathan stared down at the pitiful figure lying in the hospital bed. An IV tube was taped to Vic's left arm and the other arm was encased in a fresh plaster cast. Vic was groggy and already feeling the effect from the injection the nurse had added to the IV fluid. "You trying to make a habit out of this?". . .

Three hours earlier Vic had spotted Karen's car parked outside her boyfriend's apartment. He'd grown suspicious after she'd called from her office saying she had to work late, the second such call that week. Vic confronted he guy, heated words were exchanged and then words turned into blows. Vic won the battle but lost the war. His arm fractured, he pulled a pistol and threatened to shoot the two lovers and then himself.

Somehow Karen had managed to calm Vic down enough to convince him to let her call Nathan. By the time Nathan got directions and drove across town to the apartment, Vic was on the verge of another panic attack.

"Give me the pistol, flyboy," he said when Vic opened the door. "From what you told us in group you can't hit shit with it, anyway."

Vic was pale and gasping for breath and clutching his chest. He pointed the pistol at Nathan. "Stay back grunt, or I'll shoot your sorry ass, too."

A cold fist squeezed Nathan's gut. Was Vic so desperate or depressed that he'd really blow him away? He swallowed hard and his heart was pounding as he stared down the barrel of a gun for the first time in over seventeen years. He took a deep breath and then a slow step forward, and then another. "Go ahead flyboy, do it! Put me out of my fucking misery."

After a tense moment Vic lowered the pistol and grinned. "Fucker's not even loaded, grunt," he managed to say. "I just wanted to scare 'em shitless." Then he slumped to the floor and passed out. . . .

"It's over," Vic whispered as tears pooled in his reddened eyes. "Karen wants a divorce; said she doesn't love me anymore."

"Don't worry," Nathan said. "It'll work out. Hell, you survived the 'Nam, man; you can hack this shit."

Vic shook his head. "Got nothing left to live for. I'm a failure. Can't fly, can't hold a job, and now this. I'm going to jail, you know?" He looked up, his bloodshot eyes pleading. "What am I going to do?"

Footsteps echoed in the hallway. Nathan turned and watched a cute Candy Striper hurry past the room, and then turned back to Vic. "Don't sweat it. We'll get the jail shit straightened out. I already called George. He'll see to it. And you can stay with me again when you get out of here. For a while anyway, till you figure out what you're going to do. Quit worrying. It'll work out."

That seemed to satisfy Vic for the moment. His head relaxed into the pillow. He closed his eyes and sighed deeply. "Thanks, you're a good friend," he mumbled, and then he was asleep.

Nathan brushed his hand gently across the balding head. "You take it easy, flyboy. We'll make it through this shit. I'll check on you tomorrow."

Friday afternoon Nathan met with George Browne. Vic was still in the hospital. George had talked to Judge Wilkes. Karen had convinced her boyfriend to drop all charges against Vic, with Vic's promise not to bother them again. The good judge slapped Vic with a restraining order and gave him six-months' probation.

Dan was a no show.

"I didn't think he'd be here," George said. "His mother called again yesterday. She was all upset. He missed work all week. She thinks he's lost his job."

"Damn," Nathan said. "I guess it's partly my fault. I've been ignoring him lately with Helen and everything Vic's going through."

George shook his head. "Don't start the guilt trip again; you've come too far for that. Dan's his own person. It's his life and his responsibility."

"Yeah, but there must be something I can do to help him. Hell, he's a corpsman, he'd do it for me."

"Was. Dan *was* a corpsman. The war's over, remember? That's what we've been working on for the last past ten weeks, putting the war experience in its proper perspective and learning to get on with our lives. Or have you forgotten already?"

Nathan thought for a moment. "Yeah, but sometimes I wonder if it'll ever really be over."

"Not completely," George said. He reached for his coffee cup. "It's a part of your life experience, like school, athletics, your job, your relationships. But it's just that; only a part. Granted, it's a very important part which had a tremendous impact, but it doesn't have to dominate you anymore. You've got to put it in its proper place and keep it there. Learn from it and learn to use the lessons it taught you in a positive way. You've made a lot of progress, Nathan. You're on your way."

Nathan started to speak and then hesitated a moment. "I've started writing about it, you know."

"About what?" George sat up straight and sipped from his steaming cup. "The war?"

"Yeah, Vietnam, the Marines; you know, the whole bit."

"That's good. Journaling can be a big help sometimes. When

did you start, how much have you written?"

"A few weeks ago; I've got about four chapters done. I'm still in boot camp. It's going to be a book someday, I hope."

"Four chapters?" George raised his eyebrows. "That's great. Stick with it. It can only do you good. A lot of vets start writing but give it up."

"No, I'm going to finish it. I've already promised myself that," Nathan said. He looked out the window past the roof of the adjoining building. Billowing clouds rose high in the hazy sky and a flight of gulls glided toward the bay. "I owe it to Betz and Doc Dunn and Roberts and all the others who didn't make it back. They can't tell their story, so maybe I can tell it for 'em. Hell, I guess I owe it to myself, too. It's hard, though. It hurts to dredge up all that shit."

George nodded. "Sure it does, and it'll probably get a lot worse the further you get into it. Listen, why don't you bring me a few chapters at a time? I'd like to read it and maybe do a little critiquing, offer a few suggestions here and there. I can run off some copies for you so you'll have them when you get ready to send it out. How does that sound?"

"Sounds good, thanks," Nathan said. He paused and searched George's eyes. "Is this it for the group? I mean, with Vic's situation, and Dan's."

George crossed his legs and rocked back and forth for a moment. "Yeah, this is it. I'll be coming down every other week for one-on-ones, and Sarah's lined up some other vets to start another group. I'd like for you and me to keep working together, but this group's about played itself out."

He picked up a pencil and drummed it against his knee. "It's time. Vic's finally bottomed out. It's going to take a while but I think he'll be okay now. As for Dan . . ." George set the pencil aside. "I know it's hard to accept, but some just don't make it. He's drugging again, you know."

Nathan looked out the window. "Yeah, I don't think he ever stopped. Seems like he just keeps getting worse. I hate it. Christ, I can't stand to see him like that. He's killing himself."

"Don't let him drag you down with him."

Nathan locked eyes with George. "I don't do that shit. I don't even drink that much anymore, not since me and Helen—"

George held up a hand. "I'm not talking about drugs. What I mean is, don't get caught in the trap of feeling you have to save Dan from himself. I've seen others try to play that game, but I've never seen it work yet."

He leaned back and clasped his hands behind his neck. "You can't help someone who's not willing to help himself. You can knock yourself out trying but you'll only find yourself going in circles, and then down. It's a vicious cycle. You've come too far to let that happen. Some people just refuse to be saved."

Nathan wanted to say something, anything that would help Dan, but came up empty. He looked at George and shrugged.

George reached for his pack of Marlboros. "Remember," he said, shaking one from the pack, "sometimes you just have to save yourself."

Nathan crammed the canvas travel bag into the only remaining space inside the trunk of Vic's car. He lowered the lid and checked for clearance and slammed it shut. The broad leaves of the tall sycamore rustled in the June breeze. Summer was officially a week away but despite the wind the day was already uncomfortably warm.

Nathan retrieved his beer from the shade of the kitchen windowsill. He took a swig and said, "You sure about this? Atlanta's a big step, man. Big city life's liable to chew you up and spit you out."

Vic mopped his sweating forehead with a handkerchief and tucked it inside the sling supporting his right arm. The cast was covered with obscene graffiti, penned mostly by Nathan and Vic during their many drinking bouts the past month. He shrugged. "It can't be any worse than here." He pulled a cigar from his shirt pocket, tore the wrapping with his teeth and spit it into the air. "I need a change. There's nothing left for me here. I'm just spinning my wheels." He turned his back to the wind and lit the cigar.

"Yeah, but what about your kids? I know you're going to miss 'em. Atlanta's three hundred miles away. We're not talking next door."

The furrows in Vic's brow deepened. He puffed on the cigar and clouds of bluish smoke dissipated quickly in the steady breeze. "Sure, I'll miss 'em, but Karen's a good mother. Just because she's got the hots for another guy doesn't change that," he said with a scowl. "They're better off with her anyway. She's got a good job and they live in a nice neighborhood and the kids have their friends. Besides, I'll be coming down on weekends a couple of times a month. Karen's okay with that. Hell, it's not like I'm abandoning them."

Nathan bent over and retrieved the cellophane wrapper entangled in the tall grass. He'd need to mow the lawn soon. "Yeah, that's right. Atlanta's what, only six or seven hours away at the most. Maybe half that for a maniac flyboy like you. Guess I'll be seeing your sorry ass more often than I figured."

Despite the bravado he was sorry to see Vic go. They'd grown closer during Vic's stay, unlike Dan who had become increasingly withdrawn since allowing his son to be legally adopted a few weeks earlier. Their best efforts to get him out and about had failed miserably. It seemed the last trace of Dan's pride and self-worth were blown away when he'd signed the adoption papers. His financial responsibility was gone, but so was whatever zest for life he'd once had.

A lone gull laughed as it glided high overhead. Nathan shielded his eyes and watched it sail on the rising thermal. He sighed and thought of Helen. A month had passed since the unpleasant scene at the restaurant. When he'd called to make amends a few days later she'd seemed aloof, almost cold. And then Vic's world had come crashing down around him again. Somehow the weeks had slipped by leaving a void in Nathan's life filled only by a gnawing loneliness in his gut.

Now Vic was leaving him too, moving to Atlanta to work with his younger brother in his growing sporting goods business. Nathan crinkled the wrapper absently between his fingers and took another gulp of beer. "So, you're staying with your brother?"

Vic nodded and the bright sun gleamed off his head. "For the time being. Once I get established I'll get a place of my own. No hurry, though. He's got a three-bedroom apartment. Claims he's got more pussy lined up for me than I can handle." Vic grinned. "I'm looking forward to that. It's been a long time since I played the field."

"Yeah, well send me your leftovers. I wouldn't want you overexerting yourself. You might have a real heart attack."

Vic laughed. "I can't do that, grunt. What would Helen say?"

Nathan frowned. Helen. The name echoed in his ears. "Don't worry about that. She's history. Hell, she might be back with her ex ol' man by now for all I know." The thought had tormented him more than once.

"I hope not. She was good for you. I blame myself for you two not seeing each other lately. I've been a real pain in your ass since—"

"Screw it," Nathan said. The subject was making him uneasy. "It's not your fault. It's nobody's fault, so to hell with it. We'll either work things out or we won't. There it is."

The words hurt. He cringed at the thought of life without Helen. But if that's the way it was, he'd just have to be hardcore. It wouldn't be easy or pleasant but he could hack it. He had to hack it; he was a survivor.

Vic glanced at his watch. "I need to get on the road if I'm going to make it before dark. Frank said he'd have steaks on the grill for dinner and hot women for dessert. I don't want to miss out on that."

Vic lifted his good arm. Nathan grasped it and they hugged.

"Thanks," Vic said, his voice quivering, "thanks for everything. I never could've made it through this without you. I owe you my life, brother."

Nathan hugged Vic tighter and slapped his back. "Forget it, flyboy. I didn't do anything you wouldn't have done for me."

Vic slid into his car and awkwardly started the engine with his left hand and shifted into drive. The car eased forward. He glanced back, his eyes brimming with tears as the car rolled past Nathan. "Thanks again."

Nathan trotted and caught up with the car near the end of the driveway. "Take care of yourself, flyboy," he said as Vic steered into the street. "Hey," he shouted, "don't forget to send me some Georgia Peach fuzz!"

Vic laughed as he drove away.

"It's me," Nathan said after hearing a throaty hello.

"Hi. How are you?"

"Okay. No, that's a lie." The words came rushing out. "I'm not okay. I'm terrible. I'm miserable. I miss you. Christ, I miss you so much. I'm sorry about everything."

There was a long pause and he half expected to hear the receiver slam in his ear. Finally, Helen spoke.

"Me, too. I've acted so silly. I guess we both have. But that night, the way you reacted, I just wasn't sure you were over her. I didn't want to be hurt again."

"That won't happen, I swear. It wasn't you, it was all my fault. I could never be ashamed of you. I'm proud of you; I'm proud of us, if there still is an us. I feel like climbing on a rooftop and shouting your name to the world."

He paused and tried to collect his thoughts. "I guess I felt ashamed of myself that night. Tom's this successful lawyer and they're such bigwigs around town and all. I felt, I don't know, inadequate; like a big nothing. I felt like it would be degrading to you for them to see you with a loser like me."

There was silence for a moment, and then with fire in her voice Helen said, "You are not a loser, Nathan Henson. You're a wonderful person, as good as anyone and a lot better than most. I believe that, Heather believes it and so do my parents. It's high time you started believing it, too."

Nathan let Helen's words sink in. Scenes from his life reeled through his mind like a movie. Childhood, high school, Vietnam, Dan and Vic and Helen. It was true. He wasn't a bad person. In fact he was a pretty decent guy. He'd always tried to treat people fairly and to do his part and carry his share of the load.

He'd been a good kid, courteous and respectful to adults and never in any real trouble. In school he'd been a team player. Tom Carter may have grabbed most of the headlines, but everyone knew that a team's success depended on a lot more than individual heroics.

And Vietnam—hadn't that been the ultimate test? At nineteen he'd been tried by fire. Maybe he hadn't always made the right decisions, but who could have under such trying circumstances? He'd done his best, he was certain of it now. Sure, he'd lost some, but he'd saved others. And he'd never run away. He was no coward. Weren't the Silver Star and Purple Hearts gathering dust in his bedroom closet proof of that?

Never mind the medals—his own heart was proof enough. The close bond he shared with Dan and Vic lent further testimony to his worthiness as a person. Hadn't Vic just this morning attested to that fact; and now, Helen?

Suddenly he burst out laughing, all the pent-up misery and anguish stored inside for so many years peeling away. He couldn't stop.

Helen began laughing, too.

"What's so funny?" she finally managed between giggles. "What are we laughing about?"

"Because you're right," he said, trying to stifling his laughter, "I *am* a good person. I've been so stupid for so long for letting what other people think or say or do get in the way of my happiness. Well, it's not going to happen anymore, you wait and see." Then he broke up and laughed again.

"You're crazy," she said, still giggling. "Stop it before you pass out."

Nathan finally gained control. "Listen, I need to see you. Can I come over? I can't stand being away from you any longer."

There was a short expectant pause.

"You'd better hurry," she said, "I need a hug and a kiss real bad."

# CHAPTER THIRTY

DOCTOR PARKER CLOSED his office at noon on Tuesday, July 2, and gave his employees the rest of the week off. Helen jumped at Nathan's idea of a camping trip to Hurricane Island. The timing was perfect. Heather was in Montgomery for a week's visit with the Morris's. Nathan had worked overtime and rescheduled his few remaining jobs for the following week.

Helen arrived at Nathan's house that evening to help pack for the trip. "This is going to be so much fun. I haven't been camping in years."

"So, what do your parents think about their daughter going camping with a combat-crazed Marine?" Nathan said, only half joking.

She smiled. "They realize I'm a big girl now. Besides, for some reason Dad trusts you. Hmm, I always thought he was a good judge of character."

"Thanks; you're a real confidence builder."

Later as they were loading the gear into Nathan's truck Mrs. Ard moseyed over. When she learned of their plans she offered the use of Billy's old Boy Scout equipment.

"Thanks anyway," Nathan said, "but we've got all we can handle already."

The kind old lady insisted they eat supper with her. Around the dinner table she and Helen got along famously, making girl talk like they'd been good friends for years. As they were leaving, Mrs. Ard winked at Helen. "It does this old heart a world of good to see Nathan has found hisself a good woman. Now you come back real soon and bring Heather with you." Then she chuckled and said, "Lord, Lord, there's nothing like a fine woman and a house full of young'uns to make a man come to his senses and settle down."

"I think Mrs. Ard is trying to marry you off," Helen said as they walked hand-in-hand through the darkness to Nathan's house.

"Yeah, the poor old lady's getting senile. I've been meaning to call the Funny Farm to come get—ouch!" he said, rubbing his arm where Helen pinched him.

Tourists crowded the deck of the *Islander II* as the bow gently rose and fell as it sliced through the blue waters of St. Martin Bay. Cameras clicked and whirred as a school of dolphin followed along the port side. A raucous mob of gulls vied for bread and other offerings tossed from the stern by gleeful children and several adults. Overhead other sea birds wheeled in a brilliant blue sky dotted with cottony clouds.

On the upper deck Nathan watched Helen as she leaned against the forward rail. The warm breeze swept the hair from her face and the flowing tresses danced with the wind. She wore khaki hiking shorts and an unbuttoned white blouse over an olive halter top. The colors complemented her nice tan.

Nathan wove through the crowd to Helen's side. "Here you go." He handed her a cup filled with Diet Pepsi over crushed ice.

"Thank you, kind sir." She sipped the cold drink. "Mm that's good; want some?"

The sexy image of Helen's lips pursed around the straw excited him.

"Would you like some?" she said again, offering the cup.

He grinned and pointed at the cup. "Yeah, but not that."

"Oh, you're awful," she said and playfully slapped his

shoulder.

In the three weeks since Vic's move to Atlanta they'd seen each nearly other every day. It was as though both felt an intense urge to make up for the month wasted following their breakup on Helen's birthday. Despite several passionate interludes the past weeks, one or the other always managed enough control to stop things before going too far. Heather was certainly a factor, but there was something more. Their love and respect had resulted in an unspoken mutual agreement. Both wanted to be certain it was right and meaningful. If and when it happened, it would be special and it would be forever.

The *Islander II* slowed as it entered a sheltered inlet on the bay side of Hurricane Island. The captain steered alongside the wooden dock that extended a hundred feet into the water. A tinny voice blared from the loudspeaker above the noisy crowd:

"We are approaching Hurricane Island. All passengers on the starboard side must move away from the railing to the center of the vessel. Please wait until we have come to a complete stop and the boat has been secured before attempting to leave the vessel. The crew will inform you when it is safe to go ashore. Exit only by the starboard side gangplank. Observe all safety rules posted on the bulletin board at the pier's entrance. The *Islander II* will depart in thirty minutes for the return trip to St. Martin State Park. Additional departures will be made every two hours. Final departure for the evening will be eight p.m. It was a pleasure having you aboard. Thank you, and enjoy your island adventure."

Helen and Nathan shouldered their backpacks and stepped onto the dock and followed the push of the crowd to the pier's entrance. They found the campers' registry and signed their names and recorded their permit numbers. As they walked down the wooden steps to the beach Nathan helped Helen adjust the straps of her pack until the load rested comfortably. Then he hoisted his own and they trekked west along the beach and away from the crowd.

A short time later they paused and Nathan pointed to a high

bluff that jutted into the choppy pass at the distant end of the island. "Tomorrow night we'll sit up there and watch the fireworks across the bay."

For nearly an hour they followed the shoreline of the barrier island. At a point where the beach narrowed and then disappeared into a sheer high sandy cliff, they turned inland. Nathan led the way along the trace of a game trail that snaked uphill through scattered scrub oaks, gnarled pines and stands of saw palmetto. At the island's crest an osprey glided silently on arched wings toward the bay. To the left of the trail a doe with twin fawns were startled from browsing and bounded several yards through the low growth, their white flags waving. The deer stopped just inside a copse of oaks and turned, eyes wide and radar-like ears twitching cautiously.

Helen reached for the camera slung around her neck. The shutter clicked and the film advanced with a quiet whir. "Aren't they beautiful?" she whispered. They watched the deer for a few moments until the three whitetails sauntered off into thicker brush and out of sight.

After several more minutes of gradual climbing the terrain leveled off. The air was hot and heavy with the dry scent of pine. A thick carpet of brown needles lay underfoot. Only the rustling wind disturbed the tranquil silence. They stood for a while at the pinnacle of the island and enjoyed the commanding view. To the south lay the endless blue-green of the Gulf of Mexico. A freshwater pond sparkled in the lowlands a mile eastward. Nathan pointed out a thin black line barely discernible in the dark waters of the bay far to the north.

"That's the seawall," he said, "and you see that red over there, that flat-looking thing in those trees? That's the roof of one of your apartment buildings. And over there's Morgan's Cove."

"Are we anywhere near those pretty bluffs we saw from the cove?"

Nathan motioned toward the western tip of the island. "Over there, another mile or so. You can't see 'em from here because of the woods. We'll hike there tomorrow."

They shared a cool drink of water from a canteen and began the gradual descent to the gulf side of the island. A half hour later they stopped to set up camp in a sheltered area between wind-twisted trees and rolling dunes topped with swaying sea oats.

It was a beautiful place. A steady breeze carried the incessant murmur of the surf where fifty yards away white-capped waves rolled ashore. At the forest's edge Helen gathered dead wood for their campfire while Nathan cleared debris from a small valley between the two tall dunes. It would make a fine campsite with plenty of shade in the heat of the day and protection from the blustery wind.

He quickly assembled the telescoping fiberglass poles and pitched the lightweight nylon dome tent and secured the pegs deep in the sandy soil. Then he unfolded the twin-chambered air mattress he'd bought especially for this trip and began inflating it with heavy breaths. Normally he wouldn't have bothered with such amenities but he wanted Helen to be as comfortable as possible. When it was filled he worked the mattress into the tent and covered it with a clean sheet. He unrolled a light blanket that had been lashed to his backpack and placed it at the foot of the mattress.

Helen returned with an armload of firewood and dropped it in a heap near the tent. With his folding shovel Nathan dug a shallow circular fire pit several feet from the tent's door. Then he followed Helen to the forest's edge to gather more wood.

"How about a swim?" Helen said when they returned. They'd worked up a sweat in the July heat and the cool gulf waters beckoned. She searched through her pack and took out a handful of flimsy white fabric.

"Where's the rest of it?" Nathan said as Helen stooped to enter the tent.

She stuck out her tongue and zipped the flap shut.

Nathan watched her indistinct silhouette through the thin walls. "Need any help in there?"

"I can manage just fine by myself, thank you."

The tent door unzipped and Helen stepped outside. Nathan almost gasped aloud at the sight. She looked as if her shapely body had been poured into the thin white mold of the suit.

"Man, that is one hot-looking suit."

She blushed. "Aren't you going to change?"

He reached down and unzipped his hiking shorts.

"Nathan!"

He pulled them down, revealing his bathing suit. "Ha! Thought you were going to get a thrill, didn't you?"

"Oh, you!" she said and then turned and sprinted for the water. "Last one in is a rotten egg!"

"It's your turn," Helen whispered hoarsely in his ear.

Nathan opened one eye and squinted at the brassy sky. He'd almost fallen asleep on the blanket they had spread on the beach after their swim. Helen leaned over him and smiled; her head and shoulders shielded the sun. Freckles stood out across the bridge of her nose and tiny flecks sparkled like gold dust in her eyes. Her hair waved softly about her bare shoulders.

Nathan stretched and yawned. "My turn for what?"

"To rub this on my back." Helen handed him a dark brown tube of suntan lotion. "I can't reach it." She turned and sat up straight and offered her back.

He grinned. "I can handle that." He sat up and squeezed small dabs across Helen's back and shoulders. With both hands he massaged the lotion into her silky skin. He shifted to his knees for better leverage and with gentle strokes smoothed it over her shoulders. His head dipped and his lips lightly brushed the back of her neck. Her warm skin carried the scent of coconut.

Helen's head lolled from side to side. "Mm, that feels wonderful." She leaned against his chest as he knelt above her and continued to work the lotion into her skin. He found himself unable to resist looking down. The tops of her breasts jiggled slightly as he kneaded the delicate muscles of her neck and shoulders.

Nathan felt passion stir as his fingers drifted down and across her upper chest.

Helen lightly slapped his hand. "Hey mister, watch what you're touching."

Nathan laughed. "I am; believe me, I am."

"Oh, you," she said, and elbowed his ribs.

The campfire crackled and wavering shadows flitted along the fringes of its glow. A pine knot exploded in the embers and sent a shower of sparks cascading like a thousand tiny flares. Helen drew her knees close to her body and turned up the collar of the flannel shirt Nathan had loaned her against the night's unexpected chill. She leaned against him and rested her head on his shoulder.

"This is so nice," she said. "I could stay here forever. It feels like we're on a deserted island somewhere in the middle of the ocean."

"It probably is, at least this part of it," Nathan said. "I told you there wouldn't be many people out this way. Most people stay at the campground on the east end where they've got showers and restrooms. Speaking of restrooms, how do you like our modern facilities?" He grinned and pointed toward the slit trench he'd dug behind a thick stand of bushes.

Helen laughed. "It took some getting used to but it's worth it to be here with you."

Nathan reached for the coffee pot on the folding grill. He poured Helen a half cup and added a shot of George Dickel from the bottle he'd packed, and then poured a double shot of the good sipping whisky into his own cup.

Helen sipped the brew. "Mm, this is really good. I've never had coffee like this before." She ran her tongue around her lips and giggled. "My lips are getting numb. You're not trying to get me drunk so you can take advantage of me are you?"

"Me?" He drew back and acted shocked. "I wouldn't do that. I'll just let my natural charm work its magic."

She snuggled against him. "Well, it's working."

The full moon was a bright silver ball high in the southern sky. A mockingbird sang from a hidden perch in the branches of a nearby oak and the gulf hummed hypnotically as it caressed the shore. Almost without realizing what was happening they were in each other's arms and kissing passionately. Lips parted and tongues danced and explored together.

Nathan pulled Helen closer and cradling her upper body in his lap. His right hand slipped beneath the loose flannel shirt and brushed her breasts that were still bound by the green halter. His fingers worked desperately at the material and finally managed to push it up, freeing them. Her nipples hardened against his touch and she shuddered as he gently squeezed one and then the other.

Fire burned in Helen's loins as she felt his hardness press against her back. She gasped as his mouth left hers and found one of the erect peaks. "Wait, oh," she whispered, leaning forward to bury her lips in his hair. Fingernails raked lightly across the back of his neck. "Let's go inside the tent Nathan, please."

He forced himself from the delight of her breasts and gazed down. She was so beautiful lying there in the moonlight; her eyes were sensuous slits and her hair flowed over his arm like an impetuous wave. He kissed Helen's sweetly parted lips again and helped her stand and followed her into the tent.

Silver light shined through the netted top vent and glittered like frost upon the mattress. Blood pounded Nathan's temples as he helped Helen undo the buttons and wriggle out of the flannel shirt. She lifted her arms and slid the halter over her head and lay back. Nathan tore out of his shirt and slipped off his shorts.

He slid beside her and found her lips. The kiss intensified as he tugged at her shorts. Hesitantly she lifted her hips from the mattress as he worked them down her legs. He lay naked beside her with his right arm nestled around her shoulders. They kissed again and again as his left hand caressed her breasts and then slowly inched down across her flat stomach until it rested upon the mound of dark blonde curls.

Helen sighed and quivered as Nathan's fingers gently explored the warm wet folds and then she gasped when he traced slightly upward and began tenderly caressing her magic spot. He shifted his body until it rested against the length of her naked skin. His mouth deserted hers and again found a throbbing nipple. She was conscious of his rigidness pressing into her side and slipped her hand down to stroke him.

She moaned softly as the groundswell of passion welled within. Nathan's mouth and fingers worked faster, fanning the flame of her desire until suddenly she shuddered and clutched him tightly as wave after wave of fervent release pulsed through her.

Nathan held Helen close and stroked her face and hair until the tide rushing over her subsided. Then he eased himself above and between her legs. She parted for him and arched her hips upward to meet his initial thrust. She moaned again as their bodies united and began moving in an ageless rhythm.

Outside, the moon obligingly hid its face behind a veil of clouds that drifted slowly across the heavens. Wind whispered through the pines and the surf murmured a sweet serenade as it kissed the shore. And there, nestled among the dunes in Helen's arms, Nathan Henson made love for the first time.

Dan Matthews awakened in a cold sweat. He sat up on the side of the bed, shivering violently despite the warm July night. His head was splitting and nausea and cramps wracked his stomach.

He switched on the lamp beside the bed and found a pack of Kools. He lit one and drew the menthol smoke deep into his lungs. The nicotine calmed him. With a shaking hand he brought the cigarette to his lips and inhaled again.

Pale yellow light crept over the windowsill and across the cluttered floor. Dan noticed the window was open; he got up and stumbled across the room to close the imagined source of his chill. The full moon leered through the trees like a great jaundiced eye. A black cat emerged from the shadows and crept in silhouette across yard and disappeared into the darkness.

Dan returned to the bed. He sat down and fumbled through the drawer of the night stand until he found a syringe and small vial of liquid. He pierced the rubber cap with the needle and held it up to the light and drew the Demerol into the syringe until the vial was empty. Damn, he'd have to see Brenda Lewis soon. He'd think up some excuse to get the money from his mother.

He looped a web belt tightly above his elbow and coaxed the vein. With a well- practiced prod the needle found its mark. He placed the syringe and vial in the back of the drawer and covered them with a magazine.

Dan sighed and lit another cigarette from the butt of the first and lay back to await the escape.

# CHAPTER THIRTY-ONE

Sunday afternoon the phone rang as Nathan was unpacking and cleaning his camping gear. He'd dropped Helen off at her apartment an hour before with plans to return at seven to grill steaks and spend a relaxing evening together. Sunburned and tired from four days of roughing it on Hurricane Island, he was happier than he could ever remember being.

He hurried to the kitchen for the phone. Probably Helen, he thought, wanting me to pick up something on the way over.

"Is this Nathan?"

There was something vaguely familiar about the lackluster voice but he couldn't place it. "Yes ma'am, who's this?"

"Emma Matthews, Daniel's mother. I've tried to call you several times."

"Hi, Mrs. Matthews. I've been gone camping since Wednesday. Just got back about an hour ago. How's—"

"Daniel is dead." The voice was numb and emotionless.

A cold fist slammed his gut. Weak-kneed, he sagged into a chair.

"What? How . . . what happened?" he mumbled. He fought the urge to puke. Doc was dead? No, there had to be some mistake; this couldn't be real. He must be dreaming. Soon he'd wake up in Helen's arms in the tent between the dunes and find that this was all just a bad dream—

". . . in his sleep sometime Thursday. The funeral will be Tuesday at two o'clock at Oak Grove Cemetery. It should be a lovely service, with full military honors. Mr. Obert has been so kind during all the arrangements."

Christ, she's flipped out. Lovely service? Does she think it's a fucking wedding or something? Jesus, Doc is dead!

"You'll be there won't you Nathan? I know Daniel would have wanted you to be there."

"Yes ma'am, of course I'll be there."

His voice sounded surreal above the roar of the medevac chopper, the whirring rotors raising clouds of stinging swirling dust as he helped load the poncho-shrouded bodies of Doc Dunn and Roberts aboard.

Nathan dropped the receiver and it bounded off the floor and twisted on its cord. His mind reeled from the scene of death and the room spun.

"Nooo!" he screamed, and slammed his fist through the wall.


Thunder clapped across the heavens and the dark skies unleashed a torrent. The small crowd of mourners pushed forward to huddle beneath the maroon canvas awning as rain pelted the taut cover like the doleful drumming of a death march.

A few yards away a Navy color guard stood stoically in the deluge at parade rest. Water cascaded from their white helmets.

At the head of the grave a minister droned words meant to comfort:

"So when this corruptible shall have put on incorruption, and this mortal shall have put on immortality, then shall be brought to pass the saying that is written, Death is swallowed up in victory.

"O Death, where is thy sting? O Grave, where is thy victory?"

The preacher's words were lost to Nathan. He stared blankly at the faces of the few who had bothered to bid Dan Matthews farewell. George Browne had driven down from Tallahassee. Next to him were Vic and Karen Guerino, a temporary truce

253

called for the solemn occasion.

That must be Doc's ex-wife sitting beside Mrs. Matthews, Nathan thought, and that boy's got to be his son. He's the spitting image of Doc.

"I am the resurrection, and the life: he that believeth in me, though he were dead, yet shall he live."

Not many people here. Is this all Doc meant to the World? 'Course, most of the ones who counted with Doc are already dead.

"And whosoever liveth and believeth in me shall never die."

Never die? Then what is Doc doing laying over there in that casket? Nathan thought. Never die; what a joke, what a cruel fucking joke. Tell that shit to Roberts and Doc Dunn and Betz and so many others I can't even remember their names anymore. Tell it to the fifty-eight thousand on that black wall up in D.C. Tell it to the millions who never came back from all the wars. Tell it to the living dead who walk around pretending to be alive but who really died a long time ago on a thousand nameless, god-forsaken battlefields. Tell it to Dan Matthews!

Suddenly Nathan felt a huge fist clutching his throat. The crowd closed in. The awning lowered and threatened to cover him like an enormous body bag. He couldn't breathe. He broke from Helen's grasp. She turned to him with tear-stained face and watched as he backed away from the crowd, away from the empty words, away from the billowing tarp of death.

Cold rain stung his face. He opened his eyes to the monsoon as the years spun away. . . .

The squad of Marines moved cautiously up the hill toward the uncharted village. Suddenly gunfire erupted and a wall of tracers swept through them like a flaming scythe. The point man jerked backward across the dike with his chest blasted open and his brains oozing from his shattered skull.

From the corner of his eye Corporal Nathan Henson saw a crouching figure sprinting forward into the devastating fire.

*"No Doc, he's dead! Get down!"*

The corpsman's head exploded and splattered Nathan with its grotesque reddish spray. He couldn't tear his eyes away as the body fell and lay quivering.

*"Why'd you have to go and die on me, too? Damn you, Doc, damn your sorry ass! . . ."*

"Nathan, it's time to go." Helen embraced him in the drenching rain. "Please, it's over. Everyone's leaving. Let's get out of the rain and go home."

The wind moaned. Thunder crashed and lightning danced mockingly across the black sky. Again Nathan stared at the silver casket that waited to be lowered into the earth. He shook from Helen's grasp and snapped a solemn salute. *It finally caught up with you, Doc. Semper Fi.*

Then Helen took his arm and led him away.

# CHAPTER THIRTY-TWO

Summer finally surrendered in early October as a strong cold front swept through the Florida panhandle. Hazy humid skies surrendered to brilliant deep blue and a refreshing dry coolness filled the air.

Late Friday afternoon Helen drove into the parking lot of the Bay City Girls' Club. Heather's Brownie troop was participating in a Columbus Day weekend camping jamboree at St. Martin State Park. A county school bus idled in front of the clubhouse. A small crowd of parents and impatient teens and pre-teens milled about while a working party of older girls loaded baggage into the storage bay.

Helen carried Heather's duffle bag and added it to the pile. She kneeled and zipped Heather's windbreaker snugly to the collar. A line formed at the bus's door and the children began to climb aboard.

"Have fun honey," Helen said as they neared the door. She hugged her daughter and kissed her reddened cheek. "Be careful, and don't forget to mind Miss Land and Miss Hargess."

"I will Mommy," Heather said and returned the kiss. Then she bounded up the steps and disappeared into the throng.

An hour later Nathan and Helen were enjoying an early dinner at Helen's apartment.

"Looks like my loan's going through," he said, helping himself to another slice of roast beef. "My credit's good. The loan officer said she didn't see any problems with the application. I should hear something by Tuesday or Wednesday."

Helen smiled and brushed a strand of hair from her forehead. "That's wonderful. And you're sure the Arnolds still want to sell?"

"Yeah, I talked to Mr. Arnold again this afternoon. They're just waiting for my loan to go through so they can buy that motor home and start traveling. His lawyer's already got the papers drawn up. It all depends on what the bank says, but it's looking good."

A few weeks earlier Nathan had noticed a FOR SALE sign posted in front of Arnold's Nursery where he'd bought supplies for years. He'd stopped to inquire about it and wound up talking at length to the couple about his dream of owning a nursery and landscaping business. The Arnolds admired his zeal and plans for the future. They took the sign down as he was leaving after agreeing with a handshake to give him until the end of October to come up with the necessary financing.

Helen sighed. "It's such a big step, and so much money. But I know it'll work out for you."

"For us, you mean. Don't tell me you forgot already."

Helen flashed her tongue-between-teeth smile and lifted her left hand and admired the diamond ring. "Of course not, silly. I'm not letting you back out now. Helen Henson; that has a nice ring to it, doesn't it?" She laughed. "No pun intended."

"It ought to, for what it's costing me."

"Oh, you." She wadded her napkin into a ball and tossed it at him.

Just then the telephone rang. Helen got up to answer it.

There was a pause. "Yes, this is she." There was another pause and then, "What?" Helen's voice sounded weak and shaky. "Oh no!" She shook and turned pale as Nathan hurried to her side.

"Is she all right?" Tears were flowing now. "Yes. Yes, I'll be right there."

Nathan put an arm around Helen's shoulders and a cold chill coursed through him. "What is it?"

"It's Heather." She dabbed at her eyes. "There's been an accident, something about the bus going off the bridge into the bay." She broke into sobs and trembled.

Nathan felt nauseated. A cold fist clenched his insides, the same helpless feeling he'd experienced when pinned-down during combat. He was almost afraid to ask. "Is she okay?"

Helen sniffled and nodded. "Her leg's fractured and she may have a concussion." She leaned against Nathan and grabbed his shoulders. "They're going to operate to set her leg. I need to sign a release. We have to get there right away."

Helen ran to her bedroom for her purse. Nathan thought about calling Helen's parents, but then remembered they were out of town. He grabbed his jacket and they rushed out the door.

The emergency room was jammed. Frantic parents sought information about their children. Rumors abounded as to what actually happened. Helen was at admissions checking on Heather and signing consent forms.

Nathan stopped a young police officer in the hall. "Were you at the scene?"

"No, sir. I helped escort a couple of the ambulances that responded. I was just about to go off duty when the call came through so my partner and I picked them up and cleared traffic."

"Do you know what happened?"

"From what we know the bus had just started across the bridge when a delivery truck coming the other way lost control and jumped the median," the officer said. "We're not sure what caused the driver to lose control. He was DOA. It might've been a mechanical failure or a blown tire or possibly a medical condition. There's no way of telling until they do an autopsy and pull the truck out of the water."

The officer lit a cigarette and exhaled. The smoke seemed to calm him a little. "The truck hit the bus's left front fender and both vehicles went through the railing into the bay." He shook his head. "Those poor kids must've been terrified. I've got a couple at home myself and, well, you just hate to think about things like this happening, you know?"

"Yeah, I know," Nathan said. The thought of all those anxious parents was agonizing despite the preliminary good news of Heather having survived the crash. "Was anybody on the bus killed?"

The officer shook his head. "No, thank God for miracles. Everybody made it out. A few kids have some pretty serious injuries, but a doctor I spoke with earlier said nobody was critical." He leaned against the wall, looking drained. "They were damned lucky it was shallow where they went in. The bus landed upright but it sank to within a couple of feet from the roof. There was just enough room for a good air pocket. I hate to think what would've happened if it had flipped or those passers-by hadn't come along when they did to pull the kids out. There would be a lot of grieving families tonight."

He looked past Nathan, distracted for a moment by a gurney being wheeled down the hallway. "Those two guys were real heroes. From what I heard, they forced the emergency door open and made several trips to get all the kids out."

He took another drag on the cigarette and shook his head. "I hear one of the rescuers is in pretty bad shape. He cramped up or got tired or something. Anyway, he went under. One of our guys fished him off the bottom. They did CPR, but I don't know."

A reporter from a local television station stepped in and hustled the policeman away for an interview. Nathan returned to the waiting room. Helen was there looking for him.

"What'd you find out?" he said after catching her attention and working his way through the crowd.

Helen managed a smile. "She's in surgery now. They were able to go ahead because of the emergency consent form I'd signed earlier for the trip. Miss Hargess called the staff at the clubhouse and had someone rush the forms over here. The nurse said Heather wasn't showing any signs of a concussion, just a bump on her forehead. She should be out of the OR in about an hour. They want us to wait on the third floor."

Nathan sighed with relief and hugged her. "You want to call your parents?" The Meyers were in North Carolina visiting their younger daughter and son-in-law.

Helen shook her head. "I'd rather wait until Heather's out of the OR. There's no sense in worrying them right now."

They walked through swinging doors and down a hallway toward the elevator.

"They were so lucky," Helen said. "The bus settled upright and there was plenty of air trapped near the top, but the door was mostly under water. The kids were panicking and nobody knew what to do. Miss Land was knocked unconscious. The bus driver managed to keep her head above water until she came to. Miss Hargess did her best to calm the kids down, but you can imagine how scared they must have been."

They stopped at the elevator where a crowd had gathered. When the doors slid open the anxious crowd pushed forward and the elevator quickly filled. Nathan and Helen stepped aside to wait for the next one.

Helen gripped Nathan's hand tightly. "Some men driving by stopped and broke a window so they could force the door open," she said. "They managed to settle the kids down and then one of them took Miss Land out while the other stayed to make sure everyone remained calm. When the first man returned, they started taking the kids out two at a time. They made a game out of it; the children were wonderful despite being scared and hurt."

"Yeah, I talked to a cop about it," Nathan said as the bell rang and the elevator doors opened. They stepped in with several others. Nathan pushed the third floor button. "He said one of the guys got in trouble and nearly drowned."

"Oh, no," Helen said. "Dear God, I hope he's all right. It just wouldn't be fair."

Nathan nodded but he'd seen enough unfairness in life

already to expect much else.

The elevator stopped at the third floor and the bell dinged and the doors slid open. They walked down the hall toward the waiting room. Entering the doorway Nathan bumped into a woman hurrying out.

"Excuse me, I'm sorry," Nathan said after turning to see if he'd caused any harm.

"Pardon me," the woman said almost simultaneously.

She walked on and then stopped and turned. "Nathan?"

Nathan froze in his tracks and stared at the attractive auburn-haired woman. "Laura? What're you doing here?" he mumbled, stunned at the unexpected encounter. It was too late to avoid her or to hide.

Laura rushed forward and embraced him with her cheek pressed to his chest. "It's Tom," she said between sobs. "A bus went off the West Pass Bridge. Tom stopped to help those poor kids get out and had some kind of seizure and almost drowned!"

Nathan stood there dumbfounded with arms at his sides and Laura still clinging to him. He felt paralyzed and helpless to say or do anything for the moment. His mind raced in circles and he struggled to comprehend what was happening. Tom Carter had risked his life to help save all those kids—to save Heather? Christ, *Tom?*

Hesitantly he eased his arms up and gently hugged Laura. He wondered what Helen would think and then realized Helen was beside them and had slipped an arm about Laura's waist.

"My daughter was on that bus," Helen said with tears in her eyes. "I'm so grateful your husband stopped to help." She found a clean tissue in her purse and pressed it into Laura's hand. "Come on," she whispered, taking Laura's arm, "let's sit over here for a while."

Helen took control of the situation. Nathan wasn't sure if it was her medical training or simply the mysterious knack for womanly communication, but she quickly managed to calm Laura. Soon they were talking like old friends, alternately laughing and crying and providing one another encouragement and assurance.

Laura was relieved to hear Heather was safe but expressed concern about her injuries. Helen, in turn, convinced Laura to be optimistic and to believe that Tom would come through the ordeal and everything would be okay.

"Doctors can work wonders these days," Helen said, squeezing Laura's hand. "You'll see; he'll be just fine."

A half hour passed. Nathan still wasn't over the shock. He was glad Helen was there to handle the situation. He felt like going off by himself and getting drunk and just forgetting it all. He needed time to think. Things seemed to be closing in on him, his past and future colliding in a big mass of confusion.

Was this the same Laura who'd ripped his heart out years ago? Somehow he had trouble picturing this anguished woman as the betraying slut he'd loved and hated for over half his life. And what about Tom, his best friend-turned-Jody; the turncoat who'd stolen his love and knocked the wind out of his life; the anti-war coward who'd avoided the draft by staying in school and earning one degree after another until drawing a high lottery number. Was he the same man who had just risked his life to save a busload of children? Could the patient fighting for his life in some nearby room be the same coward he'd despised all these years? It was all so damn confusing!

"Mrs. Morris?"

Helen sprang to her feet and faced a middle-aged man in green surgical scrubs who had just come through the doorway. "Yes?"

He smiled and took Helen's hand. "I'm Doctor Elliot. Heather's doing fine. She came through the surgery beautifully." He pulled the cap off his head and raked his fingers through thinning brown hair. "Her leg was fractured in two places. We inserted a couple of pins above her ankle. She'll have about a four-inch scar but that should fade in time. She'll be in a hard cast for a month or so, but should be good as new once it heals."

Helen exhaled, releasing the tension and worry locked

inside. "Thank you." Tears pooled in her eyes. She wiped them with the back of her hand. "Can I see her now?"

"Not just yet. She's still groggy from the anesthesia and wouldn't be responsive. We'll be moving her from recovery soon. We'll let you know just as soon as she's settled in her room."

Helen frowned, and then brightened. "Thank you again. We'll be right here. Please let us know as soon as she wakes up."

Dr. Elliot reached out and squeezed her hands. "I will. Now don't worry, she's fine."

Nathan glanced at Laura and saw the anguish in her eyes. He followed the doctor into the hallway. "Hey Doc, is there any word yet on Tom Carter? The guy who helped pull the kids out of the bus?"

Doctor Elliot's smile faded. "There's no word yet. Dr. Vanovich, our pulmonary specialist, is handling the case. Are you a relative?"

"No, just a friend," Nathan said without hesitation. "I've known him since we were kids." He motioned to Laura. "That's his wife."

The doctor stepped back into the waiting room. "I'll see what I can find out about your husband," he said to Laura.

She managed a weak smile, and then the doctor turned and left the room.

For the next several minutes Helen and Laura huddled together talking quietly. Nathan couldn't stand it any longer; he had to get away for a while or he'd go crazy. He touched Helen's shoulder. "I'm going to get some coffee. Can I bring you anything?"

"Nothing for me." She turned to Laura.

"No, I don't think I could keep anything down right now."

Nathan shrugged. "Okay, be back in a few."

Hoping to avoid people, Nathan took the stairs down to the first floor. He wandered the halls aimlessly trying to gather his thoughts until he found himself standing before a door with a sign that read: HOSPITAL CHAPEL. Without thinking, he opened the door and slipped inside.

Nathan's eyes slowly adjusted to the subdued lighting. Several rows of pews stood on either side of an aisle covered with maroon carpet. A wooden cross hung on the far wall behind a simple podium. Fresh floral arrangements decorated the raised dais. He glanced around the room to see if anyone else was there and found he was alone. Choosing the last pew, he sat next to the wall.

It had been years since he'd been inside a church. Vietnam had destroyed what little faith he had in a Supreme Being. But now, sitting in peaceful silence, he wondered. "Hey God, it's me, Nathan," he whispered. "I'm not sure what I'm doing here exactly, but maybe you can help me out."

Suddenly a flood of memories rushed through him. He leaned forward and rested his arms and head on the back of the next pew. He squeezed his eyes tightly against the faces flashing through his mind like living snapshots:

Roberts, the happy-go-lucky black kid from Ohio who'd died on some pathetic nameless hill. "Why, God? Maybe he'd still be alive if I hadn't told him to walk point that day."

Doc Dunn, killed on that same godforsaken hill while needlessly rushing to the aid of a dead man. Damn it, Doc, why didn't you listen to me? Why? Why?

And Betz, good ol' crazy Betz, always ready with a joke even when the shit hit the fan; always dependable, back-to-back, his most trusted and beloved fellow warrior. "Why did you let that happen? Why, damn it? I hated you for that; I still hate you for it!"

Nathan dug his fists into his eyes. He longed to cry and purge himself of all the bitterness he'd stored for so many years, but he couldn't. The tears were dammed.

His thoughts turned to Dan Matthews. "Why did you let Doc die on me like that? The first friend I had since the 'Nam. It's just not fair. He suffered through so much and you couldn't find it in your heart to give him even a little peace and happiness? He didn't deserve to die and I didn't deserve to lose him. What kind of a god are you, anyway?"

Nathan throat was tight. He coughed and sat up and rubbed his eyes to clear them. Then he remembered Helen and Laura waiting upstairs; little Heather and her broken leg; and Tom Carter, who might have sacrificed his life for a busload of strangers.

He felt weak and helpless and empty. "I'm sorry for giving you hell like that, but I just don't understand why things happen the way they do, that's all. Guess I'll never understand. I reckon it's like Mrs. Ard says about things we can't understand—it's all in your hands.

"Anyway, thanks for letting Heather and all those other kids make it out of that bus okay. And thanks for letting Tom and that other guy get there when they did. He . . . he's no coward. In fact, that was a hell of a brave thing he did."

Nathan coughed again and swallowed hard. "Look, I'm not much good at this, but would you please let Tom make it? I know I've hated him and Laura for a long time; at least I thought I did. But somehow things seem different now. They don't deserve this. He saved those kids; that should count for something shouldn't it?"

Just then the door opened and a young couple stepped inside. They walked up the aisle and knelt before the dais. They made the sign of the cross and bowed their heads in silent prayer.

As quietly as possible Nathan stood and eased out the door.

A half hour after Nathan rejoined Helen and Laura word came that Heather had been moved from recovery to a step-down unit until a regular room became available. Helen and Nathan visited her briefly. Heather was exhausted from her ordeal and was still feeling the effects of the anesthesia and soon drifted into a deep, medicated sleep.

The pulmonary specialist, Dr. Vanovich, spoke briefly with Laura and assured her they were doing everything they could for Tom. They had nearly lost him once to cardiac arrest but managed to bring him back. The next few hours would be crucial.

Although Heather was resting comfortably, Helen refused to leave Laura alone. Tom's parents had passed away several years ago and Laura's parents were away on a cruise. Their daughter, Jennifer, made a brief appearance but Laura sent her home to be with her younger brother. Friends of the family would stay with the children until the crisis passed.

Laura insisted that Helen go home and rest, but she flatly refused. She was determined to stay by Laura's side through the ordeal. Nathan slumped into a chair and tried to sleep.

A few minutes before five in the morning a haggard Dr. Vanovich walked into the waiting room. Laura took a few tentative steps toward him. Helen hurried to Laura's side and put an arm around her. Nathan held his breath. Tension hung cold and heavy in the room.

A hint of a smile crossed the doctor's weary face. "Good news. Your husband's out of danger. It's going to take some time but he should make a full recovery."

Laura buried her face in her hands and cried with relief. She turned and embraced Helen.

Nathan exhaled and glanced up at the ceiling. "Thanks, I owe you one."

Doctor Vanovich placed a hand on Laura's shoulder. "For a while we feared there might be some brain damage from the lack of oxygen, but the CT scan was normal and his EEG looks good. All his vitals are stable. He's getting stronger by the hour. You have one tough man there, Mrs. Carter."

Laura laughed through her tears and Helen joined in with tears of her own.

"I told you," Helen said, pressing her cheek to Laura's. "I told you he'd be just fine."

Laura wiped her eyes with a tissue and blew her nose. "Thanks for everything. I can't begin to tell you how much your being here means to me."

Laura turned to Nathan and walked over and hugged him. She looked into his eyes and said, "I know Tom would like to see you when he's better."

Nathan lightly patted Laura's back but said nothing.

Laura faced the doctor and wiped her damp cheeks with a fresh tissue that Helen had given her. "When can I see him?"

"He's sedated but you can go in now for a few minutes if you'd like. Don't be alarmed by all the tubes and monitors; that's routine in a case like this. We're just keeping a close eye on him."

Helen gripped Laura's arm. "I think we'll go home now and try to get a few hours' rest. I want to be here when they move Heather to her room. Will you be okay?"

Laura smiled. "I'll be fine. Thanks so much for your support. You'll never know how much it means to Tom and me. You two go on. I'll see you in the morning." Then she turned and followed the doctor toward the ICU.

Nathan and Helen stepped from the elevator and walked quietly through the lobby. A few visitors sat scattered about. Some leafed aimlessly through magazines while others slumped in chairs watching television or trying to sleep. An early morning news broadcast heralded another day.

The heavy glass door swung open and Nathan followed Helen outside into the chilly air. They kept to the curving sidewalk for a ways, and then crossed the street to the parking lot. Suddenly Nathan felt a rush of moisture in his eyes. He stopped and turned his head as he wiped his cheeks. At long last there was room for tears.

Helen wrapped her arms around Nathan and held him close. In the pre-dawn, a cobalt blue sky capped the faint yellow horizon and the morning star sparkled like a precious jewel. She rested her head against his shoulder as they walked arm-in-arm, looking toward tomorrow.

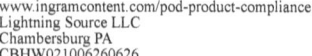